# Strange and Well Bred

SCEPTRE

*Also by Sophia Watson*

Her Husband's Children

# Strange and
# Well Bred

## SOPHIA WATSON

SCEPTRE

First published in 1996 by Hodder and Stoughton
A division of Hodder Headline PLC
A Sceptre Book

British Library Cataloguing in Publication Data

Watson, Sophia
Strange and Well Bred
I. Title
823.914 [F]

ISBN 0-340-64042-1

Typeset by Hewer Text Composition Services, Edinburgh
Printed and bound in Great Britain by
Mackays of Chatham PLC, Chatham, Kent

Hodder and Stoughton
A division of Hodder Headline PLC
338 Euston Road
London NW1 3BH

For Papa and Mama,
with my love and esteem

And with thanks to Vanessa, who more or less
adopted Esther while I finished this book

'Let us be very strange and well-bred: Let us be as strange as if we had been married a great while, and as well-bred as if we were not married at all.'

Congreve, The Way of the World

# 1

The train eased round the corner with a dull, unrelenting roar. In a few minutes it would be there, waiting implacably for the southern-bound travellers to board, an uncaring accomplice to the partings and greetings that were to come.

Dulcie felt slightly sick with unexpected nerves as she looked at her family. She wished they had not all come, although she had been pleased when the plan was suggested. The forty-minute journey into Durham had been a silent one, and there was little to say now the time for leaving was so near. Luke was leaning against a wall, whistling and bored; Benjamin was worrying at the dog who, unused to a lead or the smells of the station, whined and pulled.

'They said we should come. Silly, really,' said Sam, turning a lukewarm can of Coca-Cola in his hand.

Dulcie nodded. 'I know, I'm sorry. It seemed like a good idea at the time. There's a bin over there.'

Sam strolled over, threw the can away and came back to his sister's side. 'Well, you're the first to go. We'll know better how to do it next time.'

'I knew it.' Luke, at eighteen a year younger than Sam, joined them. 'I'll be off to Reading in a couple of months and it'll be "bye, Luke, catch the bus to the station, there's a good lad".' The three of them laughed, and Dulcie knew with a pang how much she would miss them all.

'Don't go, Dulcie.' A small blonde head butted her and Mary threw her arms around Dulcie's waist.

'Let go, Mary, the train'll go without me.' Dulcie disentangled herself from her sister and pulled a face. 'Oh Lord, look at your hand! Have I got melted Twix all down my back now?'

Mary looked worried for a moment, then smiled. 'Yes, so you'd better come home and change. You can't go to London like that.' She gave a small triumphal dance on the platform. 'Ah ha! We've got you back already!'

Dulcie gave Mary, the baby of the family at only eight years old, a bear hug. 'Bye now, pet. Be good. Remember you're the big girl now, and don't forget the chickens.'

Easy tears came to Mary's eyes. 'I won't. And – I'm sorry about the milking.' She had asked Dulcie to teach her to milk the house cow, but had proved very elusive when it came to the point.

'Don't worry about it. There's time. And I'll be back soon, I promise.'

Their mother, Molly, gently pulled Mary away from her sister. 'My turn now, Mary. We all want to say good-bye.'

'You've been saying good-bye to her for weeks, Ma,' said Ben. 'I'm surprised you can think of anything else to say.'

'Benjamin Stanley, mind your tongue,' said Molly, smiling, and turned to Dulcie. The two looked at each other and Dulcie was surprised to see tears in her mother's eyes too.

'He's right, though,' said Molly, 'I've told you more about my time in London in the past few weeks than in your whole life till now. I've probably bored you to death, and everything I've told you is bound to be out of date anyway.' She laughed. 'It's still hot news to me that Biba's closed down . . . I haven't lived there for almost twenty-five years. You'll have to rely on your aunt Carol.'

'Ma, you haven't bored me, not at all. And I'll be all right. You know I will. Don't fret.' She hugged Molly, but with half an eye was checking that Sam and Luke were not leaving any of her luggage on the platform. It really was time to go now. In every sense. There was no more to say. Except maybe to Sam.

She grabbed his sleeve as he stepped down from the train and pulled him to one side.

'Now listen to me, Sam,' she said with fake ferocity. 'I won't be here to stop you brooding, so you make sure to have a good time, won't you?' Sam, who ran the farm with his father, was a quiet boy, and Dulcie knew he needed her to bring out his lighter side. She would miss him – and worry about him – the most of her siblings. He showed no signs of wanting to leave home for university or agricultural college, saying he could learn everything from his father, and he often needed Dulcie to make him open up and relax.

'I'll be fine, Dulcie. Looking forward to the peace. Have fun.' And he gave her a quick hug and kiss.

'Ben!' Molly called. 'Quick now, Dulcie's off.'

'Bye then, Dulce. See you soon. Slim, come on.' Dulcie kissed Ben, used to his relaxed attitude, and patted the spaniel's head. Slim licked her hand and whined, as keen as Ben to leave the station. *I must let them all go*, thought Dulcie.

As the train pulled up, Dulcie turned her back on the station and looked out across the valley at the famous view. The Cathedral tower and the Castle's Keep stood and kept guard over the city as they had for so long. Dulcie willed the picture to stay in her mind's eye, knowing that it was imprinted there already. She had spent all her life here, had not even left for a far-flung university although her teachers had done their best to persuade her to try for Oxford or Cambridge. But at eighteen Dulcie had not been willing to leave her family, and had insisted on staying near home and going to what was known locally as 'The' University. In the end Durham had not proved as local a university as Dulcie had imagined: bright blonde bobs and hair bands from the south overwhelmed the minority of local students. At weekends vast numbers of southerners left to party at Oxford, where they thought they should be themselves. Occasionally Dulcie felt anger at the friendly but patronising way some of the southerners treated 'the Geordies' (a Geordie friend was as much a social necessity as a sandwich toasting machine to some students) but by the end of the first year everyone had found their own friends and occupations and Dulcie had become more tolerant, numbering students from all over the country among her real friends.

Now, for the first time, the Cathedral would no longer be a part of her life. After all these years she could still look up and suddenly see a new view of the Cathedral, see a new light shining on its tower, and feel heartened and protected. She wondered whether she might not miss the city – the narrowness of Saddler

Street which was treated as pedestrian, the curve of Elvet Bridge, the long haul of Claypath, the terraced houses of Gilesgate, the open space of the market square and everywhere the glinting curve of the Wear – more than the farm and her family.

With a faint twinge of guilt she turned back to her family, now gathering together again, the boys hauling her suitcases to the nearest door. Of course she would miss them all, especially Sam, her soul-mate and mucker. She would miss Mary, who would change the most and grow away from her. It would do Mary good, of course. She would have to help more, maybe would become less spoilt and lazy.

Last to come forward, as always, was Dulcie's father John. She hugged him, long and tightly. He was a small man, only slightly taller than his elder daughter, not given to saying much, but with a shining goodness in his face which total strangers would notice and remark upon.

'You look hot, Pa,' she said, letting him go unwillingly. Whatever the weather he wore a jacket and tie into the town and today his face shone with sweat as well as good-nature.

'Aye, well, it's time to be getting back to work,' he said. 'And you know I've always hated good-byes.' John had not said a great deal about Dulcie's leaving, but he had thought about it deeply. He hugged her again briefly. 'You'll be back, lass,' he said, but it was more a question than a statement. On one level he felt that her journey to the south was a journey away from him and back to her mother.

Molly Stanley had been brought up in the north-east, but her family had always had more southern links than his. The money with which the Stanleys had bought the land that John's family had farmed as tenants for generations had come from Molly's father. She had married John against her parents' wishes and advice, and against their expectations she had been happy. In the early years she had sometimes missed (but never longed for) London and had taken trips south to shop and stay with friends. But as the years went by the southern flights became fewer. It was hard to leave so many children, she said, and besides Newcastle's shops were better every year. Molly was old-fashioned even for her time, but had the sense to recognize it and choose a life that suited her.

And Dulcie was off to try this other life, one Molly remembered with some nostalgia and which John had never known. She was leaving the large farmhouse and family which had been the centre of her life and was going to her mother's people – family, school friends, women who had taken other paths in life and knew different ways. Molly was sure that even if Dulcie came back north she would be the better for having had the chance of a different life; she should have that chance, see where her choices lay. John, looking at his still, tense daughter, knowing her better than he did anyone except her mother, feared for her.

Doors began to slam, the station was emptying. 'Come on now, pet.' The station manager stood holding the door open, anxious that the train should leave on time. Now there was really nothing more to say, no choices left. A last hug each, a tearful Mary to be prised away from her legs once more, and Dulcie boarded the train. As it moved slowly out of the station Dulcie leaned out of the window, waving. She saw her family grouped together, all except Mary waving back. And behind them, over their heads, reared the Cathedral. The Stanleys stood in the shade of the platform while the August sun beat down on the yellow stone of the keep and the tall coolness of the tower. Although Dulcie tried to keep the family in her sight for as long as possible the little group was soon swallowed up in the shadows and she was left waving to monumental stone.

Only when the train was well out of Durham did Dulcie leave the window and find the seat Sam and Luke had saved for her. There on the table was a packet of sandwiches her mother had made and with it a cold bottle of Pils with a note. 'Mother said you could buy a drink on the train, but as you won't be at The Fleece tonight here's your usual on me. Good luck, love Sam.'

The last few days had not given Dulcie much time in which to sit and brood. It had not just been a question of packing, more of the endless conversations with her mother, reminiscences, advice, directions. It was as though her daughter's departure had opened the lock-gates of a canal for Molly who had served her own time in the capital, loved it, but had returned to her roots.

Despite the long talks Dulcie did not really know what to expect. She was aware intellectually that hers had been a sheltered upbringing, but did not understand quite what that meant. There must, she was sure, be some level of experience between her own life and that of the teenage junkies and pregnant schoolgirls of whom she read in the tabloids. She just found it hard to imagine, and nothing in her wide reading had given her a clear picture of another way of life. She had read of the middle-class 'wild child', but photographs of puffy-faced seventeen-year-olds on the arms of men many years their senior had aroused neither envy nor much curiosity in her. Night life for Dulcie was evenings at Klute, the Durham night-club, or occasionally Tuxedo Princess, its marginally more sophisticated Newcastle sister. Otherwise her evenings were spent in the college bars, at her local friends' farmhouse homes or in village pubs. She knew that at twenty-two she was old to be leaving home and was pleased at last to be doing so. But what would life be like in London? Would it – need it – be so very different? Pubs, the odd night-club, a job rather than the fluid structure of university life – what would change? Many of her friends had already started or were soon to start jobs in the capital. She would pick up with them straight away, and otherwise it would just be a question of learning her way around, presumably, and life would find its own rhythm.

Dulcie dozed for a while, ate the sandwiches and drank the beer, then returned to her novel, a Jeanette Winterson that she was reading with mild curiosity and a certain amount of admiration rather than much pleasure. Her attention was not held for long, though, and soon she was once again gazing out of the window and daydreaming.

She was to stay with her aunt, Molly's sister Carol. The sisters were not particularly close, having for years led entirely different lives, but they shared an old-fashioned (or was it Northern? Dulcie wondered) belief in the importance of family. It would never have occurred to Molly that her sister would not give Dulcie house room, nor to Carol not to have her niece. Yet Dulcie hardly knew her aunt who, especially since her parents' deaths, rarely travelled north.

Carol had married Martin Morecombe comparatively late in life, by which time she had worked in various middle-class jobs of which her father approved. She had passed time at the bookshop

Hayward Hill, at the General Trading Company, in Harrods' household linen department. All good jobs for a girl with some means who was waiting for a husband. When she married him Martin was an already fairly successful estate agent, working for a large company and earning good commissions at the top end of the market. Carol's father was almost as unhappy about this match as he had been about his younger daughter Molly's the year before. Martin was a nice enough chap, of course, was clearly going to go far, but . . . He worked hard, earned well, would on his marriage buy a small house in an acceptable part of town, but . . . But, compared especially to John Stanley, there was a brashness about him that Charles Pearsall found discomfiting. He was somehow too frank, too willing to discuss money. His suits were too expensive, yet off-the-peg; too fashionable, yet somehow wrong. There was in the end something not quite gentlemanly about him.

As a child Dulcie had heard these complaints without really understanding them. Her grandfather had made his decisions about both his sons-in-law and had not allowed the passing of the years to modify them much if at all. To Dulcie, Martin Morecombe was a genial, loving, noisy and sometimes embarrassing uncle. He clearly did not fit into their Northumbrian world, but it was not for want of trying. When he came to stay he wore expensive tweeds and drank draught beer, even went for walks – but then which farmer ever went for a walk? The Stanley dogs were as puzzled by the guest's demands as were their owners. Dulcie was fond of her uncle, though. She liked the fresh breath he blew into their farmhouse kitchen, found herself responding to his easy affection and laughing at his silliest jokes. She sensed that he was fond of her and that gave her confidence in him.

Carol Morecombe was different again. Two children were born in quick succession after her marriage – Jody, a year younger than Dulcie, and Alan. She had idled away a few years, entertaining herself during the day with other middle-class mothers and the joys of London's more expensive shops, and in the evenings with the imagined responsibilities of a company wife.

When Martin had left the shelter of a vast chain of agents and set up on his own she had been the perfectly loyal and helpful companion. Of course, being not unintelligent, she had finally tired of her way of life and taken a job. Working first for a friend, she learned the tricks of the interior design trade and by now her confident style and previously unguessed-at business sense had turned her into a successful woman in her own right. A surprise baby had been born just as Carol was beginning to make her own way but she had not allowed Piers to put her off her stride. Instead, she had hired nannies and foreign girls and invested a great deal of money and much hope in the future of her brightest and best-looking child.

If Dulcie were honest with herself – and she did not like to be on such a subject – she was not very fond of her aunt. She knew Carol would be welcoming, but feared there would be more gush than warmth in the welcome. She knew Carol would do her duty, but hoped that she would do so without too much discussion or self-congratulation. She was slightly afraid of her aunt's brittleness, her good looks, maybe even her success. But before she had even told her parents that she wanted to go south, she had known the implications and known where she must stay. So whatever happened Dulcie could only blame herself.

It never occurred to her that she could move out and rent a flat. It was just not part of her mental vocabulary. Family was family, and that was the most important single element of life.

There were the cousins, of course. Jody was all right, but Dulcie had never really known her on her own territory. Her trips to London had never been for more than a few days at a time, mostly spent travelling in her mother's wake on endless visits to old friends or shops. Dulcie hoped that she would like Jody's friends, knew that they would be thrown together more than ever before, but it did not occur to her to doubt that Jody would welcome her. Jody was not a wild child; they could get on.

On and on the train went, south to the future. In Dulcie's imagination the whole journey ran down a slight slope to its end in London. Through York and Doncaster, people with different sandwiches and different accents joined the train. It seemed to Dulcie that very few of them left it; all were bound together with a common sense of purpose, one destination – but how many futures?

She amused herself by imagining these strangers' stories.

This one was on a reprieve, a few days away from husband and children, which she would pass in spending too much money and missing her family. That one was clearly middle management, excited and worried by a big meeting in London. The tie was probably new, bought for good luck by a wife in the first year of marriage, a woman who still believed in her husband's potential and a future which included a detached house in a quarter-acre garden with a small swimming pool. Over there was a grandmother, on her way to help out a labouring daughter, bag packed with toys and sweets for the almost unknown grandchild she must succour while its mother was in hospital. There was a young woman, over made-up, overdressed, on her way to a job interview, hoping to impress, bound for disappointment. And a family of four on their way for a tourist break, a week in London to see the sights.

Dulcie dozed again, woke with a start, dozed. The countryside was bathed in the still August sunshine outside the windows and the train hurtled on through the heat. Each little person had his place in the high-speed box, each as he bought his gin and tonic, read his paper, prepared himself for his arrival, believed himself safe, inviolate, important. For each one, going to London was an aim, had a meaning. God probably minded, had each of them close to his heart. But to the cows through whose fields they were carried, to the grey-faced suburban dwellers whose window frames rattled as the train shrieked by, they were nothing, not even a nuisance any more. Lots of animate figures in an inanimate tube, rushing self-importantly nowhere.

Kings Cross was busy, loud with announcements and the slam of train doors. Big and ugly and dirty with nothing to see but rushing feet and frantic faces, it seemed a long way from Durham. Dulcie found herself a trolley, loaded her suitcases on – no cheery porters here, no 'all right, pet?' to lift her out of her despondency with a smile. Aunt Carol was supposed to meet her, but Dulcie could not see her and did not know where to wait or what she should do. The station was huge, they could easily miss each other.

Dulcie walked very slowly the length of the platform towards the main station concourse, wanting to give her aunt every opportunity to find her, not to be late. She searched every face as it hurried past her, and noticed how eyes met hers coldly and then slid away. Everyone looked on their guard. At the end of the platform she stood, dazed by the noise and tiredness and the newness of it all. Why had she come? She wanted to be home. Never had she known such bleakness.

Dulcie had not expected the streets to be paved with gold, nor had she wanted them to be. But where was the laughter she had been promised? Not on the faces of the Londoners sweeping by her.

Where were the lights?

# 2

Carol Morecombe had woken that morning with not much pleasure at the prospect of her niece's arrival, and as she was not needed at her office that day was unable to shrug off her dreary sense of foreboding until half way through the morning. For years she had more or less assumed that the day would come when Molly would ask this favour, and had known that she would have no option but to agree. She knew that Molly had entertained the Morecombe children for long stretches of summer holidays and if any of them showed any interest in farming would willingly give them board and work (but probably not much pay – the countryside did not seem to work like that) for as long as they wanted, or for ever, which ever came first. Carol felt no resentment at all about the intrusion of Dulcie into her life, but neither could she summon up much joy.

She oversaw the family's breakfast, eating melon, making sure Piers had enough, half-listening to the children discussing plans.

'I'm meeting Tommy and the gang tonight, Mum, I may not be back for dinner,' said Jody, reaching for raspberry jam.

'Jody, no. I'm sorry but you've got to be here for dinner tonight. You've got the rest of your life to go out with Tommy and the others.'

'Not true. It's cousins that are there for ever, friends you can lose. And I promised.'

'I don't care if you promised. I asked you weeks ago to be sure to be here tonight.'

'Mum!' Jody's protest was weak. She was a good-natured girl on the whole and could see the justice of her mother's demand, even if she did not like it. 'But I warn you, Mum, I'm not going to have my style cramped for the rest of my life by having to be nice to a country mouse.'

'Come on, Jode, she's all right,' mumbled Alan through a mouthful of banana.

'It's easy for you to say that, you won't have to have anything to do with her. Honestly, Mum, I don't know what you were thinking of. It's going to be a terrible squish here, apart from anything else.'

'Don't be silly, Jody, she's family. And you've always got on all right,' said Martin, ruffling his daughter's neat hair. 'Now hurry up, we're going to be late.'

Jody sighed theatrically and stood up. 'And now I've got to brush my hair again. Dad, I'm not six any more. I'm a responsible businesswoman.'

Martin laughed. Jody worked for him as a moderately efficient secretary, but had little interest in the firm beyond her pay cheque. 'Well, hurry up, or you'll miss the new sign which is going up today.'

'New sign?'

'Morecombe and Daughter. Since you're such a business-woman,' he teased. 'Now come on.' He looked at her with appreciation. Never mind Jody's business sense, she was a joy to be with and he was very proud of his daughter.

Jody was a very pretty girl, prettier than her mother had been although her looks would probably not last as long. She was tall and loose-limbed, erring towards over-large bones and a slight coarseness of feature. But for now her astoundingly clear skin, which was golden all the year round, her huge, slanting grey eyes set in thick brown eyelashes under Margaux Hemingway brows, her well defined cheekbones and dark-honey bobbed hair were a head-turning combination. She looked rather Slavic, although her size and colouring were clearly northern European. If her face and figure were not enough to encourage men to spend their time with her, her appreciation of the good things in life was. She was street-wise but never shoddy, sophisticated but never blasé. She just loved having fun, and (except on the occasional moody day when everyone, especially her close family, avoided her) it was fun to be with her. Her wit was raw, but her companions always laughed. Jody loved being twenty, loved being a Londoner, loved being herself.

She kissed her mother, waved at her brothers and settled into the passenger seat of Martin's black BMW.

'So, Jody,' said Martin after a while, drumming his fingers on the steering wheel as he waited for the lights to change. 'Are you going to show Dulcie a good time?'

'I suppose so. If she knows how to have one.'

Martin patted his daughter's knee. ''Course she will. Take to it like a duck to water, mark my words.'

'I think she only likes pubs.'

Martin looked sideways at Jody, decided she was being gloomy rather than moody, and thought she needed jollying along.

'Just because she's always lived up there doesn't mean she won't slot right in here. She's pretty enough, nice enough, she'll make her own friends soon. Probably be snitching your boyfriends if you lose your smile for much longer.' Jody grinned at the ludicrous idea. 'That's better. Look, you've only got to feel worried about her for a week or two. She starts her course next Tuesday and before long we'll be listening out for two sets of keys in the latch until all hours.'

'I suppose so . . . But Dad, you just don't get. I know we've always got on all right, but it was only for short bursts. She's different, Dad. All of the Stanleys are. Look at their clothes. And they talk differently, not just their accents; they're sort of polite in an old fashioned way. And quiet. I bet she's never even had a boyfriend. Or if she has, she'll arrive down here crying over some smelly farmhand with nothing to say. It's all right for all of you, but it'll be me that's lumbered with her.'

Martin was silent for a while, but when he spoke again his tone was sharper. 'Come on now, Jode, get this in perspective. She's your cousin, you've always got on, she's coming to live with us. You've your own life, pretty soon she'll have hers. You should be pleased you're quite different – at least you won't be stepping on each other's toes.'

It was not often that Martin remonstrated with his daughter, and when he did she responded. Jody smiled again, an unforced smile. 'Of course, Dad. It'll be all right.'

*　　*　　*

Alan and Piers left the house shortly after Martin and Jody. Alan, who had just finished his last year at school, was, like his cousin Luke, in a state of suspense, waiting for his A level results and idling away most of the summer at home. This morning he was reminded that, for reasons he could not quite remember, he had agreed to take Piers to his tennis coaching. A good-natured boy, very similar to his sister though less good-looking, he bolted his toast and bore his brother away. All the family knew that Carol was overprotective of Piers – at his age even Jody had been allowed to travel around London on buses and the Tube in the day time – but as Jody and Alan had inherited their father's tolerant attitude towards life they allowed Carol her weakness.

So by ten o'clock Carol had cleared up the breakfast, made an organised shopping list (meticulously arranged to carry her along Sainsbury's aisles in an ordered way without once having to retrace her steps) and felt the peace of the house settle around her.

The Morecombes' Pimlico house was large and in a pretty street. Many of the houses had peeling stucco but the Morecombes' money had been well spent outside as well as inside, and theirs had the whitest exterior, the most freshly painted woodwork, and the cleanest window panes. Carol felt that the appearance of their own house was important for both their careers, and Martin was not a mean man. The basement was mostly taken up with a huge kitchen, aping its country cousins as closely as possible. There was the dark green Aga (and also the state of the art convector oven), the scrubbed wooden table, the comfortable (but of course not shabby) sofa. Expensive stainless steel pans hung from butchers' hooks along a wall, dried herbs and garlic hung from the ceiling. Blue and green wall tiles were echoed by blue and green framed prints of vegetables. The essential dresser was perhaps a little small (but then the ceiling was fairly low), the china matched rather more consistently than any real farmer's would. Although the whole effect was more streamlined and expensive than the country kitchens it was supposed to emulate, the overall impression was of good cheer and welcome.

Off the kitchen, at the front of the house, was a small yellow bedroom and tiny bathroom that were to be Dulcie's. Here decoration and furnishings were pared down to the essentials, but a plain white bedspread, a painting of a summer seaside scene and blue and yellow rag rugs again gave the small rooms an air of modest comfort. No-one who saw her house could deny that Carol was good at her job.

Carol went up to her own bathroom (pale blue, shells stencilled on the wall, shell-decorated tiles, exotic shells in baskets) to fetch some sheets for Dulcie's bed. They were particular sheets of course – each bedroom had sheets bought with that room in mind and woe betide anyone who put Piers's blue striped sheets in Jody's pink room – and soft yellow towels. Carol had somehow forgotten to ask her cleaning woman Deirdre to make up the bed for Dulcie but was pleased to have something active to do towards her niece's arrival. Maybe it would help her to a more positive frame of mind.

Carol opened the window to encourage the muggy August air to move around the room. She hoped Dulcie would not feel too stifled by London after her years on the moors. Perhaps she should buy a fan for the room – but no, it would be too ugly.

Like her sister Molly, Carol was not a woman to indulge in nostalgia, but she could not help but remember her own journey south. She had left home so full of hope, so determined to have all the fun that London could offer. She could, if she allowed herself, see a great deal of the young Carol Pearsall in Jody Morecombe. The difference was that Jody already had a veneer of sophistication, an expectation of a good time, that had taken Carol some years to acquire. Where Jody assumed that men would admire her, that she was a good dancer, that London after dark was a fun-fair laid on for her amusement, Carol had hoped this would be the case. She had been sent away to boarding school, had had a share – was often a leader – in the pranks girls locked up together enjoyed, had spent her holidays in Europe with her family or at home in County Durham. She had probably had more experience of London before moving to the capital than Dulcie, because the Pearsalls owned a small flat in World's End, but she had probably had as little idea of real life as her niece. Carol had not gone to university – only very clever or determined girls did in the mid-sixties – and was just nineteen when, after a fairly dull and probably pointless six months spent in a Swiss finishing school peopled by richer girls than she, she made the World's End flat her home.

Carol sat in the blue wicker chair holding the yellow towels on her knee and, just for once, allowed her thoughts to wander back across the years. It saddened her to realise that she had changed – not just in looks, she was trim for her age and still pretty, looked after herself but was not obsessed with her appearance – but in outlook. She had been so full of optimism, looking as much for romance as for a good time. Romance, not sex, although when that had come into her life she had entered into it with verve and enjoyment. Carol had been a solitary child, more interested in sitting by the fire with a book or romantic film than in joining her sister on a ride around the countryside. She had fed her imagination with Georgette Heyer and Anthony Trollope, Mr Darcy and Mr Rochester. Although Carol looked the perfect sixties dolly-bird, her heart was hopelessly unfashionable. She could dance the night away with the best of them, jump into open-topped cars for impromptu drives to nasty pubs miles outside London, even (after a while) take and discard lovers with little thought or regret, but secretly she was always looking for the darkly saturnine stranger who would change her life. She knew of course that life was not one long musical romance but let herself believe that maybe, with the right man, it could come close to one.

Once it had come close but she did not notice the moment when it happened. Carol was the kind of girl who made real men friends, separate from boyfriends, almost closer, totally to be trusted. She flirted with them of course (she could not help but flirt, dreaded the day when age made her ridiculous), but she thought she knew how far to go, when the flirtation had to stop. Once she had misjudged.

She and Tony, the closest of such friends, were sitting in Kensington Gardens with the remains of a picnic. The sun was hot, there were not many other people around. She had been a little in love with Tony for a while, but so had her friend Chloe, a hard girl whose heart had been untouched by any of her many lovers until then. Carol did not want to lose Chloe or Tony and so had stood back and watched their affair with bemused hurt.

Tony had ended it, but by then Carol had taught herself that he was only to be her friend.

Now they sat together idly watching a squirrel being chased up a tree by a black and white springer spaniel, lazy with the after effects of wine under a hot sun. Suddenly Tony had turned to her, taken her hand and burst into song:

> I want to be your lover
> But your friend is what I stay
> I'm only half way to Paradise
> So close yet so far away

Carol looked at him and laughed, joining in:

> I long for your lips to kiss my lips
> But each time I think they may . . .

For a long time afterwards she tried to suppress the memory of his eyes flinching as he gamely sang on, turning the moment into a semi-drunken sing-along of Billy Fury's hits. She had pushed the episode out of her mind for years before she could let herself admit that Tony had loved her, that once at least in her life she had been loved in the old-fashioned way by a man who would sing to her under a summer sky, wait for her through a dreary winter.

Sitting in the little yellow bedroom Carol allowed herself to regret the lost opportunities. It had been a question of timing, she supposed, but even now she wished she could have told him that she had loved him, even if feebly, or wrongly. He had offered her romance, but maybe something even stronger than romance. She could be proud that she had inspired such love and humbled that she had failed to rise to it. Middle-aged and successful, contented with her husband, it was not wrong occasionally to remember lighter, brighter days. She wondered where Tony was now, wondered if he ever thought of her.

But enough was enough. Carol pulled herself together and pushed self-indulgence aside. She had made her choices, had a good life. It was the turn of the younger generation now – Alan and Jody, Dulcie, soon Piers. She wondered what her niece was really like underneath the quiet, considering surface. She would find out soon enough.

It seemed to Dulcie that she had been waiting a long time, but only ten minutes had gone by when she saw her aunt pushing her way through the commuters, a purposeful Londoner.

'I'm sorry, Dulcie, the traffic . . . how was your journey?' She offered a cheek, took hold of Dulcie's luggage trolley, manoeuvred it competently through the throng. Dulcie, following half a step behind, noticed how brown her aunt's legs were above the high heels, how compact her movements. Her mother never wasted a gesture, but neither did she have such jabbing energy in the smallest step, the briefest turn of her neck. Perhaps it was working in an office that made Carol's body so angry.

'Jody wasn't back from work when I left, but everyone will be there for supper.' Carol spoke over her shoulder; Dulcie nodded although her aunt could not see her. She knew the first few days would be the worst, was confident too that the long familiarity of cousinship would soon overcome the raw newness of Pimlico. She was really more nervous of Tuesday, her first day at the secretarial college, but she still wished she could sleep through this first evening and wake the next morning with the ice broken.

They drove through the busy streets, Carol driving efficiently and aggressively, keeping conversation going without much help from Dulcie. After a while Dulcie roused herself enough to pass on family gossip, messages from her mother. 'Uncle Philip and Aunt Serena are coming to dinner tomorrow, so I hope you've no plans,' Carol said. Dulcie was sure there was no malice in the remark – how could she possibly have plans so soon after her arrival in a city where it felt as though she knew nobody? Yet she felt very small and alone. Had they asked her aunt and uncle to save themselves from too many nights of polite conversation with their lodger? 'Philip rang to check when you were arriving and asked us all to dinner tonight, but I thought the train might be late, that you'd be tired,' Carol continued. 'And Jody seems to have plans,' she lied. 'Anyway, we left it that they're coming to us tomorrow.' Dulcie did not mind much – Philip was Carol and Molly's younger brother, a kind but stuffy man who farmed from a distance and waited in hope for a safe Conservative seat to be offered him. Serena, a few years older than her husband, had the ambition of the couple but not much brain. She would make a decorative MP's wife if she were ever given the opportunity and would have made a bad mother. She had had a childless six-year marriage, over some years before she met Philip, and ten years into her second marriage her sisters-in-law had given up hope of an heir to their father's farm. If Carol ever thought of Alan or Piers in those terms, she was far too wise to show it. She did, though, keep on good terms with her brother and Dulcie knew that he was as family-minded as his sisters (if less actively) and would certainly have felt it incumbent on himself to show an interest in her arrival. It pleased her that even here she had family to look out for her. How could she have felt herself neglected? Her shoulders relaxed and she settled back into the car seat. Of course her new life would work out well.

After supper Jody asked Dulcie whether she would like to come out for a drink with some friends. She asked with bad grace, suggesting that maybe Dulcie was too tired to want anything more than a bath and bed. 'No,' said Dulcie coolly. 'I'd like to meet your friends. Thank you.' And, after drying the last dish, she went to her little room to change. She sat for a moment on the bed, wishing she could just sleep but sensing that she should join her cousin when invited or she would be sidelined entirely. She already loved this bedroom – tiny and so uncluttered compared to her room at home, but peaceful and calming. It was a bit of a bore being so close to the kitchen, where the family seemed to have its base, but then it was her own: she had expected to have to share with Jody.

Wearily she washed and changed into a clean shirt and put on a bit of mascara. When she went back into the kitchen Jody was still upstairs, but as soon as she came down Dulcie saw she had misjudged the situation. She was still in jeans – clean and not torn but nevertheless jeans. Jody had changed into the smallest of A-line mini skirts, her legs long and brown beneath it, and a skimpy midriff-baring tee-shirt. Dulcie felt her heart sink but she was not going to show it. 'How did you get so brown when you're indoors all day?' she asked.

'Sunbed, of course,' Jody answered, and then Dulcie really understood the difference in their outlooks. Her own face and forearms were brown, but from having spent much of the long hot summer out of doors. She had always thought that it was only Americans, people in soap operas, who used sunbeds, not people like her.

'Are you ready?' Jody looked her up and down with some surprise, and Dulcie just nodded.

They went to a wine bar in the King's Road, all pale blue and chrome with mirrors everywhere. Some people were eating large plates of small salads, but there was quite a crowd of young people who had come on after their own suppers for an hour or so of drinking and talking. Jody relaxed a little as she reached her friends and gave Dulcie a smile. 'I'll buy a bottle. Welcome to London,' she said, and quickly introduced her to the six people sitting around a table in the far corner of the room. 'This is my cousin Dulcie, who's come to live with us. Dulcie, this is Lottie, who works with us, Jane, Giles, Phil, and of course Tommy.' She bent over Tommy and kissed him on the mouth, then wriggled up beside him on the bench. Her glance up at Dulcie clearly said, 'This one's mine, all right?' 'What are we drinking?' she looked around the table and then nodded at the waiter. 'We'll have another bottle of the white, please.'

'Make that two,' said Giles. 'Have you eaten?' The two girls nodded.

For a while Dulcie just sat between Lottie and Jane, watching the others as they talked and laughed and flirted. It was not so very different from being at home, really. The setting was not the same and was to Dulcie's eyes less welcoming, but it was still just a place where people gathered. Everyone was dressed smartly – much more than they were in the North. Looking around the bar Dulcie realised that she was the only girl wearing jeans. They all seemed so flamboyant, their gestures, especially the men's, were so much larger than at home. They opened their mouths and eyes so wide when they laughed, waved their hands about so much when they talked.

It was difficult to follow the conversation. Dulcie was tired and the others were all talking of people she did not know, events in which she had played no part. She tried to work out the relationships of Jody's friends. Tommy, Jody's boyfriend, was the most obviously good-looking, tall and blond like Jody, dressed in a loose button-down shirt. Its bluey-green brought out the colour of his eyes and Dulcie wondered if he or his mother had ironed it so perfectly. He and Jody were very tactile with each other, but Dulcie decided that they were not very much in love.

She smiled to herself – how could she jump to conclusions on so short a knowledge?

'Are you smiling at us?' Giles leant across the table and poured Dulcie some more wine as he asked the question.

'No, at myself,' she said, and as he waited for her to elaborate she went on, 'I look at people and I invent their whole lives. It's like a game really. I was just thinking how cheeky it was of me.'

'And what have you made of my life?'

She looked across the table. He was smiling but appeared to be taking her seriously.

'I hadn't got on to you yet,' she said truthfully.

Giles was almost as good-looking as Tommy – they were all good-looking, thought Dulcie suddenly; she brought the standard of the table down quite a notch. Giles had curly dark hair and slightly too small dark brown eyes. Perhaps it was his curls that made him more untidy-looking than the others, but he seemed to Dulcie less concerned with appearances than Jody's other friends. His shirt, though clean, was creased, and where both Tommy and Phil had tidily rolled their shirt sleeves back to expose brown forearms Giles had one sleeve pushed back, its cuff button straining, and the other down over his watch.

'So where are you from? The north-east, I'd guess.' Giles had let her watch him for a moment. He nearly hadn't bothered to come out tonight but was glad now that he had. He liked the look of this cousin of Jody's. She seemed a quiet girl, more a talker than a shrieker, and he was beginning to have had enough of the shriekers in his set. As the thought crossed his mind, Lottie and Jane erupted into loud giggles and Giles gave them a tiny look of disdain before turning back to Dulcie.

'It shows, does it?' she answered, wondering why he did not like his friends.

'Well, just a tiny bit around the edges of some of the vowels. I hope you don't mind—'

'Of course not. I'm proud of where I come from.' Dulcie sat up straight on the ridiculous chair and it was Giles's turn to smile at her.

'You look proud.'

'Where are you from?'

'Nowhere much, London mostly. My parents have a house in Kent but they only bought it in the last few years so it's certainly not home. I'd quite like to come from somewhere.' Giles was surprised to find himself thinking that, and realised it was true.

'Too late now.' Dulcie smiled at him and he laughed.

'Yup'.

'So what are you doing this weekend, Giles?' Jane butted in and Dulcie settled back into watching her flirting with Giles. He, Dulcie was interested to see, did not seem particularly responsive to her attentions, his body leaning slightly back as hers moved eagerly forwards.

Lottie made conversation with Dulcie, Tommy grinned at her every now and again, Phil was flirtatious in a heavy-handed way. Jane talked on and on, ever more vivacious, ever more determined to wring a laugh or a touch from Giles, ever more destined for failure. Just as Dulcie was beginning to wonder if she would find her way home alone the last bottle was finished and the party began to break up. Lottie and Phil set off together, Tommy said he would come back with Jody and Dulcie for a while. Jane, silent for the first time in the past hour, looked hopefully at Giles who said he would hail a taxi. She brightened again as they all stood waiting on the street. Her disappointment when Giles handed her in to the taxi and firmly shut the door behind her was so visible that Jody and Tommy shouted with laughter and even Dulcie could not help but smile.

Giles did not smile, though. He just said, 'If you're all walking back I'll walk with you and get a taxi from there. I could do with some air.' Jody looked surprised and Tommy nodded.

The four of them fell naturally into two pairs; Jody and Tommy first, arms around each other, their voices low and intimate, then, a few yards behind, Giles and Dulcie, walking side by side but apart.

'So what do you do?' asked Dulcie, after they had walked a while in silence.

'I work in the City – in futures.'

Dulcie smiled. 'I'm afraid that means nothing to me.'

For a few minutes Giles explained, his voice suddenly urgent and intense. Dulcie listened, but for once her mind was not on what she heard – it was too late, maybe she was slightly woozy from the wine, and she took nothing in. After a while Giles paused, waiting for some kind of response. 'I'm sorry,' Dulcie said. 'I'm not really with you.'

'Oh.' For some reason Giles was disappointed. She had not seemed an airhead.

'I wasn't really – concentrating.'

'Oh,' he said again.

They had arrived at the Morecombe house. It was clear Tommy was coming in but Giles immediately said he should retrace his steps to the main road and find himself a taxi.

'Goodnight, Dulcie,' he said. 'It was good to meet you.'

'You too,' she said automatically, but saw from his brown stare that he had meant it and smiled. Giles softened too, and added, 'Well, maybe some time soon . . .' as he waved and walked back down the street.

Dulcie, faintly shocked at Jody and Tommy, who were giggling and 'shushing' their way up the stairs together, went straight to bed where she lay for a while, too tired to sleep, and thought about her day. Aunt Carol was not so bad, Uncle Martin had been very welcoming, Piers had paid her no attention at all, Alan had been easy and relaxed and reminded her of her brothers. Jody? Dulcie wondered about Jody, who had veered from warmth to almost rudeness. She had changed the most, but Dulcie supposed Jody's life would be the most disrupted by her arrival.

She thought of the wine bar, the red laughing mouths, and wondered if she would ever fit in, become like the other girls. Then she thought of Giles, who did not laugh so much but whose brown eyes looked so directly at you, and she felt comforted. Perhaps she had already found a friend.

# 3

Carol Morecombe's business was going very well indeed. She employed two people full-time and had two part-time consultants on call. She had decorated houses from Notting Hill to Pimlico, from Northumberland to Cornwall. Sometimes she wondered when people would notice how ridiculous it was to pay someone quite so much to do something quite so simple. She did not mind working for bachelors and liked decorating a divorcé's house but found herself increasingly disliking the rich women 'rushed off their feet' doing nothing, who did not care enough about the houses they had bought or married to choose the colour of the bedroom walls. Carol had a good, if not always very original, eye, an amazing memory and feel for colour, and was an excellent businesswoman, but she sometimes wondered if her heart was really in her work. She could be as sharp and supercilious as any one of her spoilt clients, but underneath she wished she could really talk to these women, find out what they did all day while their houses were being decorated, their children entertained, their meals cooked, their gardens tended, by professionals. Sometimes she felt sad as she left a house for the last time, closing the front door on her hours of inspiration and work, wishing she would be able to see it again when it had been lived in for a while, when the colours were slightly faded, the children had kicked it about a bit. People at dinner parties told her how productive she was, how wonderful it must be to be so creative, but to Carol her job was curiously sterile. In her more fanciful moments she wished she could decorate a terraced house in Cleveland or a council house in Newcastle. It would be so much more rewarding to turn a loved but ugly house into a place of beauty than to cover yet another armchair in sixty-pounds-a-yard chintz in a third-best bedroom few people would ever visit.

This morning, though, something had happened to give Carol new interest in her work and she was full of excitement as the family sat down to breakfast a few days after Dulcie's arrival. 'I've been asked to do a house in France,' she said proudly. 'Isn't it exciting? It'd mean spending quite a lot of time out there, of course, and going back and forth, but obviously all the expenses are being paid.'

'Can we come too?' Jody was already filling the unknown client's house with her friends and planning her summer wardrobe.

Carol laughed. 'I shouldn't think so. But if you're interested in the business there's a house in Brook Green I've just taken on – you could have a go at a room if you want – the utility room.'

Jody, who was not good at being teased, scowled as the others laughed. All but Martin, Dulcie noticed, and wondered why he was looking at Carol so intensely.

'Where is it?' he asked.

Carol picked up the letter again. 'Near Albi, south west somewhere apparently,' she said. 'Where's the atlas? I'll have to check it. If I take it on – as if I wouldn't! – I'd have to go for a preliminary look-over in the next few weeks as Mr – Peterson – says he'll be away for a while after that. He says he lives in Stockholm – I wonder why a Swede's moving to France?'

Martin poked at his grapefruit, then looked up with a smile. 'Well, darling, it does sound good news,' he said. 'Uh-oh, I'm running late. Come on, Jody.'

Dulcie had never seen her aunt so animated, so genuinely excited, but she was puzzled at her uncle's reaction. She supposed it was obvious that the children would only look at their mother's absence from their own point of view, but she was surprised at how low-key Martin's response had been.

Jody, sitting beside her father in the car, was finding him uncharacteristically tetchy this morning. He sat in silence, answering her comments monosyllabically, and driving with unusual aggression.

For although Martin was the kindest, most even-tempered and tolerant of husbands he had to battle with a character weakness he despised in himself. He loved Carol, he trusted her (philosophically speaking at least), but he was very jealous. He could see her off to work with a smile, knowing that most of her staff were women, telling himself that men in the interior design world were all queer, but every now and again he would be overcome by a jealousy that made him physically sick. Weeks, even months could go by without a twinge of fear and then some chance comment, some new client, would raise the demons again and for a while overcome him.

Martin had no proof that Carol had ever been unfaithful to him physically or even mentally. In his rational moments, he would be sure that the wife he adored had remained pure every day of the twenty-three years of their marriage. But he could not be sure.

Carol was so good-looking, such good company, how could another man not want her? And how could she – so successful and sure of herself – not be tempted? She met new people – new men – all the time; Martin knew Carol was a flirt and (in theory at least) delighted in it. But even if the flirtation had not gone too far yet, it would one day. Of that poor Martin was unhappily convinced.

And so he sat, grumping at his daughter, cursing the other rush-hour drivers, and asking himself, *Who is this Peterson? Does Carol already know him? Why did he write to her at home, not the office? How did they meet? Why has he got a house in France? Why the hell can't his wife decorate it herself? Has the bastard got a wife? If not why not?* Round and round the angry thoughts churned with an occasional interruption from a cooler, saner voice: *Calm down, old chap – just a fellow with a house. We've lived through this before, we will again.*

Carol had seen the look in Martin's eye as he set off and knew what it meant. Her soul was weary as she cleared away the breakfast. She had seen Martin like this too often before, and each time, when at last his anxieties were quieted, she hoped it would be the last.

She sometimes wondered if it would not be better just to be unfaithful. He suspected her of it so often it might almost be a relief to be faced with the fact. Despite what Martin thought, though, Carol had never been tempted. She had learned how to put off importunate divorcés with a look which shut them up for good. To her way of thinking, sleeping with a client would be as bad for her business as it would for her marriage and she had no wish to risk either. She just desperately wished that Martin believed her.

Dulcie, putting the cereal away in the cupboard, tried to talk to Carol about the house in France but Carol did not give much away. Her mind was too full of Martin and the fear that she would be forced to turn down this job which she wanted so much. Her mind raced. This Peterson, who said he had heard of her through a friend, had invited her to stay for any three days in the next three weeks while she looked around the area and drew up her plans.

'I want the house to look of the region,' he had written. 'Not like Hampshire transported to the south of France. I do not know how you work but would appreciate it if you could make the time to get to know the area. My house is a *manoir* rather than a chateau, but has not been touched for more than twenty years so will need a complete working over. However I do not want it to look newly decorated. If you are interested in the idea of this project, I would like to meet you as soon as possible. I would like the house finished by the end of April, when we plan to move here full time.'

From the little Peterson said he had inspired her. Here was a challenge. To decorate a house and leave it looking as though it had been lived in for five years, to be begged to ignore the chintzes and frills that had begun to haunt her. She did not even think of Peterson. To her he was a man with a cheque book offering her an opportunity to try something new. But how could she convince Martin of that? She thought of Jody's remark and wondered if she shouldn't turn down Peterson's invitation to stay, and book herself and Martin into a local hotel but then, sighing, she dismissed the idea. How could she possibly turn up to a new job with her husband in tow? She would be announcing either that she was treating the preliminary visit as a holiday, or that her husband did not trust her. She read the letter again. There was no mention of a wife. It was all '*I* want the house . . . *I* see the house as . . .', yet at the end he had written, 'we plan to move here.' If there were a wife, it would certainly make things easier with Martin, whose fears would not be allayed but who would at least feel his corner was being guarded by an unknown ally.

In the meantime Martin had succeeded in damping down her enthusiasm, God damn him. Sometimes she wished so much that she were different, that she were a good time girl with no heart. Sometimes she wondered, what was the point of living with a husband who felt nothing – or at any rate could show nothing – but jealousy.

She thanked Dulcie for helping, but quite forgot to wish her niece good luck for her first day at typing school.

Dulcie left the house half-nervous, half-cross. She was not looking forward to secretarial college and had booked a place on the six-month course only as a means to an end. She had applied for a few jobs from Durham – tried for a training course at the BBC, sent a few optimistic letters to publishers – but had had no luck and not many more ideas. She saw her friends find jobs in banking or accountancy, and only knew that she did not want that sort of a career herself. She soon realised how little practical help a degree in English was in the real world and decided that nothing would be lost by earning a secretarial qualification (and some thinking time would be gained). Above all, it would give her an excuse for coming to London.

She hated the college as soon as she walked through its chipped front door. The secretary or receptionist who greeted her was middle-aged, middle-class and disappointed. Her greying hair was set in rigidly loose curls around her sour face, bright pink lipstick aged her pale skin and her wedding ring dug too tightly into her sausage finger.

'Yes?'

'Dulcie Stanley, I'm enrolled on the six-month secretarial course.'

'With or without finishing?'

Dulcie looked blank and the receptionist sighed, 'Without . . .' and consulted a list. 'Yes, here we are: Stanley, D.K. Room 21 – along the corridor, second on the left.'

The college was in a once-smart mews house on the fringes of

Belgravia. Its founders, Colonel and Mrs Smart, had opened it as a finishing school in the very early sixties, just as finishing schools began to become unfashionable. They had advertised themselves as parent substitutes who would guide young girls through the arts of flower-arranging, dancing, basic cooking, organising weekend house parties, etc. 'Deportment (including lessons in entering and exiting the low sports cars now proving so popular)' and lessons in precedence and etiquette were included.

Of course the Colonel and his good lady were to be disappointed in their new venture; through the years they had tried to adapt, always slightly behind the fashion, always shoring up the business with their dwindling capital. Now, disappointed and childless since the deaths of their two sons (one honourably dead in the Gulf War, the other dishonourably dead ten years earlier, a victim of the Seventies drug culture), they lived in a flat on the top floor of the college. Every now and again one of them would 'pop into' a class, where they were treated with varying degrees of disdain by pupils and teachers alike. Mrs Smart still insisted on finishing classes being on the prospectus, but nobody had applied for them for fifteen years. She did not even realise that there was no-one on her staff equipped to teach a young girl the art of sliding into a Jaguar XJS without showing her knickers.

Carol had not done a great deal of research to find a good college for Dulcie. Her sister-in-law Serena had been a friend of the dead soldier and had suggested the place to Carol as an act of loyalty to the Smarts. As the diploma was recognised and the college was within walking distance, Carol considered her job done.

Room 21 was decorated with faded willow pattern wallpaper and hung with hunting prints. A large mahogany bookcase took up most of one wall and was filled with real books, rather than bought-by-the-yard complete works. Real, but on the whole dull; 1950s light comedies and thrillers, a few dreary memoirs of military men, rows of a different coloured uniform edition of authors long since forgotten. It looked as though the Smarts had one day walked out of their sitting room and forgotten ever to come back. A sagging sofa covered with once-expensive chintz was pushed back underneath the window and the middle of the room was taken up with nasty Formica tables at which girls sat in pairs at electric typewriters. *You must learn to type before you learn to word process* was the college's philosophy; it meant fewer word processors had to be bought as the drop-out rate among students was high.

Dulcie was amazed at her co-students. She had not believed that this type of girl still existed. She had thought the Sloane Rangers on the General Arts course at Durham were as extreme examples as could now be found, but she had been wrong. There were nine other girls in the room, all talking eagerly, tossing their hair about and braying (different from the shrieking of Jody's friends; there was less enjoyment and more bossiness in these girls' collective noise). Their parents must live in Hampshire or Berkshire, Dulcie immediately decided, and they were all here straight from boarding school.

A brief silence fell when Dulcie walked in as the girls appraised each other, and then the introductions began. As Dulcie suspected, she was the only graduate, the only state school product, the only northerner. She told herself not to be chippy, and had to admit that the other girls were all remarkably friendly. They giggled and discussed the joys of boys and London life, trying to include Dulcie but marking her as an outsider. Finally, ten minutes late, the tutor walked in and the girls, good little schoolgirls that they were, settled meekly into their seats and began to type row upon row of Aa Aa Aa aaa AAA.

Dulcie did not go straight home at the end of the day. She rang Carol to say she would be late, then, using the telephone directory, began ringing bookshops. By seven-thirty she had a job in the Kensington High Street branch of Waterstone's.

So ended Dulcie's secretarial career.

# 4

Julia Yeoworthy petulantly pushed the marmalade jar away from her and looked at her husband with a sigh. She was bored again. Bored with her husband Velters, her life and her lover. Bored by her children, bored by her half-finished novel, her half-finished tapestry, her half-finished jigsaw, her half-finished life. That thought inexplicably cheered her, but nothing lasted for long with Julia. Except her marriage, which was twenty-eight years old this weekend.

She watched her husband rifling through his post and felt a spasm of annoyance. How could a man be irritating even when he was doing something as simple as opening his letters? He was so neat, so precise in his movements, and so, so predictable. He spent one day a week in the estate office, receiving telephone calls and 'showing willing' as he called it, two days a week doing his duty to his country and his ancestors by falling asleep in the House of Lords, and the rest of the week pottering. He liked them to entertain at weekends, which was a bother but Julia put up with it because she knew it was all he asked of her. He was disappointed if at least one of his children did not come home at the weekend, and as a rule one of them nearly always obliged. He loved the winter when he could hunt and shoot but was also happy to fish during the summer. He was, Julia thought, exactly as a fifty-nine year old Earl should be, exactly as she had known he would be when she had married him, so why was she so irritated by him?

Julia had been only nineteen when they married, and had seen in Velters her dream come true. He was good-looking, titled, rich, had a pretty house with a large estate in the West of England and a flat five minutes' walk from Sloane Square. He did not even have a mother. The dreams they dreamed in the months leading up to the wedding seemed perfect – a large family, life in the country, horses, friends down at weekends, holidays abroad two or three times a year. And each other. Everything had gone according to plan. The children had come a little more slowly than they had hoped, but they had spent those early years of their marriage on a round of pleasure. Once the first child arrived there had been no trouble conceiving the others. Adam, now twenty-five, worked in the City earning vast sums to increase the family fortunes but would probably leave as soon as he came into the inheritance. Ted, a year younger, was more interested in the estate than was his older brother and had offered to farm it until Adam wanted to return. But 'we have a farm manager,' his father had said, 'and tenant farmers for that.' Julia thought Velters should help Ted buy his own farm, or make one of the farms on the estate over to him, but Velters was reluctant to break up the estate and was a firm believer in primogeniture over merit or need. Finally he had agreed to match whatever money Ted could raise to help him. Then came Francis, the easiest-going and best looking of the Yeoell boys and his mother's favourite. Frank was a Cornet of Horse in the Blues and Royals and looking forward to his captaincy. He was, Julia knew, the perfect son. Finally came Miranda, about to go into her last year at St Mary's Calne, and spoilt most dreadfully by her father.

So everything had come as planned. Velters had inherited the estate and title just after Ted's birth, so Julia had been the mother of a two-year-old viscount which had made her laugh a lot for a while. She and Velters had their two or three holidays a year, had their horses and their cut flowers and expensive clothes and gardeners and cook and nanny (once Velters's own, now retired to an almshouse in which Velters had an interest). Their house – rambling late Tudor – was beautiful, their children dutiful, their income plentiful. And for some years all this had been enough.

Now it was comforting, but for Julia at least it was no more than that. When she was younger the days had been too short to fit in all she wanted to do. She had the children, the horses, the gardens, the dogs, the guests . . . and she had the nanny, the girl groom, the gardener and his wife the cook. Now, with the children all away from home, the house and garden more or less ran themselves – or were run for her. She had given up hunting after a near-fatal accident ten years earlier and riding soon after. Velters had never quite seen the point of riding for riding's sake, although they had enjoyed hacking round the estate together on summer evenings, exercising the horses and checking all was well at the same time. Another shared pastime gone by the board, she thought sadly now, although she had hardly noticed its passing at the time.

Every now and again Julia noticed how little there was for her to do, and when this happened she tried hard to fill the gap. She had taken an interest in gardening for a while, had hired an expensive garden designer and spent weeks with him, trawling around nursery centres. Then they would come back to the Manor and lay out the plants in the appropriate spots and Mr Vellacott would follow on a few hours later and do the planting. And then the garden was beautiful and Mr Vellacott kept it up and there was nothing more to do.

She went on courses now and again, hither and thither, on a variety of subjects. Quilting in Dorset, embroidery in Sussex, transcendental meditation (that had been a disaster) in Glastonbury, nouvelle cuisine in Frome, water-colours in Norfolk. Subjects or pastimes interested her for a while, but nothing really held her imagination for long. She read a great deal, middlebrow women's fiction mostly and the occasional historical saga, but when she thought about it (which was not often) she felt as though she were struggling towards something without quite knowing her goal.

'More toast, Velters?'

He looked up from his letter, smiling, still good-looking although his face was too red from good living and outdoor sports, and shook his head. When she was not irritated by him Julia supposed she still had affection for him. Sometimes she almost admired him. How could he be so contented – maybe even happy – with his lot? Why did he not notice the sameness of every day? Why did he not long for a change, for some excitement?

'I'm so lonely,' she said, without meaning to, amazed at having done so.

'Hmmph?'

'Oh, only one piece?' she said in a panic. Velters looked at her for a moment and returned to his letter. Julia did not know if he had heard her.

'Oh, there's one for you here, sorry,' he said, and slid a letter across the table to her.

Julia took it and looked for a moment at the handwriting, which was definitely familiar but which she could not place. She felt a little hope – perhaps this was the surprise, the change she had been hoping for. She opened it and turned to the signature, a momentary disappointment quickly replaced by pleasure. It held no new excitement, but maybe an old friendship was worth more.

'It's from Molly Stanley,' she said, 'I haven't heard from her for years.'

She quickly read the letter and heaved a sigh. 'About Dulcie.'

'She's your god-daughter, isn't she?'

'Mmm. Apparently she's moved down to London. Molly wants me to keep an eye on her. Invite her down here, I suppose, and introduce her to the boys. We could take her out to dinner. I'm up in London the week after next.'

'Are you?'

Julia flushed. She had not told Velters of her plans. 'I thought I would. Haven't been up for a while.' Velters looked neither interested nor suspicious.

'All right. Let's have a family outing. Ring Adam and Frank, will you, and choose somewhere nice.' Velters was generous, loved nothing more than to take his family out for expensive and delicious meals although he was not particularly interested in food. Julia nodded and stood. 'Right, I'll sort it out then. Any plans today?' she asked, knowing the answer.

'I'll go down to the estate office, show willing there. I'll be in for lunch.'

For a moment after his wife shut the door behind her Velters looked at the seat she had left. *'I'm so lonely.' What the devil had Julia meant by that? Lonely? There are people here all the time, goddammit. The house is full every weekend, she has plenty of friends, can go to London whenever she wants.* He shook his head and pulled *The*

*Times* towards him. *Out of sorts. Women's troubles, probably. So what was young Portillo's latest idea . . .?*

Julia told her daily help which beds to make up for the weekend, had a conversation with the cook about food for the rest of the week, rang the organiser of a local charity of which she was patron, then sat with the *Daily Mail* and a cup of coffee in the drawing room. Worry at her slip kept edging into her mind. Velters had not seemed to notice that she had fixed a plan without telling him, and she wondered, not for the first time, whether he was as dim as he pretended. But if he had noticed, and had said nothing, he could not really mind. And if he were dim enough not to notice, then he deserved to be duped.

Once a fortnight Julia went to London for the day without mentioning it to Velters. Once a month she spent two nights in London, the first in the flat with Velters, the second in the same flat with Archy. Archy Poole was a portrait painter with whom Julia had been having a secret and well organised affair for two years. He was married – not, of course, happily – and every couple of months Archy and Emma came to stay at Yeoworthy Manor. Emma and Velters had no inkling of the affair, at least so Archy and Julia believed. Or if they did know, they must not mind or they would have said something. So it did not matter at all. Julia did not feel guilty any more, even when she heard hopeful young couples say their wedding vows. She was sticking by Velters, after all. Cleaving only unto him in a manner of speaking. In fact, if a bit of infidelity here and there kept the marriage together it was in essence a good thing. Or so Julia now believed. She did not even feel uncomfortable when she remembered her own fiery disapproval when her friends had taken lovers. She had been a young prig. This was different, and was not hurting anybody.

In truth, except for the occasional twinge when she thought she had betrayed herself, Julia did not think very deeply about her affair. It was now as much a part of the fabric of her life as the House of Lords was part of Velters's. And about as exciting. She wondered about ending the affair, as she often had before – but why bother? She and Archy were comfortable together, good companions as much as lovers. Each gave the other something lacking in their marriages and neither was about to make importunate demands. They knew where they stood.

So Dulcie had come south. Julia cast an eye over Dempster, but as usual nowadays it was more of a press handout about little known actresses with baronet uncles than real gossip about anyone one knew. She must be twenty-one or -two by now, maybe the boys would take to her. Julia had done her godmotherly duty by Dulcie in the way of presents at Christmas, but she and Molly had more or less lost touch as Molly had retreated to her Durham farming life.

Julia had been at the same school as Molly and Carol. Her father was a doctor and could barely afford to send his only child to boarding school but he and his wife, both differently ambitious for Julia, agreed that her education must come above everything else and both blindly assumed that the more they paid the better the education would be.

Julia, perfectly intelligent, was not academic but she floated along and vaguely picked up a smattering of education. She also made some decisions about the rest of her life based on the girls she met. She knew she wanted more from life than the suburban middle class comfort she returned to at the end of term. She wanted to move south. And she wanted Things. Most of the girls at school had Things almost without realising it. They had two cars, they had dogs and ponies. They had space. They had large gardens, vegetable gardens, croquet and tennis courts. Sometimes they had holiday houses and even swimming pools. They had networks of friends which spread beyond the school and beyond the county. They had a certainty of who they were, where they were going. Julia knew that too, but in her case did not like what she knew.

There were of course other girls like Julia, girls whose parents worked hard for them and who in return worked hard. They believed in what their parents were doing for them and respected them for it, girls on scholarships, girls with ambition, but Julia did not notice them. In her eyes the world was full of families with Things, and she wanted Things too.

Her father, who had hoped Julia would eventually follow him into the practice, watched her development with a sigh. Her mother, also aware of the world of Things, looked approvingly at her daughter's growing self-assurance and blooming prettiness.

As Julia gravitated towards the richer girls, she dropped her family behind her. She was not ashamed of them, did not dislike them, was even fond of them, but they would always be there and there was a world to conquer. She found that girls' fathers always liked her and their mothers could be prevailed upon to feel sorry for her. She used her cleverness to make people like and trust her, and in return for their confidence she gave them her smiles and her humour. Without too much premeditation, Julia knew instinctively how to make herself liked.

By the time she left school Julia had been more or less adopted by two families, the Pearsalls and the Tewkesburys. The Pearsalls had taken her in first, and Carol had become her firm friend. They made each other laugh, but what Julia really liked was the atmosphere at the Pearsalls'. Charles and Jennifer never seemed to mind how many extra people ate at their table or slept in their spare rooms. Julia swore to herself that one day she would have a house like that, one filled with noise and argument and people. She went less and less often to the neat square house outside Alnwick, where the table napkins were precisely folded and the decanters of whisky, gin and sherry neatly lined up and barely ever touched.

She had hopes of Carol's brother, but he was too young and it was too soon. Julia knew that she had to act fast. Her father could not support her indefinitely and she must entrench herself in this new, bright world before she was swallowed up by the old grey one. She asked Molly to teach her to ride and, over the long hot summer after her last year at school, she and Molly rode out almost every day and forged a friendship in its way truer than the more obvious and frivolous one between Julia and Carol. Julia was truly happy that summer, perhaps because all was possible and she had not yet met the disappointment of reality.

Molly and Carol 'came out' together, and Julia, who by now was beginning to feel nervous and was spending almost as much time with the Tewkesburys (richer, with the advantage of older brothers), somehow came too. Her father hurrumphed his disapproval, her mother sent Jennifer Pearsall inappropriate presents, but Julia succeeded in staying with the Pearsalls and Tewkesburys in turn until she met Velters Exton, as he then was.

Julia's friends could never agree about how much she had planned her future, and how much she had dreamed it into reality. But those who thought, then or afterwards, that she had married Velters for his money or his title did her wrong. She was in love with him. Whether she loved him or the things he stood for first was in the end irrelevant. She walked up the aisle truly in love with her handsome viscount, truly grateful for the good things life was now going to shower upon her. As she walked towards the altar she believed in True Love, Happiness Ever After, and Velters.

Velters believed then, and believed now, in God, the Church of England, the Monarchy, the Upper House, and in his children having the same things as he had had – the same nanny, the same holidays, the same treats. He believed in fidelity within marriage and assumed that all right-thinking people believed the same. His Christianity was instinctive and born of good manners, rather than philosophical and born of the soul. He had loved Julia with the passion of which he was capable and now loved her as his companion, the mother of his children, his Countess. He was sure his mother would have approved of his wife.

Velters finished his breakfast and his post and put his head around the drawing room door to say good-bye to his wife. She looked very elegant in her pretty room surrounded with flowers, he thought. He blew her a kiss and set off, reminding himself of his luck in having such a wife. Occasionally she surprised him, though, even unnerved him a little. For instance, he thought, as he took his silver-headed walking stick from the stand in the hall and settled his cap on his head, what had she meant by that remark about loneliness? Extraordinary woman. He shut the heavy front door behind him with unnecessary force and strode off down the drive, swinging his stick. He was at home much more often than other women's husbands, always around the place for her if she wanted a conversation. He enjoyed their walks around the garden together, Julia was a clever woman and had improved the old house without spoiling it. Velters shuddered to think what any of the bright City girls Adam seemed to take up with would make of the place. Please God he would settle down and find himself a sensible girl who understood the countryside, knew a bit about horses and wasn't above a bit of hunting. A girl like Sally Webber, but with a background he could recognise.

But Julia . . . Julia had changed, he supposed. He remembered a time when they had laughed a lot together, and now they only seemed to laugh when other people were there with them. He thought back to breakfast, realised how silent it had been, supposed that it had been as much his fault as hers.

Lonely? Who were her friends these days? Molly had been a nice girl; pity they saw so little of her, although John was a dull stick. There were a few local ladies who seemed to come to lunch, but on reflection Velters realised that they were mostly duty – women with whom Julia was involved in charity work (she certainly did her share of that, he thought with satisfaction, swinging his stick at an impertinent nettle which had sprung up beside the drive).

Then there were all the weekenders – the children, of course, and their friends, the Tewkesburys, the Pollocks, the Quilpers, the Pooles . . . couldn't see what Julia saw in Emma Poole, mousy little thing he'd have thought, without a quarter of Julia's sparkle, when she had sparkle. Velters paused and leaned on a gate, looking across the valley to the river. He always paused at this spot, never failed to feel his stout heart lifting at his little bit of England (quite a large bit, actually, almost five thousand acres). But now his thoughts were more with his wife than his property. Perhaps, after all, she was lonely.

He would stop reading his post at breakfast and talk to the old girl more. That should cheer her up.

He strolled into the estate office where Sally Webber greeted him with her usual sweet smile. Now there was a girl a chap could be at peace with, Velters thought, as he prepared to show willing.

# 5

Giles Wharton nearly always succeeded in getting what he wanted. He understood that about himself and it pleased him. He was hard-working, determined and, he knew, charming. He also had an obsessive, ruthless streak which he did not recognise in himself but which was as instrumental in his success as the other factors.

And now he wanted Dulcie.

She had been out with him a few times – or rather had come out with a group of Jody's friends – and the more he saw the more he liked. He liked her quiet intelligence, her watchfulness and her self-assurance. He liked her big brown eyes, bony face and the way she held herself. He liked the fact that all his friends assumed that she was a virgin and he just knew that she was not. It would not have bothered him if she had been, and he sensed that she was no easy lay, but he was convinced that there was a great deal to discover about her and he wanted to be the man to do the discovering. He did not care whether there was a boyfriend lurking in Durham, was confident he could see any long-distance lover off in a trice, he was just determined to have her.

To his amusement he saw Dulcie beginning to respond to the charms London had to offer. She never shrieked or giggled but he saw she was after all something of a flirt, could drink steadily without appearing too much affected, could easily hold her own with the rest. Giles believed he could transform Dulcie from quiet country girl to London good time girl without too much effort but with quite a lot of fun.

He did not ask himself why he wanted to change her.

What she was attracted him, and he felt she should fit into his world.

Giles's world was one in which girls were girls and men were men. This did not mean to say that the men rode the lone prairie while girls stayed home and prepared chocolate chip cookies and grits, but it meant that when the men had all left their places of work (where other girls were as powerful as they) they gravitated towards the kinds of girls who wanted to Have Fun.

Having Fun was very important. Giles and his friends in the City worked hard, incredibly hard by anyone's rule of thumb. They were up at first light or before, bleary-eyed in striped shirts with turk's-head knot links, their heads already buzzing with figures. They spent ten, twelve, fourteen hours a day Making Money and at the end of them they were ready to Have Fun.

Drinking was Fun. Dancing was sometimes Fun. Eating small and expensive meals was Fun if done with the right sort of girl. Watching rugby with a crowd of the lads was Fun. Sex was of course Fun. But sometimes Giles wondered if any of it was really as much Fun as Making Money.

At University he had worked hard enough to get a 2:1, had played rugby and cricket, been a creature of leisure first and foremost. Now everything else – the rugby, the cricket, even the girls – came second after work. To Giles's amazement he had found himself sucked into the whole atmosphere of the City. He loved every element of it, loved the thrill and the sick fear and the buzz and the incredible high.

The sadness was that he had not even noticed how his priorities had shifted. He thought that he worked because he had to, and was still first and foremost a party animal. He did not notice how long it took him to unwind after work, how obsessively he talked about his deals and his gambles for an hour or so after he had loosened his tie or taken his first sip of beer. He often bored his friends early in the evening, but he did not notice.

'Do you work because you want to, and play because you ought to?' Dulcie asked Giles one evening in a desperate attempt to woo him away from talking about the deals he was hoping to swing in the next few days.

'What do you mean?' he asked, and his eyes were wary.

'Well, most people I know work in order to live – and if they're lucky enjoy it. But I sometimes think you're the opposite. You live to work, and in the evening go through the motions of socialising because you think you ought to.'

'That's not fair,' Giles said, and to Dulcie's surprise looked actually hurt.

'Isn't it?'

Giles did not answer for a moment; he seemed to be considering the question.

'Not quite,' he finally said. 'I really enjoy meeting everyone – having some fun after work.'

'Do you know how much you talk about work?' Dulcie sounded irritable and Giles was surprised. 'This evening probably counts as having fun, having a social life, to you. But your mind is still running on work. Look at Phil and Tommy, they've cut loose from the office now. Jody certainly has.'

'Jody is never mentally engaged in her work in the first place,' he answered, and Dulcie smiled.

'OK, maybe not. But the others are, aren't they? Giles, other people can cut loose, switch off. There is more to life than deals, you know.'

'But I love it,' he said simply, and there was no answer to that.

Dulcie, to whom the City meant Durham Peninsula, was fascinated by Giles. She was unsure how much she liked him, though. She was interested in what he had to say about his work, although she could not quite get to grips with it, liked to dance with him, thought that he was different from Jody's other friends and different from her old friends at home and University.

*I wonder how this lot would do at home*, Dulcie thought one evening when, after a couple of sets of tennis, they had gone to a pub. *For one thing they'd get a shock at the pubs*. She looked about her at the drinkers, all young, all affluent-looking, in designer tennis wear or striped shirts. She grinned at the thought of these fresh-faced young men and women transported to the north-east.

'And now what are you smiling at?' It was Giles again, his brown eyes looking hard at her.

'I was comparing here to home.'

'And?'

'I don't think you lot would last a minute.' She tried to describe the difference in atmosphere, the half-empty pubs, old men sitting quietly around in dark corners or propping up the bar and nattering. Very few women. 'The City pubs are different, I suppose, especially in term time, but in the villages, I don't know, I suppose they're more working class than here.'

'It depends where you are in London,' Giles said reasonably.

'I suppose so. But you can only judge by what you see, can't you? I don't know the East End, only this.'

'I could show you.'

Dulcie brightened in interest. But 'Giles, the pubs you'd know in the East End wouldn't be real East End pubs, would they? It's like students going to local pubs in Durham – they think they've found the genuine ones, but they never have. Because if they have they wouldn't be – do you see what I mean?'

Giles laughed. 'Almost', and he looked at her, and thought that he wanted her. 'Well, I'd like to come up north one day, see what it's really like – if you'd show me.' And Dulcie looked at Giles, who was not smiling any more, and knew what he meant.

Dulcie had not expected to become involved with anyone in London, or not for a while at least. She had left Durham fancy free, had not in fact had any real boyfriend for quite a few months. Although she was now, somewhat to her surprise, beginning to enjoy her new life, she did not think of London as home and doubted she ever would. On long telephone conversations with her mother she would hear Molly's curiosity, her reminiscences, even sometimes the smallest trace of envy, and would want to say, 'It's all right, ma, I'll be back'. But she did not, and although she had promised a weekend visit soon she kept putting off the trip. It was quite far, shift work in the book shop meant she often worked on Saturday, and besides – she was having fun. Yet she did not view any of the young men she was seeing as anything more than friends. Friends to pass the time with at that, not real friends, not soul mates at all.

Except possibly for Giles. Although she undeniably felt drawn to him, found him attractive as well as good company, something about him unnerved her. She liked the feeling that there was more to him than to the other men with whom she spent her free hours, but when she wondered what the difference was she realised she could not pinpoint anything.

*I suppose he's cleverer*, she thought. *But it's not that. He's interested in more than just having fun – isn't he? He's interested in people, I suppose. It's the way he looks at me. Does he do that to everyone? I must watch.* But when she was with him she forgot to see how he was treating other people. *He's a little like a snake*, she found herself noticing once. *When he looks at you, you can't look away, even if you want to. And I do. Sometimes. He makes me feel I have no privacy.* When she realised that, she felt a twinge of distaste for him. Until the next time she saw him, when once again he drew her towards him with his eyes and looked at her, and intrigued and attracted and unnerved her all at once.

And now . . . *He wants to see me on my own territory, take my privacy even more. On the other hand, I'd be quite interested to see how he reacts. I wonder what Pa would make of him.*

Dulcie accepted her invitation out to dinner with the Yeoworthys with interest but not much excitement. In the month she had lived in London she had already made a life for herself. She had picked up with Durham friends from the couple of years above her who had already settled in London, and others from her year were beginning to arrive. She enjoyed the book shop – her colleagues were mostly like her, recent graduates who wondered what to do next but loved books enough to find their job more than just a timefiller. Some had become friends, and she found herself fitting in to Jody's circle more and more. There was a lot to be said for London, after all. Cheap good meals on offer on every corner – Thai, Chinese, Vietnamese, Indian, Italian. About six to ten of them would meet after work in a wine bar or on a tennis court and spend the long summer evenings in idle and self-indulgent pursuit of pleasure. In some ways it was rather like being a student, but with more money.

Dulcie did not earn a great deal, but as she paid no rent what she did earn was hers to spend as she chose. Added to that, grown-up life seemed to mean that men were likely to pick up the tab so although Dulcie was very conscious of wanting to pay her way she found Giles more often than not paid for her. Sometimes all the men split the bill; sometimes Dulcie would be allowed to contribute.

Dulcie also felt that she and Jody were becoming real friends at last. The breakthrough came on Sunday morning when they were sitting sunning themselves in the small garden at the back of the house, idly flipping through the papers.

'Isn't it lovely to have this sun still in September?' sighed Jody, lifting her face to the sky.

'Indian Summer, isn't it called?' said Dulcie. 'It makes me feel as though I'm on holiday instead of starting a fabulous career.' She laughed.

'Are you liking it here?' Jody asked. The tone of her voice was offhand, but the set of her head told Dulcie that there was something behind the question.

'Yes, I am. I'm loving it. More than I expected. You've all been very nice to me.'

'Oh, I didn't mean that!' Jody laughed, flashing her blue eyes at Dulcie. 'Anyway, we haven't been *nice* – you're family, it's normal.' And for the first time she meant it. 'No, I mean – well, aren't you missing anyone?'

'Sam. Ma and Pa a bit. Not as much as I should. But if you're asking if I've got a boyfriend at home, no. I went out with someone for most of my last year, but we broke up before finals. I don't know, it seemed time.'

'And you've no-one here.'

'Jody, you'd know as soon as I did the way we live. No. No-one I even fancy.' But she was not entirely truthful.

'Is that true? I just wondered, the way you look at us. At me and Tommy.'

'Tommy? Come on, Jody, he's your boyfriend. I don't play those games with my friends.'

'No. But you couldn't help it if you fancied him, could you?'

'Well, I don't. Honestly. I'm sorry if I made you think that.'

'You're like Giles sometimes, you know.'

'What do you mean?' (And how pleased she was to have the opportunity to talk about him.)

'You look at people. I mean really look. Giles spooks me sometimes. It's as though he knows what I'm thinking.'

'Do I spook you?' Dulcie was only half-teasing.

'No, of course not. You're family.' And there was comfort for both of them in the reiteration.

So altogether an evening with her little-known godmother was an interruption to her life, rather than the diversion it would have been a few weeks before.

Giles rang Dulcie just as she was smartening up for her evening.

'Feel like a game tonight?'

'Can't, I'm being taken out to dinner.'

A pause – then, lightly, 'By whom?'

'My godmother, Julia Yeoworthy. I haven't seen her for years and she's very grand so I don't suppose I'll have much fun. Her husband's taking us, and two of their sons. So at least we won't be alone together.'

'Oh, well. What about later on?'

Dulcie hesitated, then laughed. 'Now what kind of a girl do you take me for?' Giles had crossed a line with that suggestion, and they both knew it. Although they saw each other at least every other evening, it was always with some of the others in their set. They had never yet been alone together other than on a tennis court or dance floor.

'I just thought – I could meet you wherever they're taking you and then we could go to a club.' Dulcie wanted to say yes, but was almost afraid to agree.

'Wouldn't that be a bit rude to the Yeoworthys?' Dulcie heard the weakening in her voice, and quickly added, 'No thanks, Giles. Not tonight, maybe another time.'

Giles put the telephone down and grinned.

Now he had her.

Dulcie arrived at L'Escargot in Greek Street before her hosts and sat alone at an empty table on the second floor feeling foolish and nervous. She turned down the offer of a drink as she thought it would look a bit presumptuous, and looked tentatively at the menu. This restaurant was a world away from the ethnic restaurants she normally went to, and the sight of the prices inside the menu made her cheeks freeze with embarrassment. Lord above, she was going to have to make some good jokes to be worth her supper tonight. Her mother would be able to feed the whole family for a week on what this dinner was going to cost. She had better enjoy herself.

She stood as she saw a couple make their way towards the table. Her godmother's blonde hair now had highlights, but they had been done expensively and well. Dulcie was surprised to see that Julia was less obviously smart than Carol, her clothes were well cut but dateless, not fashionable. She wore a skirt which hung in soft expensive linen folds of bluey-grey almost to her ankles. A wide belt emphasised her still-small waist. A duck-egg blue linen shirt brought out the colour of her godmother's eyes and slightly heeled strapped shoes drew attention to her fine ankles. Julia wore no noticeable make up other than a touch of mascara but she had a sapphire brooch pinned to the lapel of her jacket and an Art Deco style sapphire and diamond ring on her finger which gave her all the extra adornment she needed. She really was a lovely woman. Dulcie greeted her shyly and turned to Velters, of whom she had no memory at all. She saw a tall, good-looking, bluff-faced man in a pinstripe suit with a high-cut waistcoat. He wore a stiff-collared shirt, a heavy and worn-looking signet ring and cufflinks of lapis set in gold. He held himself very upright, and looked fit and thin. More than anything else Dulcie noticed an unquestioning kindness in his eyes, and contrary to her expectations she immediately liked him.

'The boys not here yet? Sorry to keep you waiting,' Velters said, shaking her hand. 'Good Lord, haven't you been offered a drink?'

Adam and Frankie arrived together, Adam under six foot, thin and nervy, and Frankie tall and good looking and relaxed. It was hard to believe they were brothers.

They talked of Dulcie's life since they had last met some ten years earlier and exchanged memories of childhood visits.

'And how are your brothers, Dulcie?' Julia asked. 'Still interested in farming?'

'Of course,' Dulcie answered sharply. 'We're farmers.'

'Like Ted,' Frankie put in, smiling easily.

'Ridiculous idea,' said Velters. Dulcie looked politely blank. 'Adam here's going to be the farmer in the family – right, old boy?' Dulcie looked at Adam's expensive suit and manicured nails and doubted it. 'Not that he'll be getting on a tractor much,' said Velters, laughing. 'We have a very good farm manager, John Webber. Been with us for years, would trust him with my life. Still, Adam will have to learn the ropes, show willing. Your father still running your place?' he asked Dulcie.

'Well, yes, he's a farmer.' For some reason Dulcie did not mind Velters, and even liked him as he laughed again.

'Which takes us back to Ted. Says he wants to be a farmer, happy to be our farm manager. Of course, I couldn't get rid of Webber, been with us too long. And we'd be doing him out of a house as well as a job. Ted can't see that.'

'Where is Ted?' Dulcie asked.

'Working in Devon. Doesn't really know what he's doing in life. Done Cirencester, did very well, have to give him that, now says he wants to learn about game-keeping. Can't think why. So he's working under Mortimer on Verney's estate, just the other side of Barnstaple. Wish the boy would settle.'

'He would soon enough if he had his own farm.' Julia's voice was soft, but her tone made Dulcie realise that this was a conversation which had been had many times before. She was unsure how to divert the subject, and turned to Adam. 'So do you enjoy the City?' She found herself wanting to talk about Giles, but did not.

'For now.' He was not quite rude, but clearly not forthcoming. 'Excuse me.' He stood and left the room. Velters and Julia paid no attention, but Dulcie noticed Frankie looking after his brother speculatively and wondered what was happening under the correct surface. When Adam came back he was better, attentive to his mother and Dulcie, made jokes, kept them all laughing. The food was unlike anything Dulcie had eaten before, perfect in every particular, and she found the evening slipping by, the Yeoells entertaining and warm and increasingly relaxed. *They're not grand at all, they're a proper family*, she thought, relieved.

When dinner was over Adam suggested they go dancing. Frankie was at first enthusiastic until he looked at his watch and, swearing mildly, gulped down his coffee and brandy. 'I must get back to barracks. Nice to meet you, Dulcie; some other time, maybe?'

Frankie and his parents set off in separate taxis, and Adam and Dulcie were left standing on the pavement in Greek Street. 'Well, what do you reckon?' Dulcie quickly agreed – she was beginning to have cold feet about the idea but did not want to be feeble.

Adam took her back to her doorstep at two o'clock. They had danced and laughed, and Dulcie had found in Adam a languid worldly-wise attitude which she found amusing rather than attractive. She was pleased to have made a new friend of her own, separate from Jody's circle, although she dismissed the thought as unworthy. Adam was just saying good-bye when another taxi drew up beside his and Jody jumped down.

'Dulcie!'

'Hi. This is Adam Exton. My godmother's son. Adam, this is my cousin Jody.' Despite the hour Jody looked splendid. Her hair, not her face, shone, and her make-up showed no sign of smudging or wear. She looked as fresh and pretty as if she had just dressed after a long night's sleep followed by an early morning swim. Dulcie could not help but feel dowdy and tired in comparison. And Adam, though fairly drunk, did not miss his chance.

'Jody. Dulcie's been telling me about you.' This was stretching the truth a little, but Dulcie let it pass. 'I was just hoping to pin Dulcie down for a weekend at my parents' in Somerset. It would be lovely if you could come too.' Neither was Jody a girl to miss a trick. It had not taken her long to notice not just his floppy dark hair and thin looks, but to take in every detail of his expensively rumpled appearance. She did not mind that his words were slightly slurred – it was two in the morning after all. She looked at Adam and saw a good looking clubber after her own heart. Without a trace of compunction she accepted, but she did have the grace to say to Dulcie as they unlocked the front door, 'I hope you don't mind, Dulcie, but wouldn't it be fun?'

'What about Tommy?' asked Dulcie, who had no designs on Adam but found herself resenting her cousin's assumptions.

'Tommy? I've just dumped the bastard. He's been two-timing me,' said Jody over her shoulder as she tripped up the stairs. 'Night. See you in the morning.'

An hour later Dulcie was woken by a scratching at her window. She lay for a moment, panic stricken and wondering what to do.

Finally she reached out and very carefully moved the curtain back a few inches. Giles stood there, mouthing something through the window. Half laughing, half angry, she opened the window a couple of inches. 'What do you think you're doing?'

'I wanted to know if you'd had a nice time,' he said, grinning. 'So I walked over.'

'From *Hammersmith*? At this hour?'

'Well, I felt like some fresh air, and I thought I'd better not ring first.' He paused. 'Can I come in . . . for a chat?'

Dulcie hesitated – it was her aunt's house, should she really . . .? But she thought of Tommy and Jody giggling their way up the stairs and the decision was easily made.

'I promise I'll be gone by breakfast,' he said, as he slid between her pale yellow sheets.

# 6

Carol closed the small suitcase and locked it. She would only be away for three nights and was an expert packer, so had chosen a case small enough to travel as hand luggage. She picked up the passport and ticket from her dressing table and sat down to brush her hair and put on some lipstick.

She had been looking forward to this job so much, but now she was actually about to leave for France she felt sick with nerves. Sometimes, changing to go out for dinner or setting off like this on a new job, she would be overcome with fear that she might meet someone and fall in love. She did not want to, she loved Martin, but she knew that out in the wide world there just could be someone who could turn her heart and head and ruin her life. Her love for Martin was constant and, she thought, strong enough underneath its day-to-dayness to withstand anything. But could she really be sure? Wouldn't it be – interesting – to be tested?

Martin's jealousy did not help matters. It only brought the danger to her mind more often, and made her ask herself whether it would necessarily be all bad to meet someone who would not see her as wife, mother, business-woman, but as Carol? She sometimes missed the days of the chase, when flirting was dangerous because there was a point to it. Where is the fun in flirting when both people know they will return to their marriage beds, their vows intact? Carol did not wish her life to be any different, but she knew that a part of her remained unfulfilled.

She could not entirely analyse what it was, though. She found the cheap romance of Mills and Boon and women's

magazines embarrassing, thought a dozen red roses out of
season common rather than heart-warming, hated the set-piece
romantic gestures that her secretaries yearned for so noisily. So
what did she expect of Martin? When he told her he loved her
she usually assumed that he was drunk or guilty about some
sin of commission or omission. When he was jealous she was
miserable or irritated. She wished she knew what she wanted,
but could only sporadically pine.

And now she was off again, leaving behind a silent, tortured
Martin and the three – four including Dulcie – children. Oh, they
would manage perfectly well. It was so easy – supermarkets, ready
packaged food, Deirdre coming in for a couple of hours a day. She
had left a list of Piers's movements, arranged for him to spend
one of the nights at a friend's house. They would barely notice
she had gone. Except for Martin, who would probably spend
the whole time not missing her, but hating her; not looking
forward to having her home and taking her out to one of their
favourite restaurants but imagining her sampling the delights of
some new French brasserie with a strange man.

Carol fluffed out her hair with her hands, sighing. Well, it
could not be helped. If she were going, she must leave the
house. There was just time left to ring Martin.

'Morecombe's.' She recognised Jody's voice and asked to be
put through to Martin. 'All right, Mum. Bye, have a good time,
and if you can't be good, be careful.'

'Jody!' Carol heard Martin's voice in the background. 'Put it
through now, please.'

'Martin,' Carol's voice was conciliatory, but it was no use.

'Carol, what do you want?'

'I just called to say good-bye.'

'I thought you did this morning.'

'Yes, well . . .'

'Well, have a good time. Work hard.' He could not resist the
sneer in his voice and hated himself for it. Dumb and miserable,
he gripped the telephone in a sweaty hand, longing to apologise
but unable to do so.

'Martin—' He could hear her anguish, but would not give an
inch. *If she loves me she wouldn't go. We don't need the money, she
doesn't need the work . . . swanning off with bloody Peterson, whoever*

*he might be, bloody Swede or something – affected bastard, a Swede buying a house in France . . .*

'Martin.' *So she was being gentle now, concerned and caring; well, if she cared . . .* 'Don't worry. I'll miss you.' *So why go?* 'Good-bye.'

He hung up without answering.

Carol was expecting to be met at the airport, and she was one of the first people from the flight to come blinking through the gates. Toulouse had a surprisingly small airport given its international status, and Carol was pleased at how quickly passengers were cleared by customs. She wondered if Peterson would be late, and as she looked at the clutch of people gathered round the doors felt her heart sink again. Which of these men was the one who would ruin her marriage and destroy her life for the sake of a few months' lust?

A tall, thin man with viciously receding hair and Canadian-style pilot's spectacles stepped forward. 'Excuse me, are you Mrs Morecombe?' Carol almost expected her heart to start thumping, but instead felt it relax in relief. This was not the one. This man with kind eyes and a worried brow could be a friend, she could see that at a glance, but would never be a threat.

In her gratitude to him for not being her undiscovered love she flashed him a smile of such warmth that he looked a little taken aback.

'Yes, I am,' she agreed. 'Mr Peterson? How nice to meet you.'

'Well, no – yes – well, yes, I am Peterson, but not the Peterson you are expecting,' said the man. 'I am his brother, Göstar. The owner of the house is Peter. He asked me to come so that he could have dinner ready for us. It's about forty minutes from here. Would you like a drink – or anything – before we set off?' Carol shook her head and Peterson took her bag and led her outside to the car park. Once on their way – in an old Mercedes with French number plates, she noticed – they settled into easy conversation, Peterson recapping what his brother had already told Carol about the house, and then moving on to more personal subjects.

He told her something of his brother, details Martin was longing to hear but which would only whip him into further rage. Peter Peterson was a widower whose wife had died of cancer three years earlier. She had been French, and an only child. The house was her parents', and her father had also recently died. The Peterson family (there were two children) had lived in Sweden but now that the children had inherited the house Peterson felt he owed it to them to educate them at least for a while in France so that they did not feel strangers to that part of their heritage. Gösta said that his brother was in two minds about the move, but was determined to try French life for a year or two at least. He was an architect, a partner in a Stockholm company, and was as much worried at how he could organise his working life as his social life.

Despite herself Carol found herself impressed at the sound of this man who was obviously both successful and family-minded, who could make a grand gesture to the memory of a dead wife . . .

In the overheated car she began to doze, half day-dreaming, half dreaming about a tall, handsome Swede and his laughing, vivacious, dying French wife.

She came to with a jolt as the car pulled up in front of a large rectangular pinkish brick house with long windows. The front of the house was bare except for a huge campsis vine, its tubular red flowers magnificent in the dusky light, which grew up and around a pair of windows to the right of the front door. An avenue of plane trees led up to a dusty open space in front of the house. To the right was a field of maize, to the left a small area of vines, a patch of dusty-looking gladioli and a scrappy vegetable patch.

Gösta saw her looking and explained, 'Apparently by the end the old man laid everybody off and was more or less self-sufficient. He assumed Peter would sell the place as soon as he died so didn't bother to keep it up. Sad, really. Wait till you see inside.' As he retrieved her case from the back of the car the front door opened and a man came out. Greyer than Gösta, he nevertheless had a strong look of his brother. Where Carol had led herself to expect a tragic hero, though, was a man with an arrogant air. Gösta looked more like a grieving widower than did Peter, who was dressed in well-cut green linen trousers and a white silk shirt. This was not the man either, Carol could see that at a glance.

'Mrs Morecombe,' he came forward with his hand stretched out, smiling his welcome. 'I'm so sorry I didn't meet you myself.'

'Not at all. And it's Carol.'

He led her through the door and into the hall, and all at once Carol forgot about Martin and his fears and these personable Swedes and was caught up in the house.

The hall, papered in dark brown stripes and cluttered with heavy carved wooden furniture, was smaller than in an equivalent English house, but was well-proportioned. Stairs came down in a single elegant sweep and five doors, set in pretty curved door frames, led off the hall. Through one Carol could see a large room with three full length windows, an elaborate early nineteenth century marble fireplace and beautiful plasterwork decoration – mid-eighteenth century, Carol guessed – around the cornice.

Peter followed her eyes and laughed. 'You are a true professional, Carol. Come into the music room and I will pour you a drink. I will give you a real tour of the house in the morning, but you have already seen my favourite room.'

Stepping into the room, politely accepting a glass of local white wine ('the French hate sherry, but they do make this round here, which is extraordinarily like') Carol wondered for a moment why this drawing room, which did not boast so much as an upright piano, should be called the music room. Then she saw that the plasterwork, heavily over-painted in a dirty white gloss, actually showed different musical instruments. There was a pair of violins, a harp, some kind of percussion instrument, some cornets, all bedecked with garlands and what looked like small birds. Never mind that it was papered in what looked like a fifties boarding-house grey print, or that the covers of the hard upright French sofas were torn and the carpets ragged, this was a room of immense charm and possibility. Carol looked at the Peterson brothers, her eyes shining.

'It's wonderful,' she said, and they nodded agreement.

'But remember,' said Peter.

'No chintz,' she interrupted with a smile. 'Not a hint of it. Oh, what fun.'

Martin thought that he was making a valiant effort to overcome the waves of jealousy which washed over him almost continuously while Carol was away. He joked with the girls, checked that Piers's itinerary was being followed and that he was eating properly, took Alan out to the pub for a drink while Jody and Dulcie prepared supper. He had worked hard and late that first day, sold a couple of properties which he had been longing to shift from his books. But whatever else he was doing he heard a constant refrain. *Carol's all right, wonder what he's like then . . . Peterson . . . I don't suppose she'll leave me for him, at least not straight away, too fond of the children – it would spoil everything . . . if she goes to live in France, or Sweden, it'll all be over. The children won't want anything to do with her* (he could not help a little gloating satisfaction at the thought of her misery, far from home, without her children, cut off from everything that had made her life worthwhile). *And her company . . . she won't be able to run that from Stockholm or wherever the bastard hangs out . . . and no one will employ her there, all they're interested in is white wood . . .*

So he comforted himself with the sureness of her return and tortured himself with thoughts of her infidelity. He thought of the body he knew so well sweating underneath a white, hairless, heaving Swede . . . the thought disgusted him, but he could not keep the image away.

*Not tonight*, he thought as he pulled the blankets up to his chin on the first night of Carol's absence. *She's not a tart, she won't have fallen for him quite so fast, she'll be putting up a token resistance, meeting his eyes, playing with the stem of her wineglass. She'll be flirting – oh God, how she can flirt – and he'll already know he's got her, the bastard . . .*

And so he fell asleep, and next morning, on waking, it started again. As he made toast, fried eggs for everyone, tried to make sense of the collapse of the Net Book Agreement with Dulcie, told Jody not to let him forget to ring a client about the Sutherland Street property, reminded Piers to pack an overnight bag to take with him to Jeremy's, greeted Deirdre as she arrived, negotiated the rush hour traffic, teased Jody about Adam Exton who was taking her out for the second time that night, all the time he was imagining the stage Carol and Peterson had reached in their affair.

At lunch, as he ate a Marks and Spencer cheese and celery sandwich and drank a can of Fuller's Bitter he saw Carol and Peterson eating *steack frites* and a green salad and sharing a carafe of red wine. He saw Peterson take Carol's arm as they left the restaurant and walked up the village street to the house. He saw Peterson showing Carol around the house, rushing through the kitchen, nodding at the sitting room, barely pausing in the study. He saw a silence fall over them as they made their way up the stairs, a silence born of secret desire and future guilt. He saw Peterson take Carol's arm again, saw Carol stiffen slightly – with nerves? lust? – as they approached a door to the left of the stairs . . .

'Dad!' It was obviously not the first time that Jody had tried to attract his attention. 'Dad!'

'Sorry, sweetheart,' he knocked back the warm tail-end of beer straight from the can. 'What is it?'

'Telephone.'

*So the bitch is putting a quick duty-call in first, is she?* 'Tell her I've gone out.'

'Her? It's Mr Pemberton-Jones. About the Victoria Street flat. He wants to make an offer.'

Martin looked at her blankly – *What is the girl talking about?* – and then brought himself back to his office, his work, his life.

'Shall I put it through?' Jody's finger hovered above the telephone.

'Yes, of course . . . Mr Pemberton-Jones, good morning. I'm sorry to have kept you.'

The house was everything Carol had hoped. It was well proportioned, with enough little quirks to make it really distinctive. As it stood, the heavy French furniture and dark pictures and wallpapers did their best to make the house gloomy, but Carol could see how easy it would be to let light and colour into the house. Peterson's two children, boys of thirteen and ten, had their own views of what should be done to the house, but once they were promised the run of the attic they were satisfied.

When she was decorating a house Carol always tried to find

out as much as possible about the family as a whole. It was important to her that a house should reflect the family, not its interior designer. Usually her brief was pitifully scant. 'Oh, I've three children. Emily's twelve and likes horses, Charlie's ten and he's away at school – um, I suppose he's quite interested in steam trains – and Lucy's five and likes pink. Oh, and Polly Pocket. Michael's got a collection of sporting prints he's very fond of so they'd better go in the gent's cloakroom.' And then Carol would discover that Michael's collection was a very rare set of late eighteenth century prints of tiger and elephant hunting in India which should have been given pride of place in the library at the very least.

With this job Carol had the advantage of getting to know the family and the house before she even had to begin work. She knew that Peterson wanted to keep all the dark old furniture partly because it was his children's, not his, to sell and partly because he felt that it belonged to the house.

'I don't know how well you know France,' he explained earnestly, 'or French houses at least. But they're very different from our Swedish homes, and even from your English ones. They don't seem to mind much about comfort, or the appearance of it. Everything is hard – the beds, the sofas, bare polished boards on the floors. But you'd be surprised how you get used to it. I suppose we're a bit like that in Sweden, but then we have much cleaner lines. We don't have useless things, dark things – I suppose we have our winters for darkness. They're much more cluttered than we are. Which is why I want to keep Jean-Luc and Christine's things. You can't make a house look or feel lived in when you start from scratch. And I want the boys to get a sense of their mother. They'll get it more from being surrounded by her furniture than they would from any amount of photographs.'

And so Carol began her work. She walked around the house with a notebook and sketchbook, drawing plans, writing descriptions of the old furniture, writing suggestions to herself. Occasionally the boys joined her, mildly curious at her activities, making mostly ridiculous suggestions in their sibilant, musical accents. Every now and again Peter accompanied her, his views becoming more decided as the first day went by, but his vision and Carol's were surprisingly close and as they talked their ideas solidified. It was Gösta, though, who spent most time with Carol. Silent, smiling, apologetic, he seemed just to like her company. He never offered advice or suggestions, never even asked much what she was doing, but more often than not she would find him pottering around with her. Carol felt very much at ease with him, liked his occasional flashes of self-deprecating humour, thought of him after a day or two as a friend. *But Martin would be pleased,* she thought, *he's more like a dog than a man.*

On Carol's last day Peter joined her in the kitchen, where she was inspecting the old range with a wrinkled forehead.

'It works perfectly well, we'll keep it,' he said, then added, 'I've come to tell you that I'm taking you to dinner with neighbours tonight – about twenty minutes away. Their family has lived here for ever, old friends of my wife Pauline's – as were the parents. I know I keep telling you how I don't want the house to lose its Frenchness, so the best thing is for you to see a similar house that's been properly lived in by a French family. And they're very nice. We'll have a delicious dinner and an enjoyable evening. You're probably getting bored with our company.' He spoke with the self-assurance of a good-looking man sure of his place in the world, and Carol smiled politely. She was not sure how much she wanted to be shown a pattern for the house but knew she had no choice. 'Lovely. I haven't anything very smart to wear—'

'This is the Tarn, not Wiltshire,' Gösta said scornfully. 'And you always look nice anyway.' Carol was taken aback at the unexpected compliment. *Well I shan't mention that to Martin.* 'I'll look forward to it. Now, about this range . . .'

'Martin?'

'Carol.' *Why am I so pleased to hear her voice when she's so treacherous?*

'I almost didn't recognise your voice.' *Oh God, it has, it's gone on the whole time I've been away.*

*Of course she didn't, she's listening to another voice now.* 'Oh, I've got a touch of hay fever.'

'Not again, you poor darling.' *Funny how he only gets hay fever when we have one of these crises.*

'It'll blow over, rain's forecast.' *As if you cared.*

'How are the children?' *Please stop talking with such a tight voice.*

'Fine.' *Please stop sounding so bloody bright.*

'Piers?' *Come on, Martin, help me.*

'I said – they're all fine.' *As if you've thought of us at all.*

'Any messages?'

'Nothing that can't wait.' *I'm not going to be your secretary if you forget I'm your husband.*

*This is ridiculous.* 'Martin, what's wrong?' *As if I didn't know.*

A pause.

'Carol . . . What's he like?'

And then twenty minutes of explanation, reassurance, even a few jokes, a few white lies. Until . . . 'Good-bye, darling. I'll see you tomorrow evening. Please stop worrying.' *I really think he's calmed down now.*

'Good-bye, sweetheart. See you tomorrow. We'll go out, shall we? I'll be back at six.' *Lying, heartless bitch. How could she do this to us?*

They drove the twenty minutes to Eric and Susanne Herivaux through a gloriously warm late summer evening. The light bathed the plain and the view went on for miles. Carol, feeling that this stage of the job was over and that now she was on holiday, relaxed beside Peter, drinking it all in. She felt happier about Martin than she had since leaving home and, though she was sure he was going to need another spell of reassurance on her return, was looking forward to seeing him. Maybe they should have Peter over to dinner when he was next in London. Then Martin would be able to see how uninterested they were in each other sexually.

'When will you next need to come?' Peter was asking her.

'I'll send you my ideas, swatches, samples and so forth, and then once you've agreed them I'll come back out and we'll get going. I would prefer to use my own people, because I know how they work and at what speed. They'll be easier to oversee. Of course, they'll need putting up, which is an extra expense . . .'

'It's not that I mind so much as that I was hoping to employ locals. But then I see your point . . . oh well, let's go with you

then. I've read *A Year in Provence*. We've room at the house; put
them up there if you don't mind.'

'Whatever you want. Anyway, given you approve my first
plans, I'll probably want to be back in about a month. I won't
stay with them all the time, I trust these people totally.'

'Fine. You're in charge. I would like to see everything started,
so we'll have to find a time convenient to us all. The boys are
due at their school in Sweden soon, but that won't be a problem.
I'll probably bring Birgitta with me.'

There was a small chuckle from the back of the car. 'Oh Peter,
so it's getting serious?'

Peter flashed an irritated look into his rearview mirror. 'Don't
be childish. If it were serious I wouldn't be moving here, but she's
got a right to come and see where I'll be. She's got decisions of
her own to make.'

*This is perfect*, thought Carol, listening to the brothers' bickering.
*Oh why did no one mention this Birgitta earlier . . .? Martin'll be so
pleased.* Happiness washed over her in waves. *I've calmed Martin
down. I'll be able to go back and tell him about Birgitta, beef her up
a bit if need be, and next time I'll be able to come out here without any
aggro and get to grips with this glorious, wonderful job. And maybe
Martin will have finally learned to believe me, and this will never
happen again. Maybe.*

*She sounded normal enough, didn't she? Not furtive or guilty or
distracted. Oh God, I'm a shit. How could I possibly distrust her?
Has she ever let me down? Well, I'm still not really sure about that
bastard Jewell. She swore blind there was nothing in it but that job
certainly took a fuck of a long time. For a maisonette, for Christ's sake.
And she admitted she'd had lunch with him a few times. Claimed he
was too busy to meet at the flat. Double bluff if you ask me. At any
rate he was rich enough to book a suite at the Ritz if he wanted . . .
she likes grand hotels, the sleazy bitch. I should have guessed when I
married her. . . . I suppose I shouldn't have married her. . . .*

*Oh God, what am I doing to us?*

They drove up a long drive, again lined with plane trees.

'Why are French roads lined with trees?' asked Gösta.

'Because the German army likes marching in the shade,' said

Peter, bored. 'God, that joke made my father-in-law angry. This bit of France was occupied and he was a prisoner of war. He did not see the funny side.'

Like Peter's house, Mirabeau, the drive ended in a dusty open space but here the owners had made a not-very-successful attempt at a lawn on each side, and sprinklers spurted sporadically over the yellowing grass.

Peter led the way into the house, calling out 'Eric?' as he did so. A tall man with a hooked nose, wearing a soft silk foulard and smelling essentially French – expensive scent overlaid with Gauloises – came from the back of the hall and greeted them.

'*Enchanté, Madame*,' he said on introduction and lifted Carol's fingers to within an inch of his mouth. 'I gather you are here to make over Mirabeau for Peter. It is a beautiful house, no? But it has been almost deserted for so long . . .' His English was perfect, the accent mid-Atlantic rather than French. 'Let me offer you an apéritif. But *un moment . . . Susanne? Tu viens? Ils sont arrivés*,' he called up the stairs.

At the same moment the front door opened and a woman carrying a huge bunch of parsley came in. 'Please excuse me, I just went to the vegetable garden, I forgot the . . .' she gestured at the herb in her hand and laughed, 'the word.'

'Parsley,' said another voice from the top of the stairs and they all turned.

'Henri!' Eric took a step forward, smiling. 'Let me introduce you to my neighbour, Peter Peterson, his brother Gösta and Madame Morecombe, Carol . . .'

*Oh God*, thought Carol, watching the man come down the stairs towards them. *Oh God oh Jesus, it's happened. This is it.*

# 7

They had all drunk too much on empty stomachs and then not
eaten very much of their Italian dinner and drunk some more
and decided to go on to a night-club. Even Dulcie, who had a
strong head, felt fairly light-headed by the time the six of them
giggled their way into a taxi and asked the driver to take them
to the King's Road. Still, she did not have to be at work until
twelve the next day and she felt that a good dance would work
some of the alcohol out of her system.

Giles and Dulcie were by now an accepted couple. Most of
Jody's set were surprised. Giles rarely had a girlfriend; he was
more likely to disappear with an unknown blonde he had picked
up somewhere and then not be seen around for a week or two
until he was bored. He was easily bored, they all knew. What,
then, was he doing with Dulcie, who had proved to be more fun
than any of them had expected but who was small and dark and
sometimes serious?

'She just doesn't know how to make the best of herself,' her
new girlfriends sighed. So how on earth had she managed to
catch Giles? It was an unanswerable question. 'For Christ's sake,
she can milk a cow!' one of Giles's friends had said when Giles
turned down the idea of an evening's catting, and had been
taken aback at the vicious flash in Giles's eyes as he reiterated
his refusal.

For Giles was not bored by Dulcie, nor she by him. They
still spent most evenings with a group of friends, but Giles
found Dulcie very easy to be alone with. At the weekends,
when she was not working, he showed her another side of
London. They would go north to Hampstead Heath and walk

in its almost-countryside for hours, having lunch in a pub or sometimes, while the weather was still warm enough, buying a Marks and Spencer picnic and a bottle of wine and eating and drinking under a tree off one of the many beaten paths.

Dulcie was horrified when Giles told her of Hampstead Heath's darker side – the furtive homosexual pick-ups, the beatings and the murders. How could it be the same place as this refuge for London families, where dogs and children ran so happily in the early autumn sun? London was wicked underneath, after all.

Giles laughed at her. 'Don't be silly, pet. Myra Hindley buried those children on the Yorkshire Moors. Nowhere's as pure as you'd have it.' It irritated Dulcie when Giles called her 'pet'. It was a north-eastern endearment he had picked up and it came uneasily from his mouth. She wished he would stop it.

They walked to the top of Primrose Hill, and saw London spread out at their feet and a spaniel chasing a tennis ball down the long, long slope and gallop gamely up again. Or Giles would take her to Hammersmith, where they walked along the river bank and had lunches in different pubs and saw a different sort of person – fewer families, younger couples, but older than them, looking married, probably in their first houses, thinking about babies rather than having them.

Giles loved Dulcie's habit of spinning tales around the people she saw and would encourage her to fantasise about them. 'They all look the same to me,' he admitted. 'Mostly boring.'

'Oh, but you're *wrong*. Except when you're right and then you're even more wrong.'

'You've got me there,' he said, puzzled.

'Well, of course you think a lot of people are boring, and in a way you're right, but what you mean is that their lives are boring and you're assuming that because their lives are boring, they are. But then, you see, I wonder why their lives are boring and, even more, whether *they* think their lives are boring. And if so, why do they live them as they do? Do you see?'

'A bit.'

'Well, they're doing their "boring" jobs and decorating their "boring" houses and going to bed with their "boring" wives, or maybe their "boring" secretaries, and bringing up their almost certainly "boring" children – but what's going on in their heads?

Nearly everybody has some second life, fantasies don't have to be sexual. What's interesting is what they do all these routine things *for*, what keeps them going. There must be some hope, or some passion. Otherwise they'd be just the same as ants.'

'Aren't they?'

'*No!*' But then she saw he was teasing her and she grinned. 'Well, OK, you've got me on my hobby horse. But that's why I like inventing people's lives for them – I build up a picture of their real life, and then I imagine their second, secret life. The French call it *la vie interieure.*'

Giles, who was not sure whether he had much of an 'interior life' himself, felt suddenly wistful. 'And do you give them all happy endings?'

'Good Lord, no! Where would be the fun in that?' And they laughed and held hands and were happy.

They talked a lot about each other's lives. Giles found himself envious of Dulcie's family, of the siblings and cousins and assurance that the same people would always be in the same place and always pleased to see you. He tried to describe his childhood to Dulcie. It was like so many others, he thought, but so very different from Dulcie's. The army officer father, the mother whose career was as a military wife, the endless moves, so that school sometimes seemed more like home than home. He had loved his prep school, suffered his public school (Uppingham) with equanimity, thoroughly enjoyed his university career at Exeter. He had a sister, only two years older than him, but they had never been close. Too many years spent apart early on had done their damage. He admitted that when the family was together – which probably only happened twice a year – the whole occasion invariably felt forced. 'We're so busy trying to get on, to have fun for each other's sakes, that we all show off and dislike each other for it.'

'If you saw each other more often it would be easier,' said Dulcie.

'Yes, but then none of us is motivated enough to do it. I don't know—' then he looked at her, suddenly alert. 'Well, would you mind having dinner with my sister one night?'

'No, of course not.' If her brothers had lived nearer, Dulcie would be seeing them all the time. Meeting a boyfriend's family was natural to her, meant nothing special. But seeing Giles's face Dulcie realised it meant rather more to him, and she panicked. 'It'd be a step in the right direction,' she said, as lightly as she could.

Meanwhile the evenings with the group continued, light-hearted, noisy, self-indulgent, and now here they all were, spilling out into the King's Road, arguing half-heartedly about who would pay the taxi fare, Giles and Adam Exton going through the dark doors first and signing the others in, the cigarette smoke and the music hitting them in the face like a wall. *Oh God*, thought Dulcie, suddenly sober, *why did I come?* And then Giles's brown gaze met hers and he took her onto the dance floor and she knew why she had come and wondered if she was in love with him. *I don't think so, I'd know, wouldn't I, unless maybe grown-up love is different, unless it creeps up on you, comes after lust rather than with or before it. I can't imagine wanting to marry him, so I can't be in love, but then I can't really imagine marrying anybody (God I'm hot; I need a drink) but I can't imagine how I'd like him any different, either (if only he'd stop calling me Pet). I suppose it's time I went home again – I'll take him with me next time . . .*

'Drink?'

'Yes, please. Do you want to come up to Durham with me next weekend?'

Giles was taken aback – she had been dancing as if her life depended on it, but what had been going through her mind? He thought at first that he had misheard her, but saw she was standing in the middle of the dance floor waiting for an answer.

'Yes, please,' he said, and, feeling unreasonably elated, led her from the dance floor toward the bar.

*Well, I've gone and done it now*, thought Dulcie. *Oh heck, I hope it's not too sticky . . .*

She and Giles sat at a small round table and watched Jody and Adam dancing energetically but not, in Adam's case, particularly well, which was odd. He seemed distracted, and then a man Dulcie did not know (but who Giles seemed to recognise) came up to him and gestured and Adam nodded and seemed to excuse himself to Jody who also nodded and came over to join Giles and Dulcie. Phil and Lottie came back with a bottle of champagne. 'We're celebrating,' grinned Lottie.

'Blimey, you must be. Champagne costs a bomb here,' said Jody, looking over her shoulder for Adam.

'We're going to move in together,' said Lottie, triumphant. Phil, shamefaced, muttered, 'Well, why pay two rents . . .?'

Dulcie, who did not think of herself as particularly romantic, felt unaccountably disappointed in them. *Lottie looks pleased with herself, not happy. And if you have to justify any kind of commitment as a financial deal – where's the romance there?* She looked from one to the other. *This one's really got me. Maybe that's all it is, a deal, a temporary arrangement. Easy sex, protection, companionship, sharing costs . . . It's not going to be like that for me . . . So what is it going to be like?* 'Yes, I'd love a glass, thanks' *I can't say 'congratulations' – what would I be congratulating them on?* 'Yes, congratulations!' *Well, it's what they want – and I suppose Lottie does look pleased . . .* 'So when are you going to move in? His flat or yours?' *Does this mean they're engaged? I suppose I shouldn't ask them . . .* 'Does this mean you're engaged?'

'No!' Phil and Lottie agreed.

'She's an old-fashioned girl,' Giles said, almost proudly, a proprietorial hand on Dulcie's neck.

'Sweet, isn't it?' teased Jody, snuggling on the banquette into the crook of Adam's arm. 'Got it, Adam?'

'Of course.' He grinned and handed a small piece of paper to her. 'Ladies first.'

'Come on then, girls,' said Jody, disentangling herself and getting to her feet. Lottie stood up too but Dulcie, slower, asked, 'Where?'

'The loo, of course. Come on.'

Dulcie, unsure but obedient, followed her cousin through the sweating bodies to the ladies'.

'Right, we'd better be quick. Lottie, the door.' Lottie leaned against the door and Jody unfolded the small piece of paper to show a mound of white powder. Moving quickly, she pulled a razor blade from her make-up bag and chopped swiftly on the fake marble basin surround. 'A fiver, Dulcie.' Dulcie couldn't move, just watched horrified. *'Dulcie!'* Jody hissed. 'Oh, all right – Lottie?' Lottie had the note rolled and ready, and Dulcie watched as Jody sniffed some of the line up each nostril. The girls changed places with Dulcie still rooted to the spot. Then it was her turn. Lottie passed her the fiver. 'Come on, quick.'

'I – I can't.'

'What do you mean – quick.'

'Just stick it up your nose and breathe in,' said Lottie, giggling.

'I can't,' Dulcie repeated.

'Oh, for Christ's sake, we're going to get caught.'

Dulcie handed the note back to Lottie. 'Oh well, goody goody, more for us,' she said and snorted half of the remaining line.

Just as Jody finished the last of it and was standing rubbing her finger over the surface to pick up any remaining traces of the drug, the door opened and two girls walked in giggling. Dulcie jumped and then froze with fear. 'Oooh, lucky them,' said one of the girls and she and her friend giggled again.

'I don't know what you mean,' said Jody grandly and led the way from the room with a magnificent sweep. Lottie followed, laughing, and Dulcie crept behind.

When they rejoined the others at the table it was as though nothing had happened. 'All right, girls?' Adam said cheerfully as Jody passed the packet back. 'Come on, lads.' Giles looked at Dulcie, but she would not meet his eye. He hesitated, then followed the other two out.

'Dulcie, for God's sake, what's the big deal?'

'The big deal? Drugs. Hard drugs.'

'So? It wasn't harming anyone. A little coke now and then isn't going to hurt anyone. It's not smack, for heaven's sake. It helps us to relax.'

'Relax? Bullshit. You were all as jumpy as cats afterwards.'

'OK, it helps us to enjoy ourselves. You should have tried some, you'd see.'

Dulcie faltered. Perhaps he was right, but he couldn't be. It went against everything she thought she knew to suppose that taking drugs was all right.

'Dulcie, you must have seen people take coke before. Where have you been all your life?'

'Under a cowpat,' she flashed, truly angry at his patronising tone. 'Where do you think?'

'Have you really not?' Giles looked so amazed that Dulcie could not help but forgive him a little.

'Well, no. Honestly, there were hardly any drugs at Durham. A few people smoked joints sometimes, you know, the arty crowd, but no, nothing more. Although Newcastle—'

'Oh aye, there's a big city,' said Giles in an execrable Geordie accent.

'Oh, fuck off Giles.' She flung away from him.

'Dulcie, I'm sorry.' Giles caught her up and grabbed her arm, stopping her in her tracks and turning her towards him. He had met her from work unexpectedly, knowing how angry and confused she had been when he left her the night before. She had been surprised to see him, even grateful. It was unlike him to cross London without warning, except for that first time. They usually met on neutral ground at pre-arranged places, more on his terms than hers. *I hadn't noticed that before, but it's true. Still, he is trying now – I suppose I should listen.* She relaxed and he, feeling her body change, put his arm around her shoulders. 'Shall we go and have a drink somewhere?'

'No, I'd rather walk.'

They made their way along Kensington High Street towards Kensington Gardens. The clocks had just gone back and now, at seven, it was almost dark. The shops looked bright and welcoming, the first red and green signs of Christmas beginning to appear. They walked for a while without talking. The fruit and flower seller at the corner of Wright's Lane was shutting down and Giles bought two big bunches of blue irises and handed them to Dulcie.

'I'll give you a knockdown price at this time of day,' the seller said.

'Then I'd better buy another bunch, I don't want her thinking I'm a cheapskate,' Giles said and Dulcie smiled for the first time.

They walked on, past Marks and Spencer's and Barker's and the normally beckoning row of clothes shops. At the corner of Young Street Dulcie bought some roasted chestnuts. 'Thackeray lived in that house,' she said, nodding down the street and

Giles took a chestnut, feeling companionable but not really interested.

'So maybe none of you is going to become a junkie or die or anything,' she said at last, returning to the subject occupying both their minds. 'But I just don't get it. Weren't we having a good time before?'

'Yes, and you don't mind drinking, do you?'

'No, but—'

'There isn't a but, I promise you. There really is no difference. It gives you a buzz, makes everything clearer. You *perform* better, somehow. It makes you sharper.'

'Makes you feel sharper. It's not the same.'

'Well, maybe not. But it makes you feel better about yourself.'

Dulcie thought a bit. 'Do you take it often?'

'Not very, no. If it's around, I don't say no.'

'Do you ever buy it yourself?'

Giles hesitated, but he wanted to be truthful. 'Yes. If I'm going to a big party or something. Always at weddings.' He grinned. 'Dulcie, I don't want to force you, but if you tried it once you'd see how harmless it is. Honestly.'

'And what then? Heroin?'

'No. Don't be silly.' Giles looked genuinely offended and Dulcie smiled and took his hand.

'All right.'

'All right you'll try?'

'No. All right I won't get so het up. Do the others take it a lot?'

'I don't know.'

'Jody?'

'Like me, if it's around.'

'Does Aunt Carol know?'

'How should I know? She probably doesn't think about it. Parents are good at not thinking about things they won't like, you know.'

Dulcie was not sure her own parents were quite so obligingly ostrich-like, but she did not argue. *And I have to admit (although I won't) that I'm curious – perhaps it wouldn't hurt to try . . .*

'So can you honestly say you don't know anyone who takes too much? And what about other stuff?'

'None of our lot takes heroin, if that's what you mean. I suppose most of them take E, it's easier to come by than coke, but I don't like it half as much.'

Dulcie felt numbed by all this. And then she noticed – 'You didn't say if anyone takes too much.'

He did not answer for the second time, so she guessed. 'Not Jody?'

'God, no. She's entirely recreational.'

'Well, who?'

'Oh, no-one.'

'Giles, who?'

'No. No-one.' She did not believe him, but left it at that. Her senses were bruised enough; the combination of a hangover from the night before, a sleepless night, and the emotional turmoil of the day had left her exhausted.

They stood by Round Pond and watched as a standard poodle jumped into the water, scattering geese in front of him.

'Oh, I don't know . . .' Dulcie turned away and Giles followed.

'Dulcie? Now that you know the worst about me, am I still invited to Durham for the weekend?'

'You wouldn't—?'

'Of course not.'

She smiled wanly. 'Of course you are.'

'Thank you.' He put his arm around her and they walked quietly out of the park.

And so now Carol was in the position Martin had so often foretold and she had so vehemently insisted could never come about.

She and Henri had barely talked that night, and she had been able to perform perfectly. The Petersons and the Herivaux had laughed and talked, gossiped about local life and engaged in angry discussion about politics. Carol had joined in, enjoyed herself even, but every sense was tuned into Henri. She could not understand what was happening, wondered if she had just worried herself into an emotional state where this was bound to happen. But then why Henri? Why not the dogged, friendly Gösta or the good-looking, elegant Peter? Why not Eric Herivaux or the man in the restaurant or the driver on the number 28 bus? Was this really happening or was she imagining it? *And what's going on in his mind?* She looked furtively across the table at him and caught him looking silently at her: she dropped her eyes, he did not. *Something is. He's looking at me, he's thinking about me. God, what's going on? I'm like a teenager. I must be past this. Oh Martin, why aren't you here? It would have happened anyway, even if he was here. Nothing could have stopped this. Except not coming. Oh God, I wish I'd left this evening. I could have, I've done everything I need to do. Oh shit. Never mind, I'm going tomorrow. I need never see him again. I'll just put the whole ridiculous business out of my mind. Of course I'll be able to, nothing's happened, there's nothing to put out of my mind. I'm going to go to bed with him – what? Where did that come from. Of course not. Oh God.*

And all the while she laughed and joked.

Peter drove her to the airport. They were up early and after a sleepless night and a glass too many of cognac, taken to help her sleep, Carol felt dreadful.

Peter helped her with her bag, kissed her on both cheeks, thanked her again for her 'inspiration and understanding' and drove off. Carol turned and walked into the airport terminal. Only one desk was open for checking in, and Carol walked towards it. A tall, thin figure was standing at it and the back of his neck was already painfully familiar. Carol stopped in her tracks and her heart's somersaults made her feel sick. She had to turn away, wanted to step forward, could do neither. *This is ridiculous – what am I afraid of?* Before she could force her mind to make a decision or her muscles to move, Henri turned away from the desk. Their eyes met. Carol smiled brightly and was at last able to step forward.

'Henri, what a coincidence,' she said.

'Not at all,' he answered. 'I knew this must be the flight you'd be on.'

And Carol knew that she was lost.

Where there had been silence between them the night before, there was now complete openness. They sat beside each other on the aeroplane, and talked all the way home. *It's so easy*, thought Carol, amazed, *I don't need to explain anything, it's almost as though he knows it all already.* And they laughed, and they talked some more.

They did not touch, not once. There they sat, side by side in the economy section of a small plane, and they did not so much as bump knees or graze elbows. *That will come later*, Carol knew. *God help me, I can't walk away from it now.*

She sat with a gin and tonic, pretending to read *Vogue*, her mind full of Henri, her ears straining for the sound of the front door. *He'll be back soon, and he'll want to know about Gösta and Peter. Well, that's all right, no problem there, I've nothing to hide. So why do I feel so uncomfortable? Grow up, Carol, you're as guilty as if you'd already done it. Maybe, but I haven't, have I? Who says I'm going to? I may never see him again. If I don't turn up at lunch tomorrow, that'll be that . . . but I'm going to, aren't I – (is that him, or someone pushing a freebie through the letterbox?). If it were anyone but Martin, I would just say I'd met this nice man and there would be nothing more to it. Oh Martin, I'm a bitch, it's not your fault, how could it possibly be your fault, you were right all along, you know me better than I do myself, that's all. (Shall I have another gin? I'd better not, not before Martin gets back.) Where are you, Martin? I just want to get this over with – once I've seen him, once he knows I'm innocent with Peter, innocent all round, then I can meet him in the eye and get on with it – with what? with my marriage, my life, my adultery? Adultery – oh shit, what a word, but what a thing . . . they say it's easy after the first time . . . or is that murder? Both probably. Oh God, what am I thinking of? I love Martin. I've always loved Martin, I always will – how can I even think of doing anything to destroy that? How can I not think of it? I can't not see Henri again. I have to see him. Leaving it now would be as dangerous as seeing him again – wouldn't it? Perhaps I will have that gin. I can't walk away from it, I must resolve it, and seeing him is the only way. Oh Martin, please come home—*

And there it was. The click of the door. The pause while he picked up the afternoon post from the hall table. The heavy tread of his step up to the first floor where she cowered with her gin.

'Carol?'

As the door opened she stood, and took two quick paces into his arms. 'Carol?' He tried to step back to see her but she had buried her head in his shoulder. As she hugged him she felt a surge of love for him, and she clung to him.

'Carol? You're shaking.'

Then she stepped back and looked up at him and kissed his cheek. 'I've missed you,' she said, and it was the truth.

*What's all this about?* Martin wondered. *She's normally so cool . . . it's not that bloody Swede, I hope,* but for once something in her face stopped him from asking. *No, it's not. She told the truth. She always does.* And he gathered her to him again.

'Mum?' They had both forgotten Jody. 'Hey – what's with the smooching? You've only been gone a few days. How was it, Mum?' Jody gave her mother a quick hug and her father a puzzled look. He had been tetchy for three days, getting crosser and crosser as the time for Carol's return drew nearer, and now here he was all sweetness and light . . . odd things, grown-ups, you never knew where you were with them.

'Hello, Jode. Yes, it was lovely. So what's the news round here?'

*She's not telling us much.* Martin was immediately suspicious, but then, watching her pour drinks for the three of them – *unlike her to have had one already* – he remembered all the times she had come home and he had picked arguments, accused her, cold-shouldered her . . . *who can blame her, I've cocked it up so often* . . . 'Tommy's a thing of the past, but Jody's not heartbroken, she's got someone else in tow already,' he said. *Jody must have got her flighty heart from someone,* it occurred to him, and he looked at Carol again.

'Oh yes?'

'Adam Exton,' Martin said, taking his whisky and soda and waiting for Carol's reaction.

'No! I thought he was round here to see Dulcie.'

'Mum!' Jody looked pained and her parents laughed.

'Well, why not? Julia's her godmother and—'

'You don't have to go out with your parents' godchildren, Mum. Anyway, it turns out you've known his mother for ever – why did you keep them under your hat?'

'I don't know, we lost touch – we used to go there a bit when you were little, don't you remember? Anyway, think of it this way – if you'd been childhood friends you wouldn't be romancing now. So isn't the agony of those missed years worth it?'

'Romancing? Oh, Mum,' Jody rolled her eyes in mock horror.

*What does Carol know about romance? Chucking words like that around – lust is more it, I suppose.*

'Anyway, Dulcie and I've been invited down to Somerset in a couple of weeks' time. They've invited Giles, too, which is very *modern* of them,' Jody teased. 'Separate rooms, I bet, though.'

'Jody!' Carol warned. She often had to pretend not to hear the front door slamming early in the morning. 'So Giles and Dulcie . . . I've always thought him rather nice. It's serious, is it?'

'Don't think so. Although she's serious anyway and I must admit I've never known Giles like this. Perhaps it is.' Jody sounded surprised. 'Although there was a dodgy moment the other night.'

'Oh yes?' Jody did not often sit down alone with her parents and Carol was enjoying the moment *and this is the kind of thing I'll be risking,* she thought, and an inner voice answered *You're seriously thinking of missing out on Henri for the sake of half an hour with your daughter once every two months? Don't be silly.*

Martin did not join in the conversation much – a token effort every now and again. To the outside eye he was a man relaxing at the end of the day, drink in hand, watching benevolently as his women folk gossipped. Of course it was nothing like that. He was watching Carol, not Jody – there were no surprises for him in Jody, no fears now that she was grown. When Jody was a baby, a small child, he would lie awake at night imagining the terrors that life would bring her, would envisage her death, her funeral . . . everything from cot death, through meningitis, to drowning, car accidents – ahead to a future of drugs, illegitimate babies, the Moonies. Then the worries stopped and now he trusted her; despite her carefree approach to life he felt sure she was sound, would look after herself, come to no real harm. But Carol . . .

He sensed a shift in Carol, could not really understand it. Before, he had always been so sure of himself, certain that he knew Carol so well he could tell how she would behave under any given circumstance. (Never mind that he had so often misjudged her – that was part of his temporary insanity, his jealousy. He would always push the memory of that aside.) Now, watching her, he felt at sea. She was telling the truth, he was sure – so what was going on? And why, for the first time ever, was he so wary of confronting her? *We've always been able to talk*, he thought, little imagining how his idea of talking had worn Carol down over the years. *Why can't I talk now?*

'So he was Gösta silly Swede?' he asked, out of the blue in a Peter Sellers joke voice.

Jody and Carol stopped, stared, laughed. 'Yes, Gösta silly Swede,' Carol agreed, relieved. The crisis had passed. She had got away with it. *With what? I haven't done anything.* 'And his brother Peter was Gösta heavy petter,' she added in a facetious fake sing-song, saw Martin's face darken, lighten again, laugh. *It's all right, it's over . . . and this time there won't be a next time . . . unless I make one . . .*

# 8

Giles swayed down the train aisle with his hands full of drinks and snacks. Dulcie, watching him, loved him very briefly. *Wouldn't the others be surprised if they saw him now? He does look after me, I'll give him that. And it's funny but I think he's a bit nervous. Well, he won't be when he gets there. No-one could be nervous of Ma and Pa.*

It was only the second time that Dulcie had been home since living in London and she was looking forward to seeing them all again. Looking out of the window she noticed, as she had not in the city, how autumn was making way for winter. A brisk wind swirled the piles of dead leaves, dirty and brown now rather than the fiery oranges and reds of a short while ago, under the hedges. Horses stood together under bare trees, their backs into the wind. She hoped it would be fine over the weekend, planned to get Sam to take Giles duck shooting, knew she could trust her mother not to be embarrassing.

She smiled at Giles and made room on the table for his goodies. 'You'll have to eat your dinner, you know. Ma'll have gone to town,' she teased.

'No problem.' *Oh, that fake Geordie accent again. He mustn't do that at home, I'll die.*

Giles saw her reaction. 'My dove, you can trust me,' he drawled, and she smiled.

'So what's the form?' he asked for the eighth time, and once again Dulcie described the house, warned him that there would be nothing much to do but that if he wanted to be popular he need only offer his services to Sam or her father, said they would probably go to the local before dinner the next night, Ma might've invited some people round, but to remember it was all relaxed, informal . . .

'Oh Giles, we're nearly there. Now look, you must look out of the right hand window, it'll be lit by now, oh *look!*'

Dulcie fell silent, held her breath, was still moved by the beauty of her home town. She looked out of the window with all her heart, and only when the train drew to a halt did she jump up, grab at Giles's arm, laugh, 'Come on, it'll go with us, quick – there's Sam.' And, as they tumbled off the train with their bags, she said to him, 'Well, what do you think?'

'You're right – very pretty,' and she saw that he was not looking at the cathedral and castle, lit up against the sky, but at her.

They sat around the big kitchen table, all talking at once, laughing and joking and bickering. Giles seemed relaxed, polite to Dulcie's parents yet totally at ease. John watched him, thought he liked what he saw; Molly thought him good-looking, he reminded her of men she had known in her youth; Mary flirted with him and showed off and hugged Dulcie. She had been allowed to stay up for dinner as a treat and was carried away by the whole experience. They ate lamb hotpot and red cabbage and Giles was genuinely astonished to learn that everything on their plates had come from the farm. 'That was Cindy,' Molly said as she gave Giles more lamb. 'I don't know why, but she ended up a bit tough. No good for roasting at all; she's had to go into stews and hotpots.' Giles looked at Mary tucking in happily and thought of London children who toyed with vegetarianism before they were ten.

'And I did the cream,' Mary announced as she passed the jug for the apple crumble.

'Did you?' Dulcie hugged her.

'Yes, she's doing very well in the dairy now, aren't you, sweetheart?'

Dulcie did not speak much, she was tired and happy to be home but suddenly tense to see Giles in their midst. He appeared to be fitting in very well but to her, who knew him well, he was standing back from those around him. There was a distance in his eyes that she did not like.

Her father began discussing something to do with the farm with Sam and Ben, and suddenly Dulcie saw what a load of hicks they really were. She looked again at the big scrubbed table, the stone floor, the aged Aga. Drying clothes hung from a rack pulled up to the ceiling over the range, a spaniel steamed gently and smelly beside it. The dresser was in a terrible muddle, china stacked anyhow, bills and books and packets of sheep hypodermics tumbling over each other. The sofa in the corner matched the curtains, but the print was a garish seventies design of swirling orange and pink flowers. All at once it looked scruffy and dated, not cheerful and welcoming.

And her family? Of course they were dear to her, but what would she think if she had never met them before? Looking at her mother it was impossible to believe that she and Carol were sisters. In honour of Giles, Molly had at least changed, but her old corduroy skirt was much the same murky green as her trousers had been and no smarter. She wore opaque blue tights and a green and blue jersey that had once been quite expensive. Her hair was a mess of uncared for waves, greying slightly now. Her skin was not good any more, slightly reddened and dry, but her blue eyes were bright with humour and understanding. Dulcie watched as her mother served out big platefuls of crumble. Her hands were rough, the nails short and broken. She was younger than Carol, for heaven's sake. Dulcie thought of the glass shelves in her aunt's bathroom, the expensively packaged tubes of moisturiser and cleanser and toner and revitaliser and Lord knew what lined up as neatly as in a shop. Then she thought of her mother's pot of Pond's cold cream which she scarcely ever remembered to use. She thought of the differences between their lives, their wardrobes, and smiled. She loved them both, but sometimes found herself wishing Molly were just a little more like Carol. *No wonder she doesn't come to London more often: she just wouldn't fit in. Uncle Martin's fond of her – so's Aunt Carol. But what do they talk about? They can't possibly have anything in common at all.*

After dinner Sam and John went out to check the stock for the last time that night and Giles, acting according to instructions, offered to accompany them.

'Are you sure?' Sam looked askance at Giles's suit – he had caught the train straight from work and had not yet changed.

'Well,' Giles looked pleased to be let off the hook. 'Maybe tomorrow.'

'Oh go on, Giles, borrow some boots and take off your jacket,' Dulcie urged. She did want Sam to like him. He got up with a good enough grace and followed the others out.

'Tell you what, let's go rabbiting,' Ben suggested, pushing back his chair. 'Let's take the Subaru and a couple of guns.'

The door shut behind them and Molly laughed. 'I'm not sure how much that plan will appeal to your young man. Come on, Mary, love, up to bed. I'll come and tuck you up in ten minutes.'

Dulcie had flushed at the implied criticism of Giles. 'It's not Giles's fault.'

'What?' Molly began stacking plates and Dulcie filled the sink with hot water and bubbles.

'Well, you know . . .'

'That he's a Londoner? Of course not. There's nothing wrong with that, or him. Don't be touchy, Dulcie.'

Dulcie washed up for a while in silence, but she had never been a sulker. 'So do you like him?'

Molly spoke carefully. 'Yes, I think I do. He's obviously soft on you. And he's made quite a fine lady out of you.'

Dulcie felt she was being got at, but could not resist. 'What do you mean?'

Molly looked at her, then laughed. 'I think you may have lost the last trace of your accent now.' It was not just that, though, Molly thought, studying her daughter carefully. A distance had grown up between Dulcie and the rest of them. She seemed a little detached. But perhaps that was as it should be . . . 'You feel quite at home in London now?'

'Oh yes, I love it, Mam.' *It's not often she calls me that any more*, Molly thought; *I hope she's happy.* 'But this is home.' She hugged Molly, who laughed, 'Dulcie, you're all soapy!'

Dulcie hugged her back, but her thoughts were her own. *Of course it's still my home, but I don't think I want to come back here after all. Or at any rate not yet. I want more time in London, on my own. Maybe I'll come back one day, but maybe Ma's right. Maybe I don't fit in here so much any more . . .*

Dulcie was up very early the next morning, early enough to go out to the field and bring in the house cow. With her cheek against the cow's warm flank, finding her London fingers had not lost the rhythm of milking, Dulcie had no more fears about fitting in. *Of course this is home, London is miles away – from here, from me. It's good to see Sam again. I wish I could persuade him to come down for a while, but maybe not. What would he do there? We're better off seeing each other here . . . what am I on about? He'd fit in anywhere, get on with everyone . . .*

She carried a jug of warm milk into the kitchen and put it on the kitchen table. Her mother was there, laying up for breakfast. 'I saw you'd gone out and guessed you were with Jemima. She recognise you?'

'I don't know – she seemed happy enough to let me milk her.' Dulcie went through to the stone-floored, slate-shelved larder and came back with a ham, and a bowl of stewed fruit. Together they put out the enormous feast that the men would expect when they came back in at eight thirty. They worked together companionably, talking about not much – local gossip, family talk. *Oh, she's all right*, thought Molly in relief. *There's nothing to worry about. This Giles is a nice enough boy, but he's not the one who'll take her away from here.*

The family had breakfast together, without Giles who did not make an appearance until eleven. He strolled downstairs in dry-cleaned corduroys, a thick green jersey and well-polished brogues. *Now I fit in*, he seemed to be saying, and casually fried himself an egg. By now Dulcie was livid with shame and embarrassment. 'Well, he is washing up after himself,' Molly muttered to her daughter, who was too cross to smile.

'About time for an ale,' Giles remarked, half an hour later, looking up from the newspaper which he had assumed with a proprietorial I-need-to-know-what's-happening-in-the-rest-of-the-world air. 'Fancy walking to the pub, pet?' Ben burst into laughter and left the room. Molly looked after his retreating back crossly and hissed, 'Shut up' to Mary who was preparing Brussels sprouts and sniggering.

'I don't think you'd want to,' Dulcie said icily from the sink, where she was peeling potatoes.

'Yes, let's. Take the dogs for a walk.' Mary sniggered again.

'Take the Brussels' leavings out to the pig bin, will you, Mary,' her mother said. 'Go on, Dulcie, why don't you take Giles to The

Fleece? Borrow the Cortina. Oh, I meant to tell you that Susie and Jeff said to tell you they'll be in The Victory tonight at seven. I told them you'd probably be along, we'll have dinner at nine.'

'I just don't see what I've done wrong,' Giles said, putting the drinks on the table and pulling up a stool.

'Oh Giles, really,' said Dulcie. She had barely spoken in the car, despite Giles's pleas to her to explain her bad mood.

'I've hardly said a word all morning, I've been fantastically polite to your mother . . .'

'My mother has been up since before seven. And so have I, incidentally. Breakfast is at eight thirty. After Pa and Sam have already put in almost two hours' work. No-one expects Londoners' (she put magnificent scorn into the word) 'to get up that early, but at the very least they shouldn't slop about cooking breakfast when their lunch is being prepared for them *before their very eyes*. How can that be polite?'

'Oh, I see. Yes, sorry.' Giles was subdued by this. He thought he had been doing rather well. This going to stay with a girlfriend's parents was new to him, and more of a minefield than he had expected. 'But actually, if you bother to think about it, you may remember that in the week I'm up at least as early as that. Farmers don't have the monopoly on early rising.'

'Yes. I'm sorry.' It was Dulcie's turn to apologise.

'*And* you told me to relax,' he added. 'And as you insisted we stay in our separate rooms there was nothing to tempt me to wake up.' She smiled, and he leant across the table and kissed her. 'Come on, Dulcie, it's lovely to be here. Let's not argue.'

He was right. When she was alone with him he always made agreeing with him easy. She pushed him away, but with a smile. 'Lesson number two on life in the north-east. Up here we don't kiss in pubs.'

Dulcie and Giles returned on much better terms to find lunch already on the table. 'Sorry, Ma,' Dulcie said, sliding into her place.

'Don't worry, we hadn't started without you.'

Giles, full of bitter and Bloody Mary, did not eat much, and once again Dulcie felt that he had withdrawn from them. He caught her eye and turned to Sam, who was sitting opposite him.

'So, Sam, are you staying with farming?'

Sam looked baffled. 'Why, aye,' he answered and Dulcie was overcome with embarrassment. She saw the amused gleam in Giles's eye and hated him for finding Sam funny, hated Sam for going Geordie now of all times.

'Don't you ever want to see more of the world?' Giles insisted. 'Don't you ever feel a bit limited here? I mean, you're young, you've got your whole life ahead of you.'

Sam did not answer for a minute, but he put down his knife and fork and looked at Giles thoughtfully. 'Giles,' he said, and his accent was pure Oxford with no trace of mockery. 'How many hours a day do you spend in your office?'

'Between ten and twelve, sometimes a little more,' Giles said, and Dulcie could see his adrenalin rise at the very thought.

'And how many weeks' holiday do you get a year?'

'Four.'

'Limiting, isn't it? And you're so young, there's the world to see . . . Although I suppose you could get transferred to Japan or somewhere and spend twelve hours a day in an office there.' He picked up his knife and fork again and calmly took a mouthful of cottage pie.

Giles bristled briefly, but then smiled. 'Fair cop, Sam,' he said, 'but I bet I earn more in a month than you do in a year.'

'Why, aye,' Sam said again, more Geordie than ever, 'and that's limitin' in itself, man.'

'That's enough, Sam,' John said quietly.

And Dulcie knew the romance was over.

# 9

Carol and Henri met at Launceston Place, a restaurant chosen by Carol with a great deal of thought and some trepidation. Its advantages, apart from the food, were that it was quiet and that it was far away from her and Martin's offices. Its disadvantage was that if she were seen there by anyone she knew it would only look suspicious. *But perhaps that's just my guilty mind, and why should it be guilty anyway? I haven't done anything, I'm not really planning anything, just lunch, lunch with a new friend, a friend I can't stop thinking about . . .*

She arrived late. She had not intended to – it was too much of a cliché, but she had spent so long over-making up, wiping it all off and starting again (another cliché) that it was almost twenty past one when she stepped out of the taxi. A man with a couple of cameras round his neck darted forward, and she shrank back against the taxi, horrified.

'Sorry, love, didn't mean to startle you,' he grinned. 'I'm from the *Mail* – got a tip off that Di was here. Be a doll and tip me the wink if she's already in there, would you?'

*Oh God, that's the last thing I want, the whole of bloody Fleet Street hanging around outside,* she panicked. *I can't do this, I'm not cut out for this,* but then there was Henri . . . *and if I run out on him now I'll never see him again, and I couldn't bear that. By seeing him I'm keeping my options open, that's all.*

So she braved Fleet Street's finest and made her way into the restaurant. The Princess of Wales was not there, but a fat man who might have been Pavarotti was and so was Henri, sitting at a small round table in a corner drinking a glass of white wine and reading a newspaper. Once again Carol faltered, but then

Henri stood and smiled and there was nothing to do but walk forward.

Once with him, there was no hesitation, no fear, no compunction. They sat and ate a little, and talked as lovers do, about themselves and each other and their pasts, but not too much about the present and not a word about the future. Carol told him a little about her children, he told her he also had two sons and a daughter and she was foolish enough to want to find some symbolism in the coincidence. He was a clock dealer, working for himself, advisor to various companies. He travelled between London and Paris and Geneva and New York, barely had a home, was officially based in Geneva. He was French, multi-lingual, educated, humorous, well-dressed, smelt faintly but deliciously of vetiver and vanilla, and their hands touched and Carol knew she had been lying to herself, that this man could never be a friend but was to be her lover. *Of course I knew, I didn't even come here to find out, I knew as soon as I saw him.* And Martin did not even enter her mind.

'And your husband?' she heard Henri say, and she blushed, and withdrew her hand. 'You have a husband?' he persisted.

'Yes. Yes I do. Martin. An estate agent. He's . . . he's very nice.'

Henri nodded mournfully, his eyes fixed on hers. 'And?' She knew what he meant, but was not ready to answer.

'And your wife?'

'Divorced in all but name. She lives in Paris with the children. We say it is for the education, but of course there are good schools in Geneva. And frankly Eveline – the youngest – is seventeen. She will be finishing school next year and Celeste will not be coming to Geneva. We take holidays in family sometimes, spend Christmas together . . . that sort of thing. But we have an arrangement.'

'How very *French!*'

Henri smiled. 'Maybe. But we're all happier that way.'

'The children?'

'Well, now of course the children know. They are not stupid and in plus Georges is nearly twenty-three. A man himself. But they respect it is our affair. We get on very well when we are together now – it is altogether . . . smoother.'

Carol found herself faintly shocked at Henri's description of his marriage, but chided herself for her bourgeois attitude. If it worked, after all . . . *Yes, but I'd never get that one by Martin, now would I? Nor would I want to, actually. That's not the way to be, it can't be. Oh God, what am I doing? I'm not made for this game, not at all.*

'You clearly don't work in the same way?'

'No, no, not at all.' *I can't begin to explain about Martin. How could he possibly understand. He's too – too French. And oh – the glory of him.* 'We're – we're married,' she said desperately.

There was a silence. Henri took her hand. 'So will we meet again?' he asked gently.

There was only one answer. 'Yes.'

This time it was Martin who sat waiting in the first floor sitting room. He drank whisky and soda and did not even pretend to read the paper by his side.

*So what's going on? Something. Something is very different. Maybe it is happening now. But it's not Peterson or his brother, I'm sure of it. She's different. And I'm different. If it is happening it's not how I imagined all those times. And if it is, she was innocent before. And if she was innocent before and guilty now, why? What's changed? I suppose I should talk to her, ask her . . . but I've asked so often before, and where did that get me? Here. Sitting with a bloody whisky instead of my wife. Where is she? I could ring her office . . . No, no, not that route . . . Who is it? How could this creep up on me . . . but it hasn't crept at all, has it? I've been preparing for it for years. I can't believe it of her . . . why? I've believed it before, and was always wrong, even that Jewell fellow, I was wrong there too, wasn't I?*

He stood and looked out into the street. It was almost dark, and raining. Few cars drove down this quiet road, a red one braked suddenly, windscreen wipers going at the double, and a black cat skittered across the street.

*Good or bad luck? I never know. Bad luck in Durham, I think Carol says. Good luck in the south. And I'm in the south. Where's Carol?* He watched as a taxi drove slowly down the street, but it went on past their door and stopped twenty yards further down. *It's that Mrs Bruce again, she's certainly dolled up for a wet weekday. Up to no good I suppose . . . How do I know that? (Is that what the neighbours say about Carol?) Probably been taken out to lunch by an old uncle (like hell) . . . Where's Carol? She hasn't got any uncles . . .*

The door slammed. Somehow he had missed seeing Carol, but now she was home. He heard her coming up the stairs, but he could not face her, so he stood in the almost dark room nursing his whisky and loving her. He heard her going into their room beside the drawing room, heard her opening drawers and putting thing away. *She's been shopping then. Well, that's fair enough . . . But why should she suddenly want new clothes? She bought some before she went to France, she's not usually much of a spendthrift . . . Who's she trying to impress? Should I ask her?*

The bedroom door shut and the sitting room door opened. Carol switched on the light as she came in and jumped when she saw Martin. 'What on earth are you doing standing there in the dark?' *Oh God, he knows, he's going to start on at me, and what do I say this time?*

They looked at each other, eyes locked, Carol waiting for the inevitable, summoning up all her inner resources. Now, for the first time she must lie.

*This really is it*, Martin knew and felt ineffably weary. He put down his drink. 'Buy anything nice?' he asked as lightly as he could, and turned away so he should not see the relief in her eyes.

But neither did he see the love.

Breaking with Giles had been the hardest thing Dulcie had ever had to do. How could she tell him that it was not so much him who had let her down, as herself? He had not changed, after all, he was just the same as he always had been. He was as obsessed with his work, as kind to her, as thoughtful and intelligent at one minute, and as selfish and self-indulgent another. He had not told her he loved her, and it had not really occurred to Dulcie that he might, until the showdown.

'What do you mean, you've changed? So what, of course you've changed. And what's that got to do with anything, anyway?'

'I don't like *how* I've changed.'

'Oh, don't be so fucking self-regarding. What does that mean?'

'When we went home—'

'That's it, isn't it? Home. Some kind of bloody northern pride. What was wrong? How come I'm suddenly not good enough for you? Didn't we have a good weekend?'

'Yes, but—'

'Your parents seemed to like me enough. They practically begged me to come again. Well, your mother anyway.' Giles was always truthful.

'Yes, but—'

'We all got on okay. I suppose I didn't have much to say to your precious brother, but we *got on* all right.'

'He had plenty to say to you.'

'Ha ha, so he did. Fair enough, fair cop. Oh come on, Dulcie, what's it all about?'

Dulcie struggled with herself. She wanted to be just to Giles, she was very fond of him, she was going to miss him . . .

'I suppose I was frightened.'

'*Frightened!* What of?'

'Let me finish, Giles, I am trying . . . I felt almost as though I – I fitted in with you better than them.'

'Ah-ha! My point exactly.'

'No, listen. I felt as though you and I had come in from the outside, together, in to them. I suppose it was obvious that you'd be watched, but I thought I was being watched too. And, even worse, I felt I was watching them. I don't know, I was separate.'

'That's called growing up.'

'Of course it is, I know that. But it was more than that. I mean, I want to be separate. It's high time I was. Why did I come down here, after all, if not to put some kind of distance between us? I know other people start that when they go to university, and because I was so close to home I didn't so much. But being separate shouldn't mean being different.'

'Shouldn't it?'

'Well, if not different, certainly not better. Or not thinking you are. I don't know, everything looked so shabby suddenly.'

'I thought it was wonderful.' Giles spoke with genuine warmth and Dulcie looked at him in surprise. 'I thought no wonder you're so attached to home. I thought that if I had a kitchen like that to

• Sophia Watson

go home to, I don't know, somehow that kitchen just shouted the word "home". It's wonderful. The difference between it and my parents' . . . even your aunt's . . .'

'That makes me feel even worse,' Dulcie said abruptly, thinking how she had looked at the difference and found home wanting, thought her family ridiculously, embarrassingly rural and all the while Giles, on whose behalf she was ashamed, was bowled over by them all.

'Oh Dulcie,' Giles held her in a long hug, then let her go. 'I just don't understand you. Maybe that's why I . . . mind about you.'

*You're a bloody idiot, Dulcie Stanley,* she said to herself as she walked away from him. *What the hell have you gone and done now?*

Jody had initially been invited to Yeoworthy as a hanger-on of Dulcie's but now that she and Adam were in the full throes of their affair she was behaving as though the entire weekend were due to her. Dulcie did not really mind, she was feeling more sore than she had expected in Giles's absence and was just glad to have something to do at the weekend.

The girls sat together in Jody's bedroom, talking about their packing. Jody was in a state of high excitement, Dulcie less so.

'So what do you reckon?' Jody asked, showing Dulcie a strappy black number that left her sides almost bare. 'How stuffy are they?'

'I don't know. Conventional but not really stuffy. He looks as though he is, but I don't think it's real. I suppose you should be posh for dinner. But remember it's November, you might be cold.'

'Well, I shan't be going outside,' Jody promised, rummaging at the bottom of her wardrobe for shoes.

'Adam promised some riding – won't you come?'

'Don't be silly. I haven't been on a horse since the time that little brute of yours chucked me off – what was his name? Misty?'

'Milky. Mary hunts him now.'

'Well, he must be old enough to be safe, at any rate. I thought Aunt Molly was trying to murder me.'

Dulcie laughed. 'You certainly made enough noise about it.

• 94

Well, I went out and bought a new dress for Saturday night. I haven't for ages, and Julia is so elegant.'

Jody eyed her. 'Needed cheering up? So when are you going to tell me about you and Giles?'

'Oh—'

'You're odd, you know, Dulcie. Giles told Justin who told Susie who told Sarah who told Adam who told me that you'd split up. We're cousins, Dulcie. We live in the same house. Why do you have to be so private? I promise you, it's not normal.'

'I'm sorry. I didn't think you'd be interested.'

'Come on!' Dulcie had the grace to laugh.

'Well, OK then. I just didn't feel like talking about it.'

'And now?'

'Not really.'

'Who gave who the boot? Giles wasn't saying and so everyone thinks it was you.'

Dulcie's heart sank at the 'everyone' but then what else could she expect. 'Does it really matter?'

Jody was taken aback and, for once, thought for a moment. 'I suppose not. Dulcie – are you all right?'

Dulcie looked at her cousin and was surprised – and grateful – to see the concern on her face. 'Yes, of course I am.' She took a deep breath. 'It's just possible I've made a complete fool of myself, but I'll get over it.'

'If it's any comfort, Dulce – Giles seems to be waiting for you to change your mind.'

Despite her finer feelings, Dulcie could not help but be pleased by this. 'Oh, that's not it – it's complicated. I'll explain, one day. And I honestly think that black number might be going too far.'

As always, the house was going to be full this weekend. Julia walked around the first floor, checking that all the bedrooms and bathrooms had been left as she would have done if she had had to prepare them herself. Soap, bath essence, towels, lavatory paper. Books beside each bed – the new Jilly Cooper and a Vogue history of fashion by Carol's daughter's; *The Buccaneers*, a biography of Edith Wharton and the latest John Grisham by Dulcie's; Dick Francis and James Herriot in the Quilpers', Alex's cartoons by

Adam's. Julia did not read a great deal or very widely but a standing order with Hayward Hill kept her in touch with new titles. Each room, even her sons', had bunches of flowers and the downstairs rooms were resplendent with orchids from the greenhouse and heavy with the smell of shop-bought lilies.

When she was younger Julia had adored these weekends, which were now more of a duty than a pleasure. She had loved aiming for perfection and so often coming near it. She kept books in which she wrote out the menus, her guests' favourites and dislikes, even the seating plans. She wanted her life to fulfil her dreams, and although by nature drawn to the rumbustious, slaphappy warmth of houses like the Pearsalls', she was not capable of reproducing it. Her house had none of the rigid, forbidding formality of her parents', but neither was it quite so essentially alive as the houses she had always loved. Yeoworthy was as comfortable as anywhere in England, was completely welcoming in atmosphere, but sometimes – just sometimes – it felt more like a showcase than a home to Julia. Perhaps because so much of her mind was elsewhere, even during these weekends that she hosted so admirably.

She paused a moment in the Quilpers' room. It was the best guest room, the one in which Archy and Emma Poole usually slept. *What am I to do about Archy? I'm actually glad he's not coming this weekend – but if I do finish it, then what? What'll I do in London? What'll I do down here? I'd curl up and die of boredom. But then I'm bored enough as it is. I don't know, there's no excitement in it any more. It's not much different being with Archy than with Velters, and what on earth point is there in being bored with a lover, after all? I wonder if he's bored too? Oh hell, they've forgotten the Evian water. No, he just takes me for granted – like Velters. But I suppose Velters has got some sort of right to take me for granted. It's traditional, isn't it. And Velters is nothing if not traditional. Perhaps it was a mistake to ask the Quilpers the same weekend as all the young, although Marie makes such a business about understanding young people better than anyone else . . . it's time for a change, that's my problem.* Not for the first time, she thought how impossible it was for someone in her position to have a change. *It should be easier with money, I suppose, but it ties me down . . . how could I possibly leave all this?* It was not just her husband to whom she had obligations and responsibilities, nor her children. It was the people who worked for her, the charities she helped, even in an odd way the house itself. *I've spent most of my adult life on all this,* she thought, picking a fallen petal from the dressing table. *How can I give it all up? And what would be worth it? Certainly not Archy. I suppose it's time I took a holiday. Perhaps I could persuade Velters . . . I've always wanted to see Istanbul.*

Dinner was always late on Friday night to give everyone time to come down from London. At nine o'clock eight of them sat down to carrot soup: Velters and Julia, Dulcie and Jody, Marie and Richard Quilper, Adam and Ted, the farming brother from Barnstaple. Giles had made his excuses and cancelled coming down, and Miranda would be arriving the next morning for the rest of the weekend.

'Good, good,' Velters said as he sat down, and he beamed around the table. 'Lovely to see you all here. We get quite lonely in the week, don't we, Julia my love? Two old bodies rattling around the place, always good to have people here.'

'I say, less of the old, Velters; I was just thinking how pretty Julia's looking,' Richard Quilper said with heavy-handed gallantry.

'Oh, we understand each other, my love, don't we?' said Velters, who had been trying very hard to understand his wife recently.

'Yes, we do,' said Julia from the other end of the table, behind the shining silver and glass.

And Dulcie, who had been rather enjoying herself, felt inexplicably sad.

Dulcie was delighted to hear that the local staghounds were to have a lawn meet outside Yeoworthy at eleven the next morning. This was a life of luxury of which she had only read, and never experienced. Food appeared on the table as if by magic, her bed was made by the time she had finished breakfast, life seemed given over to having maximum enjoyment with minimum effort. All this and hunting too – she could imagine finding it very easy to adjust to a life like this. Adam was going out, and Velters offered Dulcie a horse and was very pleased when she accepted. 'Don't know how much longer we've got before the buggers put a stop to it, always pleased to have some support,' he said. 'They nearly succeeded some time ago, but it seems to me God gave us stags to hunt and Exmoor to hunt them on. Have you hunted before?'

'Not stag, but fox.'

'If she's anything like her mother, you needn't worry about Dulcie, Velters,' said Julia, smiling warmly at her god-daughter. 'Molly was always out at the front, nothing put her off.'

'She used to hate fine days, said they brought out all the amateurs,' agreed Dulcie. 'She doesn't hunt any more, though. Says she hasn't the time but to be honest I think she lost her nerve.'

'It happens to women, even the best,' Velters said. 'Babies does it usually. They miss a season, and when they come back their heart's gone out of it. Sad really.'

Julia lent Dulcie the kit she needed and at quarter to eleven the house party gathered in the courtyard outside Yeoworthy. About forty horses, and twice the amount of followers, collected together. Velters, Adam, Ted and Dulcie represented the Yeoells. Miranda, a pretty girl with dark curls and a pouting mouth, arrived just in time to change quickly and join them. Jody, cold and slightly sulky at being left out, hugged herself on the doorstep and tried not to think anti-hunting thoughts. Two men arrived in a Landrover and started to film the meet with a video camera.

'Shit, the League,' muttered Adam, nodding politely. The men moved around the crowd, videoing indiscriminately. Space was made for them, a few people nodded with cold good manners, but they were basically ignored.

'Why are they here?' asked Dulcie.

'They turn up every now and again, film everything, hope they'll catch us being barbaric. Bloody idiots. Mind you, they're better behaved than the protesters in some places. They don't usually do any damage. Look, there are the Fosters, they're coming to dinner tonight, Mummy says we have to be nice to them. Let me introduce you.'

Dulcie's horse had picked up the excitement in the air and was prancing back and forth, eager to be off. This was always the worst bit, Dulcie thought, when hounds were milling around excitedly, the horses mincing and skittering on the spot. Once in full flight she never felt any fear, but the waiting was the difficult part. A little like take-off in an aeroplane. She pushed her horse through the crowd after Adam.

'Dulcie, this is Geoffrey Foster. They've just moved into the Dower House. Good to see you out, Geoffrey: this is my friend Dulcie Stanley, from County Durham. Patty here?' Geoffrey Foster was good looking in an old-fashioned, florid way and expensively dressed. His mare was beautifully groomed and turned out; he looked terrified as he tried to calm her.

'Doesn't hunt – yet. Sure she will though. And anyway,' he added hurriedly, 'our guests will be arriving mid-morning.' A thin-lipped blonde in a soft moleskin skirt and a scarf artfully tied at her neck waved to Adam, and he took his bowler off to her.

'Adam'll keep an eye on you, won't you, old boy?' Velters boomed, edging his big black mare alongside them.

'I'll try – but I can't promise,' Adam grinned.

'He does get carried away,' Velters said proudly. 'Still, you can always trust Ted. I may not last the course – getting old.'

'I promise not to need looking after,' Dulcie said, hoping for the best. A woman came round with a tray of sausage rolls and sloe gin, offering topups and collecting glasses. And suddenly the horn was sounded, the hounds lifted their heads, the followers rushed out of the courtyard to the motorbikes and four-wheel-drive cars parked in the lane and the horses moved off.

Dulcie waved at Jody and Julia, her blood rising to the sounds of the hounds and the horn, the clattering of all the hooves on the cobbles, and felt her horse respond. She thought of Pimlico and Waterstone's and Giles and laughed aloud with excitement. None of that mattered. Nothing mattered now except the chase. She had missed all of this more than she had realised.

They arrived back at five, exhausted and exhilarated. A huge tea was laid out for them, and various members of the hunt had been invited back with them. Velters, who had come back a couple of hours earlier, was already changed and longing to hear all the details.

Everyone talked at once, earnestly and totally incomprehensibly to Dulcie who had no knowledge of the area. She knew none of the landmarks or names of crosses and commons, but her face told Velters all he wanted to know.

'So you were all right?'

'Oh, it was wonderful. I can't thank you enough.'

'Were you at the kill?'

'Yes, of course.' Dulcie spoke with pride: not many had lasted the whole day.

'And you didn't mind?' Jody, who had gone antique shopping with Marie Quilper for want of anything better to do, was wishing all this talk of hunting would stop. 'I mean, I can see a fox doesn't matter, but a stag – well, they're beautiful.'

'Of course they are,' a soft voice with a faint west country burr said. 'None of us denies that.'

'Have you met? This is Colin Webber, the son of our farm manager John. Colin, this is Lady Yeoworthy's god-daughter Dulcie Stanley, and her cousin, Jody Morecombe.'

'We met today – or rather we didn't. Thank you, you were very kind about gates.' Dulcie had been grateful for the unknown young man's good manners, had noticed him throughout the day and liked the look of him. He had been unfailingly, and unnecessarily, kind, but she had seen his mind was on more important matters than strange girls and had not been surprised when he was among the twelve or so riders still out at the end of the day.

'And what about my good for nothing sons? Adam, Ted – you were supposed to be looking after Dulcie.'

'I did, a bit,' said Ted.

'I was fine,' Dulcie insisted and Ted winked at her.

'So if they're so beautiful, why do you hunt them?' Jody insisted.

Dulcie was embarrassed for her cousin. 'You'll be saying you're vegetarian next,' she said, only half joking, knowing only why she loved hunting, not quite sure why it was all right.

'We look after them, see,' Colin said. Jody looked as though she were about to interrupt, but his soft voice overrode hers. 'If we didn't hunt them, they'd disappear altogether.'

Jody shrugged. She was out of her element and she knew it.

She did not really care either way, anyway. She had just wanted to join in the conversation. She turned to Adam and whispered something and he laughed and nodded. Velters brought Ted over to Dulcie and handed her a plate of scones. Dulcie found herself in between Colin who, having said his piece, did not speak much more, and Ted, who laughed and discussed the hunt with Dulcie and the farm with Colin. Dulcie's attention wandered as they talked earnestly about milk quotas and yields, about fleece and lamb prices, and she watched them both happily. Ted appealed to her much more than did Adam. He seemed less brittle, and where Adam had ridden with a bold, flashy style of risk-taking dare-devilry Ted had seemed much more at ease with his mount.

'So what did you think of Foster?' Ted asked with a grin. 'Be honest.'

'You can't say he doesn't try,' Colin said carefully.

'Try?' asked Dulcie, her attention coming back to what they were saying.

'The Fosters are new to this neck of the woods,' Ted explained. 'Lost a lot of money in Lloyds, sold their house near Basingstoke, and they're renting the Dower House while they look around. They really want to belong, join in like mad. I suppose you have to admire them really.' It was clear he did not.

'I don't really understand about Lloyds,' Colin said. 'If they've lost all their money, and neither of them works, what are they buying that very natty mare with? Bertie Willand sold them that, and you know he drives a hard bargain. Mr Foster would've had to pay a fair price for that.'

'It's all relative.' Ted explained. 'As long as your private income keeps going and you sell your things, you're going to be all right. I suppose if they'd kept their house and tried to pay their losses out of their income, they'd have been really poor with no nice new horses. We've been lucky. Daddy never joined Lloyds, always said something about it didn't smell right, you'd be made to pay one day. And as it turns out he was right. But do you know, he's about the only one. Nearly everyone round here has been done to some degree or another. Even Mummy had a small stake, and she's been paying out recently.'

'Everyone?' Colin queried.

'Well, everyone I know.' Ted suddenly realised what he was

saying and was almost embarrassed. 'Oh, sorry, Colin, but you know what I mean.'

Colin laughed. 'I know,' he agreed and Dulcie was sure she caught the ghost of a wink.

By the time the house party had reassembled, bathed and changed for dinner, Jody was sparkling. Evenings were what she was good at, and now she would show Adam's parents the kind of a girl she was. Despite Dulcie's advice she was wearing the black dress and although few people could have carried it off she looked splendid. Her hair and eyes shone, and even her skin seemed to glow.

Velters looked at her in appreciation. *Well, what man wouldn't? Carol's girl is certainly a looker, not my type though, all flash and dash, nothing to them, though I suppose that's the kind of girl Adam will end up with and at least Julia knows her people. It could be worse. Probably will be. Molly's little Dulcie, though . . . there's a girl. I wish Adam would take up with her. Got a head on her shoulders, no nonsense about her. And by God, she can ride. Not many women I know can ride like that. Julia almost could, once . . .* He looked across the drawing room at his wife, sitting on the sofa laughing and talking to Richard Quilper and felt, for the first time in many years, the faintest twinge of unease. *I suppose I'm getting old, too – faster than she is at that. She always liked a bit of style, my Julia . . . Adam takes after her, I suppose. Miranda too. Perhaps they all do . . . no Ted's . . . steadier I suppose.*

He crossed the room and stood beside Julia, putting his hand lightly on her neck. 'How's your drink, darling?' he asked. He felt her flesh almost physically retreat from his touch.

'Fine, thank you,' she answered without looking at him, and by force of willpower sent him into retreat.

He wandered over to Miranda and Dulcie. 'All right, girls?' he asked.

'We were going over old ground – hunting ground,' Dulcie said with a laugh.

'Save that for Colin Webber – Ted insisted on asking him and as we were thirteen Julia let him. But I don't know who the devil he'll talk to.'

'I thought he seemed nice,' said Dulcie.

'Oh, the boy's nice enough, but I can't see him getting on with Patty Foster,' Velters tried to explain.

'Johnny always says he prefers fox hunting,' Miranda interrupted, going back to her last conversation.

'Johnny?'

'Oh – Cicely's brother. He was there last weekend.'

'I see,' said Velters, and he did.

'Know him well?'

'Oh you know, he's around. Sometimes he's there when I stay there, you know, just one of the gang,' she said and Dulcie tried not to smile.

'You must come again, Dulcie, any time you want to get out of London for a few days, and there'll always be a horse here for you. Are you enjoying London?'

'Oh yes, loving it. But it's wonderful to get out.'

'Johnny is like that, but he prefers leaving mid-week,' Miranda agreed, and Velters wondered at how his baby had grown, and knew that before long she would be better at dissimulating and then another stage would be passed.

The door bell rang and Julia went to greet her guests. Colin Webber was on the threshold, followed through the courtyard by the Foster party. Geoffrey had changed into a blue velvet smoking jacket, thickly frogged, Patty was wearing narrow black trousers, purple velvet slippers and a purple and black silk shirt. Five huge diamonds glittered in a row on her wedding finger. She looked small and defiant and very pleased. 'These are our guests, Robert and Laura Bedford,' she introduced them. 'Laura's an old friend of mine – from school,' she added. 'Robert, Laura, Julia and Velters Yeoworthy.' Robert Bedford had tired green eyes and a charming smile, his wife was about seven months pregnant and swamped in a green velvet maternity dress.

Drinks were seen to, small talk tackled, and then Velters had an idea. 'Julia, darling, who have you put next to Dulcie at dinner?' Julia looked surprised. Velters would occasionally ask for some particular person to be seated next to him, but otherwise paid no attention to seating plans, or anything else domestic.

'Um – let me think. Colin and Adam. Why?'

'Do me a favour and put her next to Ted.'

'Ted? Oh honestly, Velters, don't be a bore. Ted made me ask Colin and he'll be completely out of his depth but Dulcie's a nice girl and can talk to him about farming. I can't put Jody next to him, the wretched girl's had to put up with hunting all day—'

'It doesn't really matter, Julia. However you organise it, I'd like to see Dulcie next to Ted.'

'Are you matchmaking?'

'Don't be ridiculous. I just think she's a nice girl.'

Julia looked at her husband and with a sigh knew she would have to do as he asked. Why on earth had he not managed to have his bright idea at a more reasonable time of day, she wondered irritably.

Julia rang the silver bell on the table in front of her and Mrs Tout and her niece came in and began to clear the soup plates. 'Thank you, Mrs Tout, that was delicious,' Julia said, as automatically as she did every time and with as little meaning.

'I dream of you all week, Mrs Tout,' Ted said and she beamed at him.

'I know you can't resist a beetroot, Ted,' she said.

*It's all working.* Julia leaned back against her chair and looked down the long table. *Velters seems to be getting on with Patty – tiresome woman that, wants to be my best friend which is quite unnecessary. Richard told me he'd heard her telling someone that it was almost worth having lost everything to come here and make friends with us. She'd do better if she weren't quite so transparent in her snobbery. But Geoffrey* – she shot a covert look at her neighbour who was discussing the book trade with Dulcie – *now he's really very nice. Good-looking too. But I didn't know what a flirt he was until this evening. Rather jolly, that. Cheers up local life a bit. And Lord, it needs it! Pity Patty's around, really. He'd be much more fun to go around with than her. Velters was right. Dulcie and Ted do seem to be getting on very well.* 'Velters, would you carve, please?' *although I do think he could do better. She's a sweet girl, but a bit countrified still. Maybe the boys will rub off some of her edges. Those duck look good, Mrs Tout's done us proud. Marie looks as though she's struggling a bit with Colin, but he's been talking to Ted and Dulcie most of dinner anyway. When will that girl learn to serve food on the left?* 'Megan, offer the dish from the left,' she murmured as the girl passed behind her.

She turned to Robert; Geoffrey had monopolised her throughout the first course and she knew where her duties lay.

At almost the same moment Velters turned from Patty, who he liked because she was quite pretty and required no effort, to Laura, the Fosters' guest. She began telling him about her stepchildren and he nodded gravely. 'You worry about them just as much when they're grown up,' he said. 'I worry that Adam's not interested enough in Yeoworthy, and that Ted is too much. We're on a smaller scale than Longleat, of course, but we don't want to end up like the Thynnes. All that bickering among brothers does an estate no good at all. Poor old Henry Bath . . . I wish my boys would find themselves some nice girls.'

'Do I gather that the blonde – Jody – is Adam's girlfriend? She looks very nice.'

'Oh yes, she is – but what would a girl like her do down here? Julia's clever, she's arranged everything well – but even she, sometimes . . .' *Why am I talking like this to a complete stranger?* he wondered, but looking at Laura saw genuine interest and even maybe some understanding.

'It can be almost more difficult when you've arranged everything too well,' she said. 'It leaves you with nothing left to do.'

'Oh, she *does* lots of things – um, you know, embroidery and such-like. I think – she said something to me a while back – I think she finds the house very *big* sometimes in the week.'

'Empty.'

'Yes.'

'I feel like that sometimes when the children are with their mother. And of course, our house isn't even big. If it's any comfort, you can be very lonely in Fulham.' There was a pause, then she said hurriedly, 'Well I mean, not now, not any more—'

'Is this your first child?' he asked, to ease her embarrassment.

'Yes, well – no.' She smiled. 'It's complicated. There are my husband's children, of course, and we have a daughter we adopted eight months ago. Ho-Min, she was called, we call her Minnie. She's very nearly two, she's Chinese. She's utterly lovely.'

Velters looked at her and thought how pretty she had suddenly become and hoped Miranda would be as happy and as lucky. He looked at his daughter and heard her say earnestly to Colin,

'Johnny says if everyone became vegetarian it would ruin the economy,' and he chuckled. 'My daughter's in the throes of young love, and thinks we haven't noticed.'

'With the man next to her?'

'Lord, no. That's the farm manager's son. Nice boy, sound, friend of Ted's. He works on the farm too, and his sister's in the estate office. Nice family, been here for years.' (Laura realised he was talking in terms of hundreds, not tens of years.) 'Miranda's young man's the brother of some girl at school, I gather. We haven't met him yet. Doubt we ever will. But we certainly hear about his opinions. It's all innocent enough. Adam? Be a good boy and fetch that bottle of claret from the sideboard, would you?'

Mrs Tout went home after serving the coffee and Dulcie, going into the kitchen on an errand to fetch more cream, found Adam and Jody giggling and preparing lines of coke. 'D'you fancy some, Dulcie?' Adam asked. 'I've got lots – can't get through a weekend at home without it. I'd have been very rude to that ridiculous Foster woman if I hadn't been kept sweet.'

'Oh, she won't,' Jody flicked a look of contempt at her cousin. 'I think she thinks it'll turn her into Dr Jekyll or something.'

'Dulcie?' Adam ignored Jody and looked at Dulcie.

For one moment she hesitated, then she thought of Giles and temptation and experience and – *what the hell*!

'Mr Hyde, actually,' she said. 'People always get it the wrong way round. And yes, please, Adam, why not?'

## 10

'It was nice to see Laura and Robert again, it's so easy to lose touch.' Patty spread a piece of toast with Vitalite and looked longingly at the honey.

'Um,' Geoffrey put his plate of fried eggs and bacon on to the table and hunted ineffectually in a cupboard for the pepper pot.

'Cupboard on the right behind the Marmite,' said Patty, who had had to find her husband's tie and the pepper for him every morning for the twelve years of their marriage.

'She went on a bit about her baby, though,' he said, as he settled down to eat.

'Yes, well . . . Do you know, I'm really glad we went to dinner at the Manor on Saturday. I do want our friends to know we're all right.'

'How do the Yeoworthys prove that?' asked Geoffrey.

'Well, you know, that we've made new friends, that people here don't mind about our – troubles.'

'I would have hoped,' he said, with heavy-handed irony, 'that they would see we were "all right" from coming to see us together in our own, albeit rented, home. I don't see why seeing us accepted by the locals would make any difference.'

'Oh, come on, Geoffrey. You know perfectly well what I mean. Not just the *locals*, not any old locals—'

'But the Yeoworthys. The Earl and his good Countess. Patty, you shouldn't let it show so much.' He chased the end of the yolks around his plate with a piece of bacon, and mopped up the last traces with a piece of bread.

'Oh Geoffrey, I wish you wouldn't do that,' Patty grimaced.

'Afraid I'll let you down in front of your smart new friends?'

'If I can't talk to you, who should I be able to talk to? I haven't always got some piece of totty trailing round after me to confide in.' Patty had only recently learned the word 'totty' and had been looking forward to having the opportunity to use it. Her relish took away some of the bitterness of the remark.

Geoffrey sighed, gave up the effort of finding more cholesterol on his plate, and pushed back his chair.

'I thought we'd finished with all of that. I thought that one good thing was going to come out of everything, and that was that all this would stop.'

'What do you mean *you* thought?' Patty gave up the struggle and spread honey – and butter – thickly on her next slice of toast. 'It's up to you, you know it, it always has been.'

'In the past. This is the future.'

'Don't be so idiotic. I don't know why we ever thought there could be such a thing as a future. No matter where we go it's always the present. And there'll always be some piece of totty.'

'Oh, balls, Patty. Give it a rest, will you? I admitted, I made a few mistakes in the past, understandable – you said so yourself – even forgivable. But that's happened. It won't happen again.'

Patty's eyes filled with tears, her good mood of half an hour earlier entirely evaporated. 'Oh Geoffrey, how can you, you know it's only because I love you, how can you deny it?'

'Deny what?' Geoffrey was resigned. His wife had indeed forgiven his infidelities and a lot else beside – his business failure, his rough treatment at the hands of Lloyds, his sterility. But forgiving and forgetting bore no relationship to each other in Patty's mind and every now and again (not that often any more) for no apparent reason, Patty would exact a little revenge. Oh well, he had no office to go to, there was nothing to be late for, nothing he could do would stop the inevitable scene.

'Deny how dreadfully you were flirting with Julia on Saturday night? Not just Saturday, now I think about it – always. You flirt with her *always*.'

Despite himself, Geoffrey laughed. 'Are you implying that your new best friend the Countess is a *bit of totty*?'

Patty flushed darkly, uglily and twisted her rings on her

wedding finger. 'No, I'm not. But you just can't help yourself, can you?'

'Well, no. Flirting I can't and won't stop. And neither do you. You flirted with Adam and he's half your age, and you always flirt with Robert.'

'That's different. Obviously. Adam's not much more than a boy. And Robert – well, he's in love with Laura.'

'I'm sure Julia loves Velters.'

'Don't be silly.' Perhaps the idea was ludicrous.

'So it's all right to flirt with someone who loves their husband?'

'Of course it is. Everyone knows no-one means it.'

'But that takes away half the fun, if you look at it like that.'

'Oh, *Geoffrey*!' Here came the tears, no longer threatened but pouring down her cheeks. *How ugly she looks when she cries. Her nose seems to swell to twice its normal size and her skin goes all blotchy. I wonder what Julia looks like when she cries.* 'Geoffrey, promise me, promise me you won't . . . I can't take any more, I really can't . . . Just as we're all settled down here, and you've got your horse . . . I really like it here now, really I do . . . I don't mind leaving Hampshire any more, and we can manage here even if Lloyds takes more . . . I haven't bought any new clothes for *weeks*, and we go to dinner with the Yeoworthys, which will show the Laings . . .'

'Patty, for God's sake. What is all this about? Do you think I'm having an affair with Julia or are you still cross that you never cracked high society in Basingstoke? Tell me the problem and we'll sort it out.'

Patty tried to pull herself together. 'Well, the Laings would never have us to dinner although you took guns on their shoot, bloody expensive too if you ask me and a filthy lunch to boot. Nor the Goudges, nor any of those nice people round there that we used to meet at drinks parties. They thought we weren't good enough for some reason, looked down their noses at us—'

'Maybe they just didn't like us,' Geoffrey suggested, but luckily Patty did not seem to hear and continued.

'And now we've lost all our money, but people don't seem to mind, they ask us anyway. We used to give those huge dinner parties, Saturday after Saturday, it used to kill me, and now we seem hardly ever to have people over, but everyone's friendly. And if you spoil it all by following your dick over to Yeoworthy, I – I – I don't know what I'll do.'

Geoffrey was hugging her now (she always ended up in his arms on these occasions, they usually ended up in bed, he forgetting her blotchy face with the same time-honoured reassurance) and she clung to him, whimpering slightly every now and again. He looked over her head, out of the window on to the kitchen garden. *She's an odd girl, really. I think she minds more about where she stands than anything else. I wonder if she cared about the affairs because of the infidelity or because of what it made her friends think of her. I suppose I went a bit far having a fling with Izzy, best friends and all that, but did she mind the social betrayal or the sexual more? She doesn't want me to have an affair with Julia because she doesn't want to stop going to dinner there. If only I'd been able to give her children, it would have been different. She'd have had other things to worry about. Poor old Patty . . . what a mess I've got her into . . . I must try not to seduce Julia, I really must try . . .*

*Let it be said for Julia, she doesn't muck about with her food.* Velters watched approvingly as Julia took a second sausage and poured some more coffee. 'Another weekend over and done with then,' he said cheerfully. He was still trying to talk to Julia more, but often there was nothing to say.

'Yup.' She reached for the *Daily Mail*.

'Who's coming next weekend?' he said desperately.

'Oh, well the Pooles were meant to be coming, but I think I'll chuck them.'

'Why? It'll be a nice quiet weekend if it's just them, and you're always pleased to see Emma.'

'Emma.' Julia's lip curled and Velters was suddenly deeply uneasy without knowing why. 'Frankly, Emma bores me. She comes down here time after time, sits on the sofa with her endless tapestries, witters on about her blessed children. To be honest, I've had enough. She just doesn't contribute.'

'Always seems a pleasant little thing,' Velters said feebly. 'And she laughs at jokes.'

'Exactly. She's pleasant and she laughs at other people's jokes. It's not enough. She should make some of her own.'

'You're being very harsh all of a sudden. You can't just drop old friends like that, Julia. And what about Archy? You can't deny that you get on like a house on fire with him.'

In the tense little silence that followed Julia was flooded with panic. *Oh sweet Jesus, he knows.* She pushed her plate away, the scrape of china covering the stillness.

'Yes, yes I do. But she drags him down.' Now she could meet his eye and realise that no, he did not know, it had been an innocent enough remark. Velters, seeing her changing expressions, but not quite interpreting them – wariness? relief? triumph? what was going on? – suddenly began to understand. But as soon as light began to show through the chink in the door that had just opened, he took a mental step back, slammed the door shut, reached automatically for *The Times*.

'Yes, well, darling. Do whatever you want. Perhaps one of the children will come down. Frank hasn't been for a while, has he?'

*Why can't he stick the idea of a weekend alone with me?* Julia drank her coffee and looked at *The Times* which shielded her husband's face from her. *He'd rather have Archy and Emma here – even them – than sit and face me alone for one meal more than he has to. I don't understand it. He doesn't know, doesn't even suspect* (but there at last she was wrong), *probably doesn't even care. As long as I don't let down the Yeoells, the family name, the ancient title . . . is that really all there is to his life? The house and the title? Oh, and I suppose the children. He does love them – as much as he can. Oh God. But if he doesn't know, and I don't bore him – I don't suppose he'd notice being bored – then what is it? Why do we always have to have people here?*

*I'm going to have to see Archy, I suppose. Velters is right. I can't just cancel the weekend and never get in touch again. Oh God, what will I do without Archy? But then what do I do with him? It's gone on long enough, it's as sterile as every-thing else. There's no point going on just for the sake of it. And I'm certainly not leaving Velters, not giving all of this up for Archy. A clean break. We've been friends long enough. He'll understand.*

'Shall we take a holiday?'

'What?'

Velters lowered his paper a fraction and looked at his wife as though surprised to see she was still there.

'Don't you think it's time we went away together? We haven't for such a long time. And we don't see that much of each other.'

'We're together most of every week!' Velters looked almost horrified and Julia laughed. After a second he joined in, a warm rich laugh that came straight from his belly. Julia reached across the table and touched his hand. 'Come on, Velters, I'd like a long weekend in a good hotel in a beautiful city. No guests, no friends, no family, nobody we know. Just us.'

'And P.G. Wodehouse,' he said. 'Can't go abroad without P.G. Wodehouse.' And they laughed together again.

Carol drank orange juice freshly squeezed by Martin and ate a croissant. Martin ate All-Bran and a banana. Jody and Dulcie ate Shreddies and toast and Molly's raspberry jam and an apple. Piers ate three Shredded Wheats. Alan was still in bed. Nobody spoke. Finally Jody broke the silence.

'Well, Mum, since you ask, it was a wonderful weekend, wasn't it, Dulce? It's the nicest house I've ever been in and seriously luxurious. Honestly, Mum, you should have seen the size of the towels. Well, actually Saturday was a bit boring and I had to go antique shopping with this frightful woman who was training as a youth counsellor or something and wanted to practise – on me, I ask you – but Saturday night was brilliant, wasn't it, Dulce?' (with a wink) 'We played this brilliant game where you chuck billiard balls around – it was so funny – how're your fingers, Dulce?'

'Frieda, I think,' said Carol.

'What?'

'That game. You hurl the balls at other people's fingers across the table? I haven't played that for years.'

'We don't know many people with billiard tables,' said Martin. 'Or only professionally,' he added sourly.

'Adam took me hunting. Or Velters did.'

'Or Ted,' Jody said meaningfully.

'Well, the horse was Velters's.'

'And who saw you home? Velters was back in his cardy by the time we got to the house.'

'Colin, actually,' said Dulcie, surprised at the memory.

'Colin? Oh yes, but he doesn't count.'

'Why ever not? He was nice, quite funny when he warmed up.'

'Yes, that's true. He was much better after Julia went to bed.'

'Perhaps he's scared of her.' Both girls considered the possibility.

'Of Julia?' Carol made an effort. Everything was an effort now. Every bit of her normal life – her family, her work, conversation, cooking, driving – took an impulse of will. Everything except her secret lunches. Two hours every other day or so the minutes flew by her, she felt as though she were swimming in a clear, cool, limpid stream, fast-flowing, bright. The rest of the time she was in a thick fog, blind and deaf to her present, her mind dwelling on the last meeting, her heart yearning towards the next.

'No one could be frightened of Julia.'

'She can be very grand, you know.' Dulcie thought of how Julia had talked to Colin, how she did not really talk to her staff, how you could sometimes see her making a monumental effort to turn on her charm. 'You can see her being a hostess, if you know what I mean,' Dulcie said. 'She didn't do it to me at all, but I could see her doing it to those people who came with the neighbours, you know, Laura. And to Patty Foster. Perhaps it's just to women. You can see her deciding when to make an effort, but then when she makes one she forgets she's making one and it becomes natural. I think she's quite nice really.'

'You sound surprised.' Martin put his bowl into the washing-up machine.

'No, not really. She's obviously nice, I just can't work out how nice she is *underneath*. She's hard to work out, don't you think?' She looked at Jody, but Jody never wasted much time trying to work people out, so she shrugged. Dulcie looked at Carol, who was back in her fog (*what is the matter with her these days? Something's on her mind. I hope she's not ill*) and then at her uncle.

'Well, I'm glad you both had a good weekend,' he said hurriedly to try and cover up that he had not been listening.

'Well, anyway.' Dulcie threw her core into the bin. 'I

don't have to be at work until late today. Anything I can do?'

'We must go, Jody,' said Martin, and Jody sighed and picked up her tiny pink knapsack.

'OK. I'm ready.'

'You could do my spelling, I've got a test today,' suggested Piers.

'That sounds as though you've left your homework until too late again,' said Martin. 'If you haven't done it by now you'd better do it on the bus on the way to school. Bye all, see you tonight. Bye, Carol, doing anything special today?' His attempt at casualness was pathetic, they all noticed it, even Jody.

Carol jumped, moved nervously towards the sink, looked more alive than she had for days. 'Me? No. I've got to get my plans off to Peter Peterson by the end of the week, and somehow I've got behind. I may be home a little late. There's another new house to look at in Richmond, and I may leave that until the end of the day.'

*She's lying*, thought Martin, looking at her back and he turned and left the room.

*She's lying*, thought Dulcie, *but what about? Perhaps she's ill, has to go to the doctor.*

*She's odd*, thought Jody, *she should loosen up, Dad should take her away somewhere*, and she followed her father from the house.

'Mum?' said Piers when they were alone together. 'Mum? Have you got time to test my spelling before you go?'

And Carol, recognising something she could do, even in her fog, sank on to the sofa and opened Piers's school book.

Dulcie sold yet another copy of *Sense and Sensibility*, this time to a middle-aged man in a pin-striped suit of mediocre cut, and turned to the child who wanted help in spending her book token. This was an aspect of the job she normally adored (maybe she should think harder about becoming a teacher, but the idea of other teachers depressed her too much) but today she could not engage her mind. The child went away with its mother, perfectly satisfied, but Dulcie knew she had been lazy and unimaginative. Roald Dahl, Noel Streatfield, Rosemary Sutcliffe, Henry Treece – she had made no effort at all. She made a mental note to read some more up to date children's books again soon. It was about all she was good for at the moment, her thoughts were so preoccupied.

Firstly with Giles, who she missed and wanted to ring but did not dare to in case of rebuff, or in case he assumed she wanted to take up with him again. All that rubbish about staying friends never worked, at least not at first, not for a while, not if you had been remotely fond of the person. And yet she so badly wanted to see him, to talk to him. He had been a real friend, and she had let him go. Perhaps she should never have gone to bed with him, but then the friendship could not have survived that either. Oh hell. She wanted to tell him about the cocaine, needed to de-brief with someone who knew how she had felt, who she could have a real conversation with – but what could she do? She could hardly ring him up and say, 'Hey, guess what, you were right. I took coke and it was fun and I'm still alive. Next party it's E all the way.'

Because it had been fun. After the embarrassment of actually taking it (supremely undignified, she could not help but feel) she had really loved it. She had loved the sensation, the whole experience, even (although afterwards she despised herself for this) loved the surprise on Jody's face, the immediate feeling of acceptance. 'Now I am one of the gang,' she had said and they laughed together.

Giles was right. It did no harm. It helped turn a perfectly pleasant evening into one filled with jokes and laughter and good spirits. Afterwards, on going back into the drawing room, she had found it easier than ever before to talk to the comparative strangers around her, and laugh and make them laugh (and they had not taken anything so she must have been as witty as she felt). They had taken more, later, as they played Frieda, (without Colin and Ted – Adam said that Ted was a killjoy and Colin was almost certain to disapprove) which was probably why she had not felt the pain of the ball smashing her thumb until the next morning when she woke to find it almost twice its normal size.

So as she filled up the Penguin 60s dump bin Dulcie reconsidered her stand on drugs. *It's self-indulgence, obviously, but that's all. And self-indulgence is clearly wrong, in the strictest moral sense, but only a little bit. Did I hurt anybody else? No – although Adam hurt me with that blessed ball. We all enjoyed ourselves, nobody who would have minded even knew, it helped the party go with a swing. So why do I still feel a bit guilty? Giles would say it's because I'm too puritanical, which I suppose is true. I'm trying not to be, though. Would I take it again if I was offered? Yes, of course I would, if I was going clubbing or anything. And anything else? E? Well, it's a bit scary, isn't it . . . people seem to die of it, something to do with water . . . and if coke's that nice then why bother with anything else? . . . on the other hand, I didn't know it was that much fun before, so perhaps I'm missing out . . . steady, one drug at time, oh I wish I could talk to Giles.*

The other thoughts to preoccupy her were on the subject of Ted, and those she did not want to share with Giles. She had liked Ted a great deal, sensed that they had a lot in common. He was an agreeable cross between his parents, she thought, with his mother's easy charm and his father's good manners and, Dulcie was sure, a deeper kindness. Dulcie enjoyed being with Adam, she was very pleased that his romance with Jody had brought him into their circle, but she was not sure how much she actually liked him. He made self-indulgence a way of life, an art form, and occasionally it occurred to Dulcie that maybe he went too far in his pursuit of pleasure.

'I know I play hard,' he had once said, 'but you don't see me working, and I promise I take that just as seriously. Anyway London's here to make money in and have fun in. Until the day when I have to go down to Yeoworthy for the rest of my life.' Dulcie had not then been to Yeoworthy since her early childhood. 'Is it that bad?' she had asked. 'The house is all right if you like that sort of thing, but it's the country, Dulcie, it's so – not even provincial – so aggressively rural. I honestly don't know how you could have stuck it for so long. So come on, let's order another bottle and have fun while we can.'

Ted on the other hand understood all about the country. He and Dulcie did not need to discuss farming or hunting or anything else – it was immediately obvious to Dulcie that they understood each other. On the strength of the last weekend, Dulcie thought Ted a perfect mix of town and country; he had none of the snobbery of the town but had a veneer of sophistication that was inherent, not learned.

Dulcie hoped she would see more of him, but then there he

was in Barnstaple (she had looked furtively in a West Country guidebook and found it was even further than Yeoworthy) and here she was in London and that she supposed was that. For a brief moment she allowed herself a romantic daydream involving a large Somerset farmhouse, a row of children, hunting three times a week, freshly churned butter, a big book lined room as her refuge, a teasing, smiling man who looked just a little like Ted . . . but then a woman asked her for the biography section and she pulled herself together. What was she thinking of? She had only just got going on this part of her life.

## 11

Henri had been very good about not pushing her, but Carol knew that sooner or later she was going to have to make a decision. The lunches were bliss, all her romantic dreams (the dreams she had pushed aside as unworthy over the years) come to fruition. A good-looking man, flirtation, eyes meeting, fingers touching, everything said and nothing said. Was this love? There was deep attraction, but more than that. 'Our minds speak to each other,' she said once, full of wonder, and he had just smiled. She had not felt like this for oh so long and it was wonderful. She had reached the point where she felt no guilt, or at least none when she was with him. Seeing him made her so happy that she could not believe she was doing anything wrong. It was her secret vice, but no worse than eating too many chocolate bars. No-one knew, she was not hurting anybody.

The problem was that while she could justify, or excuse, or ignore the implications of the uneaten lunches, the locked eyes, the constant daydreaming, she was not yet prepared to make the big jump. She could argue now that she was not being unfaithful to Martin, but the minute she went to bed with Henri the situation would change. Somehow seeing Henri three times a week, thinking about him almost exclusively, yearning for him to touch more than her hands, her arm, her cheek, was all right, forgivable – not even a sin. If only everything could continue in this delicious way, if she could be lost for ever in this half-world, it would be all right.

'I understand you, really I do,' said Henri one day, sipping at the cognac he had only ordered to make the meal last longer, 'but you must understand that what we are doing now is the same as sleeping together.' He was beginning to be a little impatient, a little tired of trying to coax Carol out of her near-virginal fears.

'It's not, not really,' she said.

'Oh, but it is, really,' he echoed. 'Carol, *ma chère*, if your husband knew where you spent your time and with whom, do you think he would see the difference between doing the act and thinking about it? Of course he would not. Anyway, the Pope says it is exactly the same – wishing as doing – so why not have the fun of doing if you are going to commit the sin of wishing?' He tried to speak lightly, and Carol tried to smile, but she hated this conversation. 'This is a fine time to bring the Pope up,' she said. 'Anyway that can't be right. You must get some credit for resisting temptation.'

'But you're not resisting temptation. Or the Pope would say not enough. After all, here you are with me.'

'Yes.' Carol looked miserable. She did not want that pointed out. She was doing perfectly well inside her own head.

'Carol, I'm not trying to send you away, I'm trying to bring you closer. I suppose you need to see the whole picture, and I am part of your whole picture now – aren't I?'

She nodded dumbly.

'So now you have to think. Why am I here with this man? Because I need him – as he needs me. Why? Because there is something missing in the rest of our lives, and when we are together that wound is cured. We do not want to hurt anyone else, of course, so we will be discreet. But to be happy with them – the others in our lives, also important – we must be happy in ourselves. And here is Henri, who loves me—'

'Oh Henri, you sound like a woman justifying leaving her children with a nanny while she disappears after a career.'

'Well, you did that and no one suffered,' he said, totally reasonably.

'That's unfair. It's different.'

'Not at all. Then you take your time away from your family, and to some degree your heart and mind. This way you just add your body to the things you are sharing. And oh, what a body . . .' And he grinned and reached for her hand and wished they could stop these games, stop fooling around with courtship, and begin the affair which he knew was inevitable.

'It's different for you. You are separated from your wife, you owe her nothing – and you've done it all before. How many times? Where do I come on the list?'

'I owe her respect,' he said sharply. 'And affection. And Carol, it is not like you to be bitter. I'm just trying to help you. If you cannot stand it, just say to me "go" and I will go. You will never hear from me again, I will respect your decision entirely. But I think that would be wrong and sad and a waste of our feelings, our true feelings.'

They sat in silence, Carol staring blankly over his shoulder at a couple of power lunchers earnestly discussing contracts. The bill arrived and Henri put down his credit card, and still they did not speak.

'Do you want to?' he said finally.

'Of course I do,' she answered.

'Then we must. And we will enjoy it,' he added with a gleam.

Carol smiled wanly. Yes, she wanted to, and yes, she would and she would shut her eyes to the possible consequences. But she could not bear to think of the planning, where they were to go, what lies she would tell to cover herself.

'You will be happy,' Henri said gently and she nodded.

As they left the restaurant Henri took her arm. 'I have to go to Geneva tomorrow, I should have gone earlier, but . . . I can't put my business off any longer. I will be gone a week. I'm sorry I did not tell you sooner, but I have been trying to avoid it . . . Shall we say lunch here tomorrow week? And then . . .' He smiled and kissed her on her mouth for the first time, fleetingly, but with so much promise. There on the street she clung to him, willing him to stay, not to change anything by leaving her and coming back and asking for more. Then she remembered where she was and pulled herself back. 'Yes, Wednesday week,' she promised, frightened by his threat of withdrawal, the reminder of his other life. He could so easily disappear, go back to his clocks and his smart French women. She would not even know where to find him. If she loved him she would go to bed with him ('and if he really loves you he won't ask you' her mother's warning voice came suddenly through the decades; wasn't that what mothers through the ages had told their young daughters in a doomed attempt to keep them virtuous?).

She watched him walk away from her, her heart full of love. He was right. They had to be together. Discretion was all. Everything would be all right.

Martin found Carol no easier to understand as the weeks went by. Something told him she had changed, but he could not see how. All he sensed was her withdrawal. It was in no way cold, there were moments when they talked as easily as ever, laughed, enjoyed themselves with friends or the children. Whenever Martin decided to spend time with her, to try and unravel whatever problem it was that was creating a wedge between them, she seemed to respond. There was no feeling from her of dislike or rejection. It was just that her mind seemed always to be elsewhere, except when he reached out and grabbed for it. He kept buying her presents, for which she thanked him prettily, but they seemed not to be the answer. They never were.

One Sunday afternoon when Dulcie and he were alone in the house he felt an impulse to go outside, find some fresh air. In spite of the January cold he suggested that Dulcie come with him for a walk. She was surprised.

'It's very cold, Martin, and it'll be dark soon.'

'Don't worry, it was just an idea.'

'No – no, I'll come. Just a minute while I get my coat.' Slightly reluctantly she put her novel aside and went downstairs for her things. Martin looked so sad these days, not edgy as he had when Carol had gone to France, just somehow rather pathetic. The last thing Dulcie wanted to do was to tramp around in the freezing streets, but if Martin needed company it would be cruel to ignore him. He did not ask for much – for anything, now she came to think of it – and she could not bear to see him looking so lonely.

They slammed the door behind them and set off at a brisk march, Dulcie keeping pace with her uncle, neither of them talking.

At last Dulcie, thinking she should try to be a companion and with no idea of his trouble or of what to say to him, said, 'Where are we going?'

'That, my dear Dulcie, is a question we should all be asking ourselves every day of our lives.' He had meant to sound jocular, but all his customary bluster was gone and to Dulcie he sounded only hollow.

'I meant now,' she said gently.

'Yes, I know. I'm sorry, love. It was foul of me to ask you to come out with me. I don't know which is the worse, the weather or my mood.'

'I don't mind either. But I wish I could help you. You've not been yourself recently.' She hesitated, unsure how far a niece could go but wanting him to feel that she was on his side. He wondered if anyone else in the family had noticed his agony and, self-pitying, doubted it. He stole a look at Dulcie striding along beside him, her cheeks and nose pink with the cold, her dark eyes fixed firmly on the pavement in front of her. He sighed.

'This isn't much of a place to walk in, is it?'

Dulcie adapted to the change of conversation, following Martin's lead as she did his pace.

'Oh, I don't know. It's quite comforting to feel all those people cosy in their houses, digesting their Sunday lunches, reading their papers, getting on with their own thoughts. We don't walk much at home, you know. People in the country don't unless they're actually going somewhere.'

He laughed. 'So you spot Londoners by the way they "go for a walk".'

'Something like that.' She paused then, encouraged by his laugh, went on, 'When we were children we used to think your walks were really funny. And best of all was how surprised the dogs looked – going for a walk with no purpose.'

'You should have told me.'

'Oh, we liked it. I liked it. It was always nice going walking with you.'

The silence between them was more comfortable now and after a while Martin, encouraged by the realisation that Dulcie really did like him, said, 'Dulcie, do you think your aunt's all right?'

'No.' They were both taken aback at how strongly the word came out. 'Not really.' She tried to soften the impact, but it was too late. 'Well, anyway, I don't mean there's anything wrong but – well, she's not normal. At least not most of the time.'

'No. Dulcie, I'm worried about her. I don't know what to do.' What was he doing, confiding to Dulcie – a child? And how could he explain, anyway? He could not tell her of all his fears, of his jealousy, of how he had accused and been wrong and accused and been wrong again and yet now . . .

'I don't suppose you can talk to her doctor?'

'Her doctor?' Dulcie was crazy; even Carol would never look at old Porter, nearing retirement, balding, bearded, deaf, impatient. 'Her doctor?'

'She seems really worried about something, and I'll bet it's not work.' Dulcie misread his reaction entirely, and went blindly on. 'She talks about work – seems all right, doesn't it? From what she's said. But maybe – I don't know, I wondered if she was ill and didn't want to say anything. 'Cos if she is, the worry will only make whatever it is worse. That's why I wondered, you know, about talking to her doctor.'

Martin wanted to hug Dulcie for her innocence, her purity and above all for the flood of relief that was so strong he almost staggered. *Ill, that's what she is – of course. Why didn't I realise, why did I doubt her? She's been seeing a doctor and is too worried to tell me. Oh God, I'm a fool. I knew it was different from before, I knew I had something to worry about and all those other times, well I had nothing to worry about then, did I? Oh Dulcie, you're a dream, I've never felt so happy in my entire life.*

Dulcie, keeping step with Martin, could not see his face and mistook his silence for worry. She tried to reassure him. 'It's probably nothing serious, Martin. Ma had a lump and didn't tell anyone anything about it, not even Pa, until it was all over and they found it was benign. In some ways they are quite alike, you know, Carol and Ma. I didn't see it until I lived here, but you know that although Carol's more outgoing than Ma, I think she's just as much of a thinker, and maybe more of a dreamer.'

'A dreamer?' Martin was holding fiercely onto his line of hope, but Dulcie's words brought him back to earth. 'Carol, a dreamer?'

'Yes, don't you think? I see her sometimes and she's not there, at her desk or wherever, but somewhere quite different. It's like all her energy has gone into her head. You look at her, and she's quite still, but her eyes are laughing, or – I don't know . . .' she tailed off, embarrassed that she might have overstepped the mark. 'Anyway, I mean that she can keep herself to herself,' she finished. 'And usually when people are like that it's because they have something they want to keep separate.'

Her last words could have – perhaps should have – alerted Martin's worries again, but after nearly twenty odd years of unnecessary panics he was only too pleased to seize the idea Dulcie had fed him and make it his own. They turned towards home, silent again, Martin chiding himself for his lack of faith, his insensitivity to Carol's fears. It was only as he put his key into the lock of number 27 that a new panic overcame him. He turned to Dulcie, voice lowered in case Carol and Piers had returned. 'Dulcie, sweetheart, don't say anything to Carol, or the others, will you? I'll talk to her. I'll pay for her to see the best man in Harley Street, the world. And when she's better I'll buy her that cottage in the country she's been thinking about . . .' Dulcie shrank a little. Martin always thought that money would solve everything. But then he added, 'Dear God, I hope it's not serious,' and she felt the misery behind his words and forgave him.

'Giles? Hi, it's Jody.'

'Jody? Is Dulcie OK?'

Jody laughed. 'Don't sound so panic-stricken; of course she is, she's fine.'

'I just wondered.'

'She misses you. You should come out with us one night.'

'Yes, sure, well, maybe.'

'Actually, Giles, I was hoping you'd have a drink with me tonight. I – I want to talk to you.'

'What about?' He sounded wary.

'Please, it's hard over the phone. I, well I think I've got myself in a bit of a mess and I don't know who to talk to.'

'What's wrong with your cousin?' and now he sounded cold, slightly aggressive.

'Please, Giles, she wouldn't understand, you know what she's like.'

'She's good at listening.'

'Yes, but she's too – oh look, never mind.' She was about to hang up but something in her voice had made Giles realise the degree of her desperation.

'Jody? Are you still there?'

'Yes.'

'This isn't a silly game, is it? No tricks?'

'Of course not.' Jody was too wrapped up in her own troubles to bother with fooling around with other people's, and Giles sensed that.

'All right, Jode, of course. After work tonight? Where do you want to meet?'

She told him the name of a wine bar off their beaten track, and he knew that she really did not want to bump into any of the others. As he hung up he had an inkling of what was to come. *Poor old Jody. Well, at least she's realised in time. I hope.*

It took a great deal to shake Jody's calm, but as soon as he saw her Giles knew for sure that she was worried about more than an overdraft or a decision about a party. Her normally clear skin was blotchy, her eyes looked sore and somehow shrunken. She did not usually wear much make up, and her attempts to repair her damaged skin only made her look worse. She would not be very good looking in middle age, Giles realised, when her hopes and excitement at life had gone.

He ordered a bottle of Sauvignon, lit her cigarette, loosened his tie and after a few moments' preliminary small talk, waited. Jody gabbled a bit to fill the silence, then ground to a halt. Giles poured more wine.

'It's Adam,' she said at last. Giles said nothing

'I thought, well, you know both sides of him. You see him at work, you've known him for ages. Oh Giles, I'm worried.'

'What about?' he prompted, pushing an ashtray towards her.

'It's the coke, the dope, I don't know . . . At first I thought it was just a bit here and there, but he seems to take something every night. You know me, I don't mind something every now and again, a bit of E, some coke . . . but I can't keep up. What am I to do?'

'Have you tried talking to him?'

'Yes, I have, but he just laughs. He says I'm getting up-tight, who does it hurt, just a bit of self-indulgence to help him relax . . . I just think it's getting out of hand.'

'Why don't you just leave him?'

'I *can't*.' The cry was one of pure pain and Giles looked more closely at her. 'I can't,' she repeated more quietly. 'I – he needs me, he needs someone to help him sort it out, I can't just walk out.'

Giles looked at her again, taking in her exhaustion, her misery. Was there even fear there?

'You're serious about him, aren't you?' he asked; they did not use words like love in their circle.

'Yes, I suppose I am. He's such good fun, he makes me laugh, we get on so well together. It's just . . . does he take the drugs at work?'

'I don't know. I honestly don't. But to tell the truth, rumour says he does. Not often, but sometimes. They say he was nearly caught once but managed to bluff it out.'

'Will he get the sack?'

'No, no reason to at all. He's doing his job well, so far.'

'So far? Be honest, Giles, are you worried?'

Giles thought a moment and wondered whether he was or not. 'Well, *I'm* not. But maybe I should be.'

'You mean maybe I should?'

'I mean that I'm all for a bit of fun, relaxation or whatever. I'm all for self-indulgence. It's just that it can be taken too far. I suppose if the only person you're going to hurt is yourself, it's fine. But when the effects will be felt further afield . . . it looks to me like you're in danger of being hurt.'

'And his parents.'

Giles was surprised Jody should think of them. 'They wouldn't be, not in the same way. If he loses his job, their pride will be hurt more than anything else.'

'Have you met them?'

'No, I was meant to go down for the weekend the first time you went, but it was just after Dulcie and I split up so I cancelled.'

'You do see why I couldn't talk to Dulcie about all this.'

'Yes, I suppose so.'

'Although she is lightening up. D'you know, she tried some coke that weekend.'

'Dulcie did?'

'Yes, it was almost like she was accepting a dare. She was fine about it, said she'd just got on her high horse about the drug culture and found it hard to get off.'

Giles laughed. 'That's Dulcie all over,' but he was a little sad.

'But that's what I mean about Adam. You know, he won't let it drop. He wants everyone else to be like him, or else they're not having fun or being fun or something. It's a bit like those keen people who go to church.'

Giles wondered whether Adam were to blame, or he himself, and whether Dulcie would ever admit to him that she had tried the drug and liked it.

'Dulcie going out with anyone now?'

Jody hesitated long enough for Giles to notice. 'No.'

'Which means?'

'No,' more forcefully. But she could not resist adding, 'But I think Adam's brother fancied her.'

'Frankie? I wouldn't have thought she was the army officer type.'

'No, the other one, the farmer.'

'Oh, the farmer.' Well, he could not compete with that.

'Will you talk to Adam?' Jody was back with her own problems.

'No. I can't, Jody. You must. If he's serious about you he'll listen to you. Or he's more likely to, anyway.'

'Please.'

'Jody, the best I can do is this: if I find out he's doing drugs at work, or if I even have good reason to suspect it, I'll talk to him. But out of work hours it's over to you. And I'll keep an eye out, OK? Now come on, let's finish this bottle and move on. Do you fancy a film?'

# 12

They had met as though the week apart had been a month. In that week the relationship had moved into a new phase. Henri's absence had made Carol realise how empty her life would now be without him, and the fact that he could leave her even for a while made her realise that he could leave her for ever. They were to be apart for another week as Carol had to go back to the Petersons' house and this added urgency to their reunion.

Henri clearly thought that the courtship had taken long enough and it was time for consummation. Carol, feeling his hand in the small of her back as he guided her to her usual seat in Launceston Place, agreed. She was a grown-up now. The mooning and spooning had been delicious, but lust was taking giant strides forward. Mooning and spooning were no longer enough.

They barely talked during lunch, Carol nervous of what lay ahead, Henri not wanting to shift the change in balance which he sensed in her. Under the table he held her leg between his and she had no thought for Martin or her home or her children. All that mattered now was Henri.

She refused a pudding or cognac. 'Just coffee please,' she said to the waiter with a smile, and then when he had left said, almost matter-of-factly, 'I've no appointments this afternoon'. And then, in case he had not quite understood her message, 'I told the girls I would not be back at the office this afternoon.' In fact, still unsure, she had only said she might not be back, but then she had also cancelled her meeting for the afternoon, just to keep her options open.

'You mean . . .?'

Shyly, she nodded. 'But where? We can't go to your friends' flat.'

Henri grinned. 'I am not staying with them this time. I am in an hotel.'

'You were that sure of me?'

'I could only hope,' he smiled again, a little gleam of triumph in his eyes which Carol chose to ignore. He called for the bill.

'But your coffee, your cognac, sir?'

'I've changed my mind. Let the cook drink them. I owe him more than a cognac.' And he rushed through paying, positively bundled Carol into her coat and out of the door.

'Where are you staying?'

'Five minutes away. Come, *ma chère*.' He tucked her hand into the crook of his arm and set off, a happy man.

Now that the irrevocable moment was so near, Carol was frightened again. Her body sang with the thrill of soon-to-be-fulfilled lust; through their two coats she was aware of his body beside hers, her hip close to his thigh, her head so near his chest, but her mind was crowded with fears. Would he notice her stretch marks? Would he mind? Her figure was good enough but her body was irredeemably that of a woman in her forties who had borne three children. And what was she to do about Martin? Would he notice? Would something about her give her away as soon as he saw her? She had had a friend who had been brought up to believe that a father could tell as soon as his daughter lost her virginity. They had all hooted with laughter and persuaded the poor girl that it was nonsense, but now for the first time in years the memory came back to her. Could a man tell if his wife had been unfaithful? Would she look different, feel different? Would their lovemaking be different?

She held tightly on to Henri's arm, anchoring herself to him to prevent her own flight, looking blindly ahead at the Kensington High Street crowd surging around her. She wished this walk, which already seemed so much longer than the promised five minutes, were over. She was sure that once this first time were over and done with, the decision made and acted upon, life would be easy again.

Then she saw a face she knew coming towards her in the crowd. She gasped, clung closer to Henri, then pulled herself away from him. He looked at her, surprised, and followed the direction of her eyes. She was staring at a young girl, small and dark with wavy hair and big brown eyes. The girl seemed to be window shopping, and was not looking at them at all. But as he watched, he saw her look at Carol, surprised, and make as if to speak. Then her glance slid from Carol to him, and he saw comprehension in her eyes. She looked back at Carol who had stopped in the street and stood as though petrified. Then the girl shifted her eyes into the middle distance and walked past them, only the width of a pavement away.

Henri re-engaged Carol's arm and moved her on without saying anything. She struggled with herself for a while then said, in what she hoped passed for a normal voice, 'Did you see that girl?'

'Yes.'

'She's my niece, the one I told you about who is living with us. I'm idiotic, I never thought – she works at Waterstone's, a book shop down the road from here. Why didn't I think?'

'Why does it matter?'

'Henri! She saw us!'

'*Et alors*? We were walking down a public road.'

'Together.'

'Yes.'

'I had my hand in your arm.'

'It is a cold day. Friends often link arms. We are friends.'

'Henri, she knew.'

'Carol, in case you have forgotten, there is really very little to know. As yet. We are friends who have had lunch together. If you prefer I could be a client.' It was the first time that Henri had been impatient with her and Carol shivered more at his displeasure than at the cold wind which blew bitterly into her ears and around her ankles.

'She saw me, she looked at me, she nearly spoke to me. She looked at you and she walked past. I was cut by my own niece!' Her sudden sense of outrage made Henri smile.

'Sensible girl. She saw we did not want to be interrupted.' He walked on calmly, determined she should see this through but half wishing he had never become involved with such an unwilling lover. And yet he could not resist her, coveted her and lusted after her and maybe even loved her. He could not let her go, not now. He was in blood so steeped . . . he smiled to himself, a prickle of pride at his own grasp of a foreign language interrupting his thoughts.

Carol, looking up, catching his smile, misunderstood and tore her hand from his arm. 'Henri, what are you smiling at?' Before he could answer, she stepped back and said, 'I'm sorry, Henri, not today, I can't . . . I can't have Dulcie knowing what I'm doing, I can't—' and before he could stop her she had turned and half run into the road. 'Sorry,' she shouted as she hailed a taxi and leapt in, and then 'Sorry' again as she pushed down the window and leaned out, tears running down her cheeks. 'I'll ring when I get back. Sorry.' And the black cab pulled back into the stream of traffic and took her away.

So that was it. Carol was not ill at all. How incredibly naive she had been. Dulcie flushed with shame at herself. She really had not learned much, had she? Thought the worst thing that could happen was an illness, a benign tumour. Carol was not ill, she was in love. Dulcie did not doubt for a moment that he was her lover. She had never seen her aunt look so stricken, like a rabbit the second before you shot it. *I'm not very grown-up really,* Dulcie thought sadly as she reached Waterstone's and took her coat off. *I still expect grown-ups to behave properly, as they told us to when we were little.*

Then she thought of Martin and she felt sick. Thanks to her interference he now thought that his wife was dying of some unspecified illness, when in fact she was trolling around with strange men in Kensington. Oh God, what had she gone and done? And the worst of it was that she could not undo the damage. 'Oh by the way, Martin, Carol's quite all right. She's not ill at all, she's having an affair. Unless it's the doctor, and then she's ill *and* having an affair.' What an idiotic, well-meaning, interfering fool she was. Why had she opened her mouth? Other people's marriages were their own, should not be known about or discussed or presumed to be understood by anyone else. If a marriage was not private, what was? The worst part was realising that she had been so nearly right – had seen that Carol was worried, nurturing some secret. She had just presumed to know what the secret was. Oh hell.

'You all right, Dulcie?' The manager of the book shop was hovering over her.

'Yes. Why?'

'Only there's a customer who's been trying to get your attention for five minutes.'

'I'm sorry. How can I help?'

The woman wanted an 'X-Files' book and Dulcie, wishing that everything, even Jane Austen, were not sold on the back of a television series, led her to the piles of books. The woman made an impulse buy of a Delia Smith book and thanked Dulcie sweetly for her help, leaving Dulcie feeling lower than ever.

She was sure Carol had seen her, and wished she knew whether or not she had done the right thing in ignoring her. It had been so clear that Carol had not wanted to be seen, but then having seen her should she not have said hello, pretended everything was normal, not shown quite how clear it was that Carol was looking furtive?

Dulcie wondered who the man was. She had certainly never seen him before. He was tall, dark, not especially good looking. He had an *amused* look in his eye which Dulcie could see was attractive, and something about his swept-back hair and hooked nose had given him a faintly foreign air. His long dark coat looked expensive and business-like. Perhaps he was just a client, one of the divorcés Carol joked about who were suddenly thrown on to their own resources and had no idea about where to buy anything from sofas to pots and pans. Having already jumped to one wrong conclusion, Dulcie tried to stop herself from reaching another on as little information. But this time she was sure. That man had been no client. He had been a threat. A threat to Martin, a threat to Jody and Alan and Piers and even in some senses a threat to Dulcie. He was a threat to the established order of life and Dulcie did not know what to do about it. Nothing, she supposed. All she could do was brace herself to look her aunt in the eye when they met this evening.

'Carol, my love, I think we should talk.'

It was not the first time in their marriage that Carol had heard those words and it was many years since she had learned the agony that always followed them. Jewell, Ackroyd, Peterson, had been just a few who Martin had accused Carol of sleeping with and her innocence had made no difference to him. This time, with something to hide, she could do nothing but wait. She was frightened, defiant, penitent and unrepentant all at the same time. She was also very angry with Dulcie. Angry with her for having been in Kensington High Street, angry with her for having realised the situation and pretended not to in such a gauche way, and livid with her for having told Martin.

So, on the pretext of chopping onions, she turned her back on Martin and said nothing. If he was going to be so ungentlemanly as to insist on going into everything, it was up to him to make the running.

'I think,' he went on, 'that you're keeping something from me and I just wish you wouldn't.' Still she did not speak – what was there to say? – so after a moment he went on. 'Carol, my darling, I know you're trying to protect me and I love you for it, but please, know that we'll be stronger if we fight together.' *What on earth is he going on about?* 'You know we can. I know my weaknesses, but give me the credit for my strengths. Let me in on this and it will make it easier.'

'What if I don't want to fight it?' she asked, looking up from the onions, grateful that they gave the alibi for tears.

'Don't want to? Of course you must. We must. Whatever it takes we can fight it.'

Carol was dumbfounded. All these years of ranting about nobodies and now he was facing real danger he was talking like a Crusader off to face the Saracens.

'Punch-ups aren't your style, I would have thought,' she said. Sometimes she had wished they were. A half hour's outburst of vicious temper must be easier to live with than a month's smouldering and brooding.

'No, which is why it's probably easier to deal with when it's something you can't punch. Carol, tell me about it, just telling will help. And then we'll look at the possibilities and the options and work out our approach.'

Carol wondered whether this time he was not more deeply mad than all the other times. What did he want, a full confession, a *mea culpa*, a forgiveness scene? She was not ready for that, was not prepared to commit herself to abandoning Henri.

'I don't know why Dulcie had to open her mouth and blab,' she said bitterly. 'None of it has anything to do with her.' She slid the onions into the pan and, on automatic drive as far as the cooking went, began chopping bacon with shaking hands.

'It wasn't like that, I sort of led her on, she was just concerned. You know how walking makes you talk? I asked her to come with me.'

What on earth was Martin talking about now? Walking? Talking? When? Dulcie was not back from work yet. Carol had come straight home and when Martin had also come home early she had explained that she had left work because of a dreadful headache. What had Dulcie done? Rung him at work? Carol found it hard to believe, yet how else did he know? And what was all this about walking?

'Don't you sometimes think you'd be better off without me?' she asked, although she had never really contemplated leaving.

'No! Carol, no, I love you. But you've been so unapproachable recently, I've been so worried. And I have to admit all the old demons began to resurface although I tried so hard to keep them away. Then on Sunday, when you were picking up Piers from badminton I felt so low, so utterly alone. I asked Dulcie to come for a walk with me, and it was just the way the conversation turned, you mustn't blame her. Blame me if anyone.'

Carol turned and faced him. *Sunday? What does he mean – Sunday? Dulcie did not know anything on Sunday – couldn't have.*

They faced each other, he misunderstanding her incomprehension. Then he said, very gently, 'Carol, darling, would it be easier for you if I went and talked to your doctor, let him explain? Don't you see, I must know. I love you too much to be excluded.' And suddenly all that he had said fell into place and she understood.

'No. Don't go to my doctor,' she said quickly, too quickly, trying to think on her feet but numb with confusion.

'Then you must tell me, Carol. You've got to tell me, you've got to help me to help you.' To her amazement she saw Martin's eyes fill with tears – could the onions be blamed? Almost certainly not. He moved round to her side of the kitchen table and gently took the knife from her hands before hugging her tightly. 'Carol, I love you so much. I'm so frightened for you. I've got to help you. I couldn't bear . . .' To her horror he seemed to be crying. Carol stood rigid in his arms, her mind racing. What now? What next? A lie, of course, she had dug herself in so far that all she could do was to lie.

'It's all right, Martin, it's all right.'

'What do you mean?'

'I'm not ill. I'm fine.'

He searched her face, uncomprehending. She took a deep breath. This was where the lying had to start. 'I don't know how Dulcie knew, I've not talked to her. But in one sense she was right. I – I have been ill . . . Or I thought I was. And I didn't want to face up to it. To the implications. But it's all right now.'

'I don't understand.'

She was going to have to do better. 'Martin, it was gynaecological stuff. You know. I thought things weren't right and I was worried, but anyway it's turned out that everything's all right after all.'

She met his eyes, praying that such a sketchy explanation would do, daring him to question her further, not knowing what she would say if he did. Maybe she would have to tell him the truth after all. Maybe it would be a relief if she did.

'Carol.' He was very serious. 'If ever anything like this happens again, tell me at the beginning, not at the end. When you're worried, not when you know it's all right. I would make it easier for you, I promise I would.' He hugged her again and this time it was Carol who had to squeeze her eyes tightly against the tears. 'Promise me,' he said into her hair and Carol, not quite knowing what she was giving her word to, promised.

# 13

Carol left for Toulouse in an entirely different frame of mind from that of her first visit a few months earlier. Then Martin had been silent and glowering, now he was loving and gentle. Then her worry had been his unreasoning jealousy, now it was his reasonable kindness. *Perhaps he's got a lover?* she thought, and smiled. *Well, that's the tables turned on me.* She knew he did not have a lover. *Well, you can never be sure . . . Yes, I can be sure of Martin.*

She drank the bitter cup of coffee the air hostess offered her and looked out of the window at the blank blueness all around her. She was thankful to have a week away from home, away from Henri and Martin and Dulcie.

She had wondered what to say to Dulcie and had in the end decided that silence was the best policy. It seemed she had no other choice – if she faced her niece she would either have to lie or tell the truth and throw herself upon the girl's mercy. The first was impossible, the second unthinkable. If she totally ignored the issue maybe Dulcie would begin to doubt her own eyes. That first evening had been hard. Dulcie had walked in from work, forced herself to look her aunt in the face, shrunk and looked shifty. Then Martin had come dancing in and told Dulcie it was all right, Carol was fine, worried by a false alarm. Carol, trying not to sound tight-lipped, thanked Dulcie for her concern – what else was there to do with Martin there, grinning idiotically? – and offered her a glass of wine. As Dulcie took it their eyes met, and Carol saw everything she needed to know. Dulcie had judged her guilty and been made miserable by it, but would say nothing.

*Why couldn't it have been Jody who saw us?* Carol wondered. *She's so relaxed, so uninterested in other people. She wouldn't have minded, would probably have laughed, made a joke. Actually, she probably wouldn't even have picked up on anything.* Maybe that was the difference between Jody and Dulcie. Maybe it was not so much that she would not mind, as that she would not have noticed. Dulcie was a little too straitlaced about things, always had a view and was always prepared to defend it, but she was interested in people. She minded about them.

Carol picked up the paperback she had bought at the airport but her thoughts drifted from it after the first couple of paragraphs. For the first time she wondered why it had been her niece, not one of her children, who had seen the signs that something was up. Piers was too young of course, just a child, and Alan was off at university now, an occasional weekend visitor with nothing more than home cooking and laundry on his mind. But Jody – Jody was a girl, a woman really by now. They lived in the same house, laughed at the same jokes, ate together, sometimes watched television together . . . Jody was her daughter – how could she be so self-absorbed? She should be beyond the selfishness of teenagerhood by now, was meant to be a fully functioning adult. Perhaps it was time she left home, although when Carol and Martin had discussed it before they had always felt it to be an unnecessary expense. She did not seem to want to go, they gave her plenty of leeway in her private life, closed their ears to stairs creaking and front door slamming early in the morning. All that was expected of her was good manners, which included a sense of discretion. And golden Jody drifted on through life, never asking for anything but always getting what she wanted.

And now she was involved with Adam Exton. Carol did not know if her daughter was in love, but now she thought about it she realised that Jody had been slightly subdued recently, had begun to look flaky and tired, was not quite so shining as she had been. What was the matter with her? Adam seemed attentive enough, she was never left looking longingly at the telephone. If anything she was out more often than ever. Martin had not said anything, but then she and Martin had hardly talked about anything recently, her mind had been so full of Henri . . .

Carol brought herself up short. *So who's being self-absorbed? Jody or me? Both, maybe, but I'm her mother, I'm the grown-up in the relationship, always will be to her. I should be watching out for her, not wondering why she isn't watching out for me. And something is the matter with her. I should have noticed, I would have before . . . before Henri. What is the matter with me? Where is my sense of perspective?*

The seat-belt light came on; the short flight was nearly over. Carol put the unread novel back in her bag, clipped on her safety belt and checked her face in her hand mirror. It looked the same, there was no sign that the last few months had changed her. *Why should they have? I've done nothing.* A little lipstick, a quick comb of her hair and there was Carol the business woman, ready to meet Peterson and turn her mind to the job.

A blonde of about Carol's age was with Peterson at the airport. He introduced her as Birgitta, and said he had been taking her sightseeing in Toulouse that morning. The two women smiled and shook hands and Carol remembered how relieved she had been to hear of this woman's existence and what little difference it had, in the event, made. Birgitta was tall and striking, just on the tarty side of glamorous. She explained that she was an anchorwoman on Swedish television, that she had only recently landed the job, an enormous boost to her career, that she was a divorcée, that she could not yet uproot herself but that she so much wanted to see how Peter would live, to be able to imagine them all. It was very different from Sweden, yes, very foreign, she did so hope they weren't making a mistake, although she quite understood, of course she had never met Pauline . . . on and on she went, garrulous and friendly and behaving as though Peter were not there. It suited Carol admirably. She could sit in the back of the car nodding and smiling where it seemed appropriate, pretending to admire the view but lost in her own thoughts. And she had a week in which to think. A week she badly needed.

The boys were friendly and pleased to see her, both said they liked the designs for their rooms – in fact they were the only rooms in the house where she had been totally conventional. They had simple, classic wallpapers, one with a faint blue and green stripe, the other the same paper in green and yellow, heavy plain green curtains, green paint work and large, framed posters. The posters were a clever mix of accessible modern art and the boys' passions – motor racing for one, anatomical drawings for the other (medical posters and prints of Stubbs's drawings did the trick there). It was a clever ruse, which would make the rooms easy to alter when the boys' tastes changed, without costing too much.

Had Carol been honest with herself she need not have spent more than two days at the house this time; the decorators were already there, she knew and trusted them implicitly, but she had been grateful for the excuse to escape and had argued that it would save making another trip too soon.

She wandered around the house, notebook once again in hand, checking that the paints matched the samples, that the curtains (made up in England, arriving in batches almost daily) were hanging correctly, had been measured and made properly. The rooms that had already been decorated were waiting, clean-smelling shells, for her to arrange; and under her eye pictures were hung, furniture aligned exactly to her instructions. In many ways this had been an easy job: Peter had told her he did not want to throw furniture or pictures away, wanted nothing new bought unnecessarily, so there had been very little trawling around antique shops to be done. He had even insisted that where possible curtains should stay or, if moved, be re-used. This was not, he insisted, out of meanness, but part of his effort to let the house keep as much character as possible, to stop it looking as *arriviste* as he was but his sons were not.

Carol avoided Birgitta as much as she could, but found her talkative presence at meals a distraction, and even began quite to like her. She would have found Peter heavy going without his bewildered brother as a companion; they had nothing in common except the house, and having spent all her days on it Carol welcomed a change in the evenings.

Whenever her mind was not busy – and Carol kept it as busy as she could – her brain filled with thoughts of Henri. Henri, and the impossible mess she had got herself into. Luckily there were no memories of him in this house, of him or of Martin either, so it was easy – or as easy as it would be anywhere in the world – to try and be objective.

What did she want from Henri? From Martin? What had been missing in her marriage that had pushed her so fast into the arms, if not yet the bed, of an unknown Frenchman? Sometimes she began with Henri, sometimes with Martin, but wherever she started she could not see her way to a conclusion. She knew that one solution, perhaps the best, was to go ahead, have an affair, work the whole thing out of her system, keep it quiet, go back to Martin without ever having left him. In some ways that would be the most honourable thing to do. But to her that route did not address the problem. Carol was a fair-minded person, and she would not allow herself to be unfair to Martin. That would be too easy.

She loved Martin. She loved Henri, but that did not stop her loving Martin. She still loved him without having to think why or how, but nevertheless she forced herself to add it all up. She loved him for his generosity, his relaxed approach to life. She loved him as father to her children, she loved the drive, the hard-working will to succeed which they both shared. She loved the way he took her family on board as his – the way he had never questioned the absolute right that Dulcie should make her home with them, for instance. She loved him on holidays, when they seemed so perfectly in tune that they barely needed to discuss whether they felt like visiting a bar or a beach or an art gallery, they just knew. She loved him in spite of the ferocious jealousy which had at times been so hard to live with. She loved him in spite of, maybe even because of, the way he could sometimes get things so wrong, misjudge a situation, be too loud, too obvious, be a little bit the wide boy or 'not quite a gentleman' as her father had described him. All those presents recently – she had accepted them gracefully because she had known they came from his love, but she deplored the assumption that money could buy her back.

And so? What had she missed? She had a career, children, a nice house, a loving and loved husband.

She had had too much for too long, that was the problem. The only excitement in her life had come from Martin's jealousy, and that was not an excitement worth treasuring. She had missed romance, flirtation, the thrill of the chase. She was too contented. She wanted to be courted, frightened, challenged, woken up. She wanted to be romanced.

Was that all this was, this feeling for Henri? Was it just that she was still the young girl who had dreamed of Mr Darcy and Mr Rochester, despised Angel Clare and William Dobbin, seen why Amelia Sedley loved George Osborne, despite his weaknesses? Had she spent too many years finding romance in old love songs and books and memories of long-done-with affairs?

Which was partly Martin's fault. He could have romanced her a little, organised the occasional – not too embarrassing – surprise. *Oh hell, what do I expect him to do? Run through London with an umbrella, singing his love for me?* Briefly she thought of Tony and 'Halfway to Paradise', but *no, that's what I've been doing all these years, living well in the present but harking back to my past. And that's idiotic. But oh, it's bliss to be wanted, to be desired as a treat rather than a right. If he thought of it, Henri would sing to me, I'm sure. And in a way he does sing, all the time. Oh God, what am I to do? And Martin's face, when he knew I wasn't ill. How can I think he doesn't love me? He loves me so much, more than I deserve. I don't want to leave him, don't want to risk it. Without him I'd be nothing. Oh, I'd manage all right, there's some money still and there's the business, but he's my home, my husband, he's been my life for all these years, we've got years more, why am I even thinking like this?*

*But I am, and I'll probably do it, and I desperately want to do it. If I can without spoiling everything else. And I can't. Even if I'm never caught – and that's thinking like a child – I'll have spoilt it all in my head. I'll know. And every time afterwards when Martin goes on one of his rants, I will be guilty as charged. Maybe not that time, with that person, but in essence.*

*But Henri, oh how can I leave him, now – if he'll give me another chance after the other day. And he will, I'm sure he will. If I don't go to bed with him, I'll always regret it, I'll never know . . . it's love, not lust, I'm sure of that, although of course lust comes into it, quite a lot, but that's not what's driven me – so why am I so scared? Because if it's love why am I not prepared to leave, to ditch everything, to run off with him? Not that he's asked me, he'd probably be horrified at the thought . . . he wants me to play his game, and I'm just not used to it . . . but it's not just a game to him now, I'm sure of it – well, maybe just a little, but he wants me, he loves me, in his way, he must do . . .*

Round and round it went – Henri, Martin, love, lust, fidelity, infidelity, passion, security, romance, familiarity. *What is so wrong with security and familiarity?* she asked herself more than once, and *nothing, but wouldn't it be heaven to find out if anything is really wrong with romance?* And all the while Birgitta talked and talked at her, and the boys joked and even got her to play table tennis and Peter walked around the house and watched his dead wife's possessions being moved around and smiled and looked happy. *And that's all it would be, a shake-up, a rearrangement, nothing more pernicious than that . . .*

'The Herivaux are coming over tonight for dinner, do you remember them? The couple we went to dinner with when you were last here?' Peter said on the morning of her last day with them.

'Oh yes, of course. They were very nice,' Carol finished lamely.

'They've been very keen to see what I – you – have been doing here; so I thought it would be fun to ask them over while you were here, see the work that's been done and we could talk them through what remains. If you don't mind,' he added, wondering suddenly about artistic temperament.

'No, of course not,' Carol said with what felt like an immense effort. 'It's your house,' she added, and immediately felt she had sounded graceless.

'I'm going to send all your boys down to the restaurant in the village,' Peter said, referring to the decorators who were still swarming through the house. They always ate apart, but there was no denying they were a noisy and definite presence. *Still, that was his decision*, thought Carol, wondering if she was expected to foot the bill. 'I've told them dinner's on me, but they'll have to pay for their drink,' he added, reading her mind. Carol thanked him prettily, knowing it was to her that they would all come complaining about being forced to eat fancy foreign food and the impossibility of finding a proper cup of tea on the continent and what was the point of being in bloody Europe if they couldn't learn anything . . . They'd been living off sandwiches and the occasional stew or cottage pie Birgitta uncomplainingly made them. Every now and again they would disappear to the village and come lurching back, noisily drunk, laughing and cursing good naturedly. 'I'm gutted, fucking gutted. I'm in love, in love with that girl, I'm fucking gutted,' Carol had woken one night to hear one of them bawling at the moon. The others had shushed him, laughing, slipping on something, almost as noisy as he. 'Which one?' 'That fucking lovely one in green. I'm in love, I'm fucking gutted' and she had heard them, thumping unevenly up the stairs to their attic rooms, chorusing 'fucking gutted' in counterpoint to his howling protestations of love.

Which is what it kept coming back to, everything, the conversation, her thoughts, life, reality, dreams . . .

'I hope they don't come back too noisy,' Carol said, smiling, and Peter, who had shown remarkable restraint, smiled back and shrugged his shoulders. 'They always start work on time,' he said, 'and they've given the villagers some colourful theories about English workmen. They don't do any harm. Tonight Birgitta's going to prepare a special Swedish dinner for us all, she thought it would be nice, show what we can do. I hope you don't mind,' he said again.

'I'd love to try Swedish food.'

'I meant about showing the house before you are finished. I should have asked.'

'I honestly don't care two hoots,' she said and left Peter laughing at the new English expression.

She did not care two hoots about the house, but she did about the Herivaux. What did they know? What, if anything, had Henri told them? Oh God, today was going to be long.

In fact it flew by; it was her last day at the house and she had to be sure that the decorators knew exactly what they were doing over the next couple of weeks before she was due to come back. She was very pleased with the shape the house was taking, and Peter seemed to be as well. She had rediscovered its clear, straight lines, let in the light, opened up an enfilade that went the length of the house and had unaccountably been blocked by a heavy armoire. The dark furniture was still there, giving the house a certain melancholy gravitas, but somehow now it worked. The bravest thing she had done was in the music room, where she had had the delicate plaster work on the ceiling picked out in bright colours. It was a shock to eyes accustomed to white plaster, but the room was wonderful, humorous and elegant and lyrical. It was the one room from which Carol had succeeded in banishing the dark bourgeois pieces that were everywhere, and had bought a few smaller, more delicate, bits of eighteenth century furniture.

Every now and again the consciousness of something unpleasant, or at any rate uncomfortable, to come tickled at the edge of her brain, but it was not until she was up in her room, changing for dinner, brushing her hair, carelessly checking her make up, that the thought really took hold. It had not occurred to her that she might see the Herivaux, the thought had not even crossed her mind. She had never even discussed them with Henri, had no idea how close a friend of theirs he was. They had too much else to discuss to bother with such peripheral things. Well, she would just have to play it by ear.

Carol wandered down the stairs, loving the sense of the house changing around her, and delighted to be staying it in as it did so. She had more feeling for this house than for any job she had undertaken for months, and it had given her back faith in her work. At least something good had come from all this mess. She found Birgitta in the kitchen, stirring something on the range which had been restored to all its former glory.

'Can I help?'

'That's kind. Give yourself a drink, first. There's some white wine and some vodka in the fridge. If you don't mind laying the table that would be a help, but it's the company more than anything, isn't it, someone to talk to while you're cooking.'

Someone to talk at, more to the point. And off she went, wittering on about her mother's cooking, her aunt Kristina, someone called Lars Poynsson who Carol had never heard of before but who seemed important in some way – television? Carol completely lost track. Carol laid the table methodically for six, three courses, three glasses, until she heard Birgitta, saying, 'Oh sorry, I completely forgot to tell you, it's one extra, they're bringing a friend,' and her heart stood still. *It can't be, he wouldn't, he knows I'm here, what am I to do? He wouldn't.*

But he had.

\*  \*  \*

'A great coincidence,' Susanne Herivaux repeated innocently. 'Do you remember Henri Durand, he was staying with us when you came to dinner? He rang us yesterday morning.'

'Another self-invitation,' Henri apologised with a small bow.

'*Mais bien sûr* – you are always welcome and only you know when you are free. You are much more busy than us,' Susanne said, again with no mockery or irony. *She really is a sweet woman,* Carol remembered, *she won't suspect a thing. Well, what do I mean by that? That I'm in with the bad boys now?*

Henri held out his hand and looked her in the eye with the faintest smile. 'There is no reason for Carol to remember, but of course I do,' he said and raised her hand. *So that's my cue, he hasn't said a word. What's he here for then, if he's not asking them to collude with – anything?*

'Now that is why I like the French,' said Birgitta. She was particularly sprightly tonight – the responsibility of entertaining, no doubt. 'The most effortless flattery, so sincerely.'

'No flattery at all, madame,' Henri said severely, loosing Carol's hand and taking Birgitta's. 'Most genuinely meant.'

'You see?' she laughed. 'I'm Birgitta Bjornsson. How nice to meet you.'

'I believe last time we met you were being introduced to this house,' Henri turned back to Carol, 'and now we are here to see the consummation of all your plans. I am privileged.'

'I don't know,' Carol's voice came out in a feeble bray. 'It's not at all finished yet, it looks very different but not finished, you know what I mean? But you haven't been here before, have you, so it will not look very special to you.' *I've gone and done it now, oh shit, they'll notice.*

'Now talking of flattery, I'm flattered you remember,' he said smoothly. 'No, this is my first visit here but I will be interested to see your work.'

'Are you thinking of buying a property yourself? I've never been to Geneva.' *Oh shit I've done it again, what's wrong with me, I'm a total idiot.* 'Or was it Berne?' she gabbled. 'Or Zurich? Oh Lord, I'm so pea-brained about abroad, but I'm sure you mentioned Switzerland.' Eric Herivaux looked surprised, and Henri's eyes sent her a stern warning.

'Yes, Geneva,' he said. 'No, I'm not buying anywhere myself.

My present arrangements suit me very well. In most particulars. But I am interested in the idea, if you understand me, of interior designers. If you will forgive me, I have always considered it a peculiar kind of a job.'

'Yes, well, before anything else what would you all like to drink?' Peter said. 'I have some very good champagne I thought we could christen the house with – prematurely perhaps – or vodka? Gin?' Carol was already drinking Absolut Citron on the rocks and, guessing it was probably a mistake she would regret, stuck with that. The others all took glasses of champagne and, leaving Birgitta in the kitchen, followed Peter through to the music room.

Carol felt she should stay behind too and offer her services, but she did want to see Henri's reaction.

She could not have been better rewarded. An indrawn breath, a short silence, then *'Ma chère* – Carol – it is wonderful,' said Henri, and the Herivaux joined in the praise wholeheartedly.

'I've only brought back the room's own elegance,' Carol said modestly, so pleased she almost forgot the embarrassment of her situation. Until she met Henri's look and her heart sank again.

*Is this a punishment? I suppose he could have told them; in some ways it would have been a relief, would have been fun to play at being a couple, but that's all it is, isn't it, play? A bloody game, and one I don't seem to be very good at.*

In some ways it was like the evening they had first met: once again Carol laughed and joked, almost unaware of what she was doing. She helped Birgitta serve and clear the dinner, discussed food around the world and its relative merits, the European Union, the marriages of the British Royal Family, the place of church in society, promised to visit Sweden, to bring her husband, but all the time all she was aware of was Henri. His eyes seemed never to be off her face – why did the others not notice? – a taut thread seemed to connect them. This time was worse, though. This time there was no doubt that the attraction was reciprocated, but there was fear. Fear that she would give something away, fear that he had come here to punish her for running out on him, to torment her further.

After dinner Peter took Eric into his study to show him some plans that had been drawn up for some new planting. Carol led the way into the music room, but found that only Henri had followed her.

'Susanne is helping Birgitta with the coffee,' he said as he carefully shut the door behind him.

'Why did you come?' she asked, backing away from him, longing to go into his arms.

'Because I had to see you. Our last meeting was rather unsatisfactory.' He smiled but there was a hardness in his eyes Carol did not like. 'And I wanted to give you this.' From his pocket he produced a tiny box.

Despite every instinct warning her against doing so, Carol could not resist taking it and opening it. Inside lay a beautiful pair of smoky topaz and crystal earrings. 'They're wonderful, Henri, beautiful, but I couldn't.'

'Don't be ridiculous. I saw them and could not resist them for you. I wanted to give them to you before, but . . .'

'I know. I'm sorry. Oh, Henri . . .'

She took one out of its box and turned to the mirror above the fireplace.

'No, don't put them on now,' he said sharply, and she realised that the others might notice.

'Yes, of course, I do see,' she said humbly and put the jewel back on its bed. Sadly she closed the box and handed it back to Henri. He put his hands behind his back and grinned, suddenly looking mischievous and very attractive.

'When would I ever wear them?' she said sadly. 'If not here, where no-one knows me, where?'

'Oh, you'll be able to find an occasion,' he said easily. 'And won't it be fun just knowing you've got them? You'll only have to look at them and we'll be together. I would have thought that wearing them would be almost an extra.'

*That's it, that's where he's got me. The romance of the gesture, the word. He just has to look at me and I know what life is about. And he's right, this is all an extra. But essential now.*

'Oh, Henri'. She put her hand up to his cheek and his face came down to hers and in the kiss everything was asked and everything promised and everything inconvenient forgotten.

Footsteps crossing the hall drew them apart and by the time the door was opened Henri and Carol were sitting on different chairs discussing Pat Barker's novels with remarkable composure.

'Well, Henri,' Susanne said as she passed him a cup of coffee, 'do you know yet whether you are staying another night? Did you succeed in talking to the airport?'

'Yes, I'm sorry, I should have told you. There's room on a flight tomorrow.'

Carol could not help but smile. He had arranged to fly back with her again, which meant a few more hours of his company. *And when we get to Heathrow, no-one knows what time I'm due back, as long as I'm home by dinner . . . we'll be able to spend a whole day together, lunch when we get back, an afternoon . . .*

'But not until the afternoon,' he was saying, and he was not even looking at her. 'So if I could possibly stay for lunch?'

'Well, of course,' Susanne smiled, and addressing Carol added, 'Henri did want so much to be back in Paris in time for dinner. It's my sister Celeste's birthday tomorrow, and Henri does spoil her rather, don't you?'

'Celeste?' Carol said blankly.

'His wife – did you not realise that Henri was my brother-in-law?' Susanne said, looking Carol straight in the face. And Carol was sure that behind the clear eyes lay a warning, or even a threat, and as she smiled back her fingers closed tightly around the little box that she had jammed into her jacket pocket and her blood ran cold.

# 14

'Now, darling, let's try Laura Ashley, they always have pretty things,' Julia said, backing dangerously out of the courtyard into the lane. 'And maybe Monsoon; their clothes are always in very good colours.'

'Oh Mummy,' Miranda wailed, clicking her seatbelt into place. 'They're so dreary! It's a party, not a job interview.'

'You said you liked the clothes I bought you for Christmas; they were from Monsoon. Geoffrey said you looked very nice in them.'

'Yeah, well, they were nice. But their party things, Mummy, they're all for people who've had babies.'

'What do you mean by that?' Julia had determined that she and Miranda were going to enjoy this day out together, and she was not going to be drawn into an argument about clothes if she could help it.

'Well, you know, long and formal and *tidy*.'

'All right then, Laura Ashley.'

'No, Johnny says they smell odd.'

'Laura Ashley?'

'Yes, all its clothes. It takes a year before you can wash the smell out and by then you're even more bored with them than you were when you started.'

'It's true. Laura Ashley shops all smell exactly the same. I'd never noticed it before. But it's not a bad smell.'

'It's still a smell. And everybody's mother makes them wear Laura Ashley and they either look like sailors or ballerinas. Honestly, Mummy, I won't.'

'Right.' Julia took a calming breath. 'So do you have any idea where you want to go?'

'No, I don't know Exeter, do I? I thought you were going to take me shopping in London.'

'Yes, well it didn't work out like that. I can't come traipsing up to London at a moment's notice because you've decided you want to go to a party. A party I'm not even sure I should be letting you go to. Geoffrey said he saw a picture of that party last year in the *Daily Mail* and all the children were necking.'

'Johnny went to it last year and said that it was just a small group who were drunk, and that it was fine. Anyway I don't know what you're fussing about. His mother's letting him go.'

'He's a boy. It's different.'

'Cicely isn't.'

'No, but she's going with her brother. And we don't all have to bring our children up in the same way. I'm still not convinced it's a good idea. Paying for parties, going where Lord knows who else will be there – there's no security, anyone can buy a ticket.'

'Mummy, it's all organised. Someone's mother gives us dinner, a group of us go together, we're taken and picked up. I don't know what you're fussing about. Half of my class is going.'

'I know, and the other half isn't. Anyway, I've said you can go and I won't go back on it.'

'Johnny says you should never go back on your word.'

'Exactly. Although I was talking about just that with Geoffrey the other day, and his point was that you can't make hard and fast rules about moral questions. There is a moral absolute, but its application need not be absolute. Or something.' She trailed off vaguely. 'He lent me something about it, must get round to reading it.'

'It's lovely being lent books, isn't it?'

Julia looked at her daughter out of the corner of her eye, amused. 'I don't have you down as much of a reader, darling.'

Miranda flushed. 'Well, you know, if someone you like lends you a book and you read it then you find out a bit what they're like and it helps you understand them better.'

'And what has Johnny been lending you?'

'Well actually, yes, he has lent me some books as a matter of fact. He lent me some Wilbur Smith.'

'Oh yes, and?'

'And what?'

'And what did you discover about him?'

'Not him, so much as Africa. They made me see why he wants to go to Africa so much, and they made me want to go too.'

'Mm, I was surprised that Geoffrey is bit of a philosopher. He read Philosophy and Italian at Oxford, so he's really frightfully clever.'

'Johnny's clever too. They want him to go to Oxford but he wants to have a couple of years off first, maybe join some charity or something, you know, do a bit of good.'

'Languages are always useful when you travel. Geoffrey said he couldn't have got by in Portugal without his Italian. If they spoke very slowly to each other they could usually understand. French was no use at all, of course.'

'Apparently some African countries speak French instead of English, so he'd have to avoid those. He wants to give something back, you know, he's been so privileged, Eton and everything.'

'He says that schools should teach German before French, the way the world's going, but look what happened last time. Mind you I suppose if it comes to that his Italian will be as useful as anything else.' Julia laughed.

'He likes reading about hunting big game, although of course he wouldn't dream of doing it. But he says that to understand the way the continent's – er – become, you have to understand the people who came before. He's thinking of doing Anthropology at university, but they say it's not a proper subject, it's something you do later. They just don't understand.'

'Yes, it's funny about understanding things, isn't it? Geoffrey says none of his old friends can understand that he really is happy, although he's lost so much – almost everything, really. He says that it makes them uncomfortable so they shut their eyes, or their ears or something, to it. After all, if they're still working away to keep everything together, and can't face up to the final crunch, they want to believe it's all worth fighting for, that they really can't do without it.'

'All the working away for money's pointless anyway,' Miranda volunteered.

'Really? That's very rash.'

'Well, Johnny says what's the point of working so hard for so much? If you're really responsible you'd give away all the unnecessary extra money you make. So it's better not to make it at all and then the other people can make it themselves and have a bit of self respect.'

'That's astoundingly simplistic,' said Julia who really quite liked having more money than was strictly necessary.

'Johnny says that you should always look at the simplest answer first as it's nearly always the best.'

'I'm getting just the tiniest bit tired of hearing what Johnny has to say about everything.' Julia was beginning to regret the trip, doubting whether she could bear to hear Johnny's name through all the clothes shops in Exeter, lunch, and back to Yeoworthy.

'Sorry,' Miranda said huffily. 'I won't mention his name again.' She stared moodily out of the window while Julia pretended to concentrate on overtaking a lorry. 'Anyway,' Miranda added almost, but not quite, under her breath, 'I'm pretty bored with hearing Geoffrey this, Geoffrey that all the time. And,' she said, her courage growing, 'I should think Daddy is too.'

'I beg your pardon?'

'Nothing.'

'I think that implication was really rather impertinent.'

'There's no implication at all. You said I talked too much about Johnny, and I just said you talked a lot about Geoffrey.'

Julia did not know how to react. Perhaps it was true, perhaps her mind was running on Geoffrey these days. Well, she had seen a lot of him – of them – recently. They were so near, and had got into the habit of dropping in on each other. Patty had gone to stay with her father in Kent for a fortnight while he was ill, and Geoffrey had come over for dinner or lunch almost every day.

'Not Foster again?' Velters had finally said. 'I don't think we need to see him quite so often, Julia. Surely the fellow can rustle himself up a steak?' So the next day the two of them had gone out for a pub lunch and giggled their way through prawn cocktail and chicken in a basket.

'Well, I suppose we've seen quite a lot of him recently, with Patty being away and everything,' she admitted. 'And you're right, Daddy did get a bit fed up. You know what he's like, he doesn't like having to make conversation too much.'

If she had hoped to disarm her daughter, the attempt failed.

'Perhaps he just felt left out,' Miranda said, feeling very grown up to be having such a conversation with her mother.

'Well, then he should make more of an effort,' Julia said tartly. 'Anyway, darling, it really isn't anything to do with you, is it? Now, who is it that's giving the dinner before the dance? Do we know them?'

The conversation with Miranda made Julia think. Yes, it was true that she had been seeing a lot of Geoffrey, but that was all there was to it. They were, to use an old phrase, 'just good friends'. They certainly flirted with each other, teased and laughed and talked endlessly, but that was all. And to Julia that was nothing. She found it ridiculous and irritating that Miranda should get into such a stew over a few lunches. After all, if Velters did not mind . . . But that old refrain did not work quite as well as it had through the Archy years and before, when there had been Jerry Mantel and Benjy Shelley to keep her young and her loneliness at bay. In the mildest possible way Velters had shown that he did mind, that he at least had seen enough of Geoffrey for a while and even, when he met her coming back from the pub lunch, that he thought she might have seen enough of him too. Well, Patty was due back today so of course they would see less of each other, get back to a more formal come-to-dinner-on-Tuesday sort of footing. She would miss him, though.

Never mind, she was off to London next week, where she would see Archy.

Her heart sank at the thought. She no longer looked forward to seeing him, and that was the truth of it. *I'd be happy enough if we were just good friends, too. Although it would be a different kind of just good friends, wouldn't it? It would be good friends with a past rather than good friends with a future . . . so is that what Geoffrey and I are? I'm not sure it's a good idea, he's too close, even Velters might spot something was going on if it were right under his nose . . . although Archy's been to stay often enough . . . but then Miranda's noticed something, and nothing is more self-obsessed than a teenage girl . . . except a teenage girl in love. Stupid of me to have been squishing about her wretched Johnny, but then it's bad enough to have to listen to one's own children's half-witted views without having to take their friends' into account as well. Anyway she's at school most of the time so it doesn't matter. Perhaps I should invite her Johnny next time she's home for the weekend and then she won't have eyes for anything else anyway. And we can have a gander at him at the same time. Although I pity any boy who has to deal with Velters. He may not care what I do, but no one's going to be good enough for his precious daughter. Well, that'll keep them all occupied.*

*I don't need to keep them occupied. What am I thinking about? But I might, mightn't I? Soon? Oh, life is exciting, after all. I think I had better talk to Archy when I see him on Wednesday. It's time I stopped thinking about it and did it. Time for a break.*

Velters walked down the drive to the estate office swinging his stick with slightly less vigour than usual. Suddenly life seemed rather more complicated than it had in the past fifty or so years. Something was different, something in the air that felt vaguely threatening, and he did not like it much. Outwardly everything was the same: the house parties, the regularity of his trips to and from London, the children . . . and Julia. Although was Julia the same? Everything ran as smoothly as ever, she seemed normal enough. Visited London less often these days, and for slightly shorter visits, but that was entirely her own decision. When he had vaguely asked her why, she had just said there was nothing on at the theatre that she wanted to see, which was odd because she had not seemed to go to the theatre that much anyway. She seemed cheerful enough, seemed to be making an effort to get on with Miranda, which was a relief; the two of them had been barely able to say a civil word to each other recently. So what was it?

*She's unsettled, that's what it is. Women's problems, probably. Can't be serious or she'd have told me. Needs a change. It's not good all this suddenly falling out with old friends, not that I shall miss the Pooles much. Emma's a nice enough girl, but Archy's frankly not much of a fellow. Doesn't quite dress like a chap somehow, always hanging around Julia in an agreeing, spoony sort of way.* And again, that little tickle on the edges of his mind, ignored rather than scratched. *And now she's suddenly made best friends with these Fosters, nice enough, Patty's a poor little thing, always looks sad, can't see why, Geoffrey looks after her . . . it's Geoffrey she gets on with better though, the fellow's been hanging around too much, can't cross my own hall without bumping*

*into him. Don't really mind him but he's not much of a chap either,
everything's too new which is odd when he says he's got no money.
Not much of a seat either, although I'll give him credit for nerve, can't
quite see what Julia sees in him . . . oh Lord . . .*

And for the first time a thought crossed his mind which every
bit of him wanted to push away, to ignore, to deny. *Julia's not
like that. She's my wife, she can't be – getting fond of the fellow.* Velters
stood quite still, not seeing the view he loved so much at all,
not seeing anything but a series of images flashing in front of
his eyes. Julia laughing across the table with Geoffrey, at some
joke he had missed; Julia seen from the drawing room window,
walking across the lawn with Geoffrey, not touching, but their
heads bent close together, talking intently; Julia coming into
the hall with a wave and a laugh behind her, seeing Velters,
starting, saying casually, 'Oh sorry I didn't catch you before I
went out, I've just been down to the Yeoworthy Arms for lunch,
did Mrs Tout tell you?', Julia jumping to her feet as the door
opened, smiling, hands held out to Geoffrey. And Velters heard
Julia's voice, telling him what she and Geoffrey had done, what
Geoffrey thought, pitying Patty for her failure to adjust to life in
the real country. He remembered sitting through a lunch with
Miranda and Julia, both talking without listening, and realised
now that they were more similar than either realised, that both
were infatuated women.

*It's got to stop. This isn't the way to behave. She's married. So's
he, come to that, no wonder Patty's been looking bitter. But of course
I'm being ridiculous. Not Julia. Never Julia. She's lonely. She said so
herself, didn't she? Extraordinary. She's looking for friends and for
some reason the Fosters fit the bill. Foster. Geoffrey Foster.* He set off
walking again. No swing to his stick now. *Whether it's true or not,
and I don't think it is, I owe her doubt at least, it's got to stop before
it becomes true.*

*A holiday. She said something about a holiday. We laughed. We
were going to read PG Wodehouse. And then what, I don't know.*

He reached the estate office and paused a moment. *Got to pull
myself together. Can't let Sally see I'm bothered, it wouldn't do at all.* He
stood with his back to the office door, wondering where it would
all lead. *Nowhere. It won't lead anywhere. We're safe at Yeoworthy.*

He shook his shoulders briskly, like a dog coming out of a lake.

*It's just a load of nonsense. Women's trouble, that's it* and turned and let himself in.

'Good morning, Sally.'

'Good morning, Lord Yeoworthy. Lovely morning.'

'Well yes, I suppose so. Sally, I want to take Lady Yeoworthy away. Look into – er, Rome, will you? Four nights, good hotel – in the centre somewhere. Better not be this weekend – the next one. Cancel anything we've got on then. And be a good girl, don't say anything to Lady Yeoworthy, will you?'

Sally smiled. 'Of course not. A surprise. How nice, Lord Yeoworthy. I'm sure it will do you both good.'

And did he imagine it, or was there the smallest bit of sympathetic understanding behind the open smile and the clear, frank gaze?

'Lord Yeoworthy's taking Lady Yeoworthy away to Rome. A surprise,' said Sally, cutting thick slices of white bread and putting them into the pan of sizzling goose fat.

'Oh yes? Good thing too, I'd say,' said Colin, coming out of the larder with a tray of eggs in his hands and putting them down beside his sister.

'Now then, Colin,' John Webber was sitting in an armchair by the Aga, reading the day before's newspaper and waiting for his breakfast.

'Well, she's certainly taken a shine to Foster, from all accounts.'

'Gossip, Colin,' John remarked mildly.

'A bit of gossip never hurt anyone.' Sally flipped the frying bread. 'So what have you heard, Col?'

'They were in the pub a week or so back, all over each other, so Josey White said.'

'Come on, Colin, that'll do. That's where gossip hurts. Josey said they were very friendly, nothing about all over each other.' John got up from his chair and sat at the table.

'So you were listening, Dad?' Colin laughed, pouring tea.

'Couldn't help but hear. She was telling everyone who came in. Told us what they ate, what Lady Yeoworthy was wearing, you'd have thought she'd never seen her before. Can't see what the fuss was about.'

'People have been talking about the Fosters since they arrived,' said Sally. 'I never knew anything like it. And that poor soul, Mrs Foster, she doesn't look too happy. Can't have children, so they say. No wonder he's ready to look elsewhere.'

'Sally,' John was beginning to be cross now. 'Don't talk about what you can't know about. Unless Mrs Foster has taken you into her confidence? In which case you should respect that.'

'Of course she hasn't, Dad, I was just wondering.'

'Didn't sound like wondering to me.'

'Or unless Foster's put the mark on you. Been after you, has he?' Colin grinned.

'And that's not the way to talk to your sister,' said their father, worry at the notion superseded by the knowledge that Sally was no fool and could look after herself.

Sally dished up breakfast and the three of them sat down together and began to eat.

'So why's he doing it, anyway? They've not been off together for Lord knows how long. And he's been looking down recently, not his normal self.'

John agreed. 'We went over to have a look at the Witches' Walkway yesterday. No interest at all. And all that planting was his idea. Had some friend to stay who knew all about trees, got all fired up, barely looked at them when we went up there. And they're coming on a treat. First signs of Spring up there now.'

'He's master unhappy about something. Not like him at all,' said Sally.

'Your mother and I went down to Torquay once, last minute, sent you two off to your aunt's,' said John, cutting himself another slice of ham. 'Just the weekend, but she looked so tired I knew if I gave her time to think about it she'd find reasons why it was impossible. So I didn't. Rang your aunt Joan, packed the bags, told her we were going.'

'That was nice.'

'Exactly. We had a happy weekend. We didn't go because we didn't like each other, or liked other people more. We went because we liked each other, despite you two and work and everything else, and wanted to spend some time together.'

'But you, Dad, are different,' said Sally, kissing his head as she passed his chair.

'Yes. There may be nothing going on between Lady Yeoworthy and Foster, but it's no good Dad pretending Lord Yeoworthy's taking her away because he wants to be with her. Marmalade, please, Sal.'

And John, watching his two children, wondered where they had learned to be so worldly wise.

# 15

'Telephone, Dulcie!' Carol called down the stairs.

'Thanks,' she shouted back, and went to pick up the kitchen extension.

'Dulcie? It's Ted here, Ted Yeoell. Adam gave me your number.'

'Ted. Hi, how are you?'

'Fine, fine.' Silence. 'I'm coming up to London this weekend – a friend's stag night – and wondered if you'd be able – like to – meet for a drink.'

'I'd love to, but we're – Jody and me – going down to your parents this weekend.' *And I'd been hoping he'd be there, what a bummer.*

'Oh, well, actually the stag night's on Thursday and I'd been planning to stay on, but Mummy did want me to go down for the weekend. Um.' There was a slightly embarrassed pause and Dulcie smiled down the telephone. *So he's thinking of changing plans, that's good, well I won't push* . . . 'Er, did Daddy say anything about hunting?'

'No, but Adam said he'd ring and find out where the meet is on Saturday. Jody's hoping it's the other side of the county.'

'Well, perhaps I'll join you. I haven't been out for a while, been working too hard – helping out with the lambing – but as I've got the time off . . .' Dulcie smiled again

'Yes, well. Maybe I'll see you then. Pity about the drink,' she said smoothly.

'What? Oh yes.' Then he laughed and came clean. 'Well, we'll drink Daddy's instead. I just thought I'd like to see you again.'

'Thank you. Have a good stag night.' Dulcie hung up and

could not resist giving a little skip. Ted was undoubtedly keen.

'Forgotten Giles already?' came a voice from behind her and she jumped and turned. Jody was leaning against the doorway and laughing at her. 'Ted, was it?'

'How did you know?'

'Well, there you are skipping about like a spring lamb, and he rang Adam – which he never does – and oh-so-casually asked for the number here and Adam decided it would be quite a good joke not to tell him you were already booked this weekend so we could see how keen he was.' Dulcie blushed. 'So he did change his plans!' Jody said gleefully. 'Ah ha!'

'He said he thought he'd quite like to go hunting,' Dulcie said, and they both laughed.

'Well, it's worth another boring day at Yeoworthy Towers while you all go off. Goody goody, what fun. We must get him up to London more often. Oh but what'll I do all day? I feel I've been to every antique shop within thirty miles, and it was dull enough the first time.'

'Take some books,' Dulcie suggested. 'Or go for a walk.'

Jody rolled her eyes. 'Oh come on, just because things are going well for you, there's no reason to be cruel! You'll be telling me to take up embroidery next. Now come on, are you ready? I said we'd be at The Glove a quarter of an hour ago.'

Velters was delighted when Julia told him that Ted had said he would come that weekend. 'Time one of our boys settled down, and he could do a lot worse than Dulcie,' he said. 'Good seat on a horse, fine nerve, pretty girl, no airs and graces. Make sure you put them together at dinner.'

'Velters, you're jumping the gun a bit you know. They've barely met.'

'I know, but they've got to start somewhere, haven't they?'

Julia looked at Velters. He had been very cheerful recently, trailing around her like a spaniel puppy, talking a lot. She could not make him out. Only a few days before he had been irritable with her for inviting Geoffrey so often, now he did not so much as ask her where she was going, often just volunteered to come with her. That she had been put on the spot more than once by this renewed companionship irritated her, but she had her own revenge by willingly agreeing to his coming too and then dragging him for hours around a nursery garden or the linen department of a local shop. He did not seem put out, though, just said it was pleasant to spend more time with her, that they had both been too busy.

What was he up to? In one sense he was acting as though he were suspicious, but at the same time he seemed as though he were keeping a secret of his own. What could it be? Velters never had secrets, he was not that kind of man. And now he was matchmaking. Well, Dulcie was a very nice girl and Julia liked her too, but it seemed a little hasty to rush her into marriage with Ted. They were only babies, for heaven's sake – she pushed back the thought that she was already married by Dulcie's age.

Meanwhile, despite Velters's vigilance, Julia had still managed to spend some time with Geoffrey, and the strength of their attraction continued to grow. Nothing had been said yet, but Julia knew that she was tacitly encouraging him to make a move. She had been to London and cleared the decks as far as Archy was concerned – a much easier job than she had anticipated. He had seemed unhappy, but she had been brisk, pointing out that theirs had always been a no-strings-attached sort of arrangement, and adding that Velters had begun to be suspicious. She did not say that his suspicions were over an entirely different man; what would have been the point? She had said that of course they would remain in touch, nothing should spoil their friendship, but it would be better if he did not come down to Somerset for a while. She knew that Archy, rejected lover, would be much more likely to sense the state of affairs between her and Geoffrey than anyone else.

Surprisingly, she did not miss the thought of Archy at all. He had been a part of her life for three years, but now he was gone he had left no scar, no shadow behind. *Oh Lord, perhaps I'm turning into a hardened old bitch*, she thought, doubting it. *But what can I do? If I don't miss him I can't make myself, just for the sake of it. It's his fault for being so feeble. If he'd made more of a mark on my life I'd be missing him more. He was a good companion, a good friend, a bit of a convenience, I suppose. A bit like a best girlfriend, but with sex thrown in. Ideal, really. Except this time – this time it feels different. I don't remember ever being so excited about Archy. With him all the excitement came from the danger of being caught, from the risk. With Geoffrey – well, he's exciting. I feel alive when I'm with him. I've got to decide what to do. I could still put a stop to it, but I won't be able to for much longer. There's a limit to flirtation, and then it must either stop, or move forward. It's a dangerous game, and I've always played it well, always been in control. This time I'm just a little frightened that I'm losing the upper hand. If only I could decide . . . is it worth the risk? It would be if I knew I could get away with it . . . what's the answer? I must decide.*

She had gone to bed with Archy one last time, for friendship's sake. Perhaps he had thought he could succeed in persuading her to stay with him in bed better than he had over a restaurant table. *But even the sex is companionable now*, she thought as she dressed afterwards. *I'm right in getting out now.* And she had kissed him good-bye and left.

Now she was entirely focused on Yeoworthy. Velters's attentions irked her a little, but she was trying to respond – on her own terms. As long as she could do what she wanted to do she did not mind being nice to Velters in between. When he was not irritating her they got on well enough, they had the children, the house, the past in common. Sometimes it seemed enough.

This weekend Ted and Adam would be here, with Jody and Dulcie. A small, family-only house party which was a nice change. The Fosters were coming to dinner on Saturday, and Jamie and Sarah Robinson from near Bridgwater. Perhaps she should ask them to stay the night; it would mean they could drink without worrying. Velters was hunting on Saturday, the boys and Dulcie would almost certainly go too. Miranda's horse had gone lame which left them a mount short but with a stroke of genius Julia had asked Geoffrey to lend Ted his horse, which would give him an honourable alibi from the hunting field. A flicker of anticipation interrupted her train of thought. *Maybe this weekend will be it, it can't be long now, I can handle it, we'll be discreet, no one need know . . . but there's Jody. Damn and blast. Why couldn't Adam get involved with a hunting girl, someone like Dulcie . . . I'm as bad as Velters . . . I can sort something out if I need to . . . I've always been a good manager . . .*

\*     \*     \*

The meet was ten miles away, the horses had been boxed over, Dulcie and Jody were given a lift by the Fosters. Geoffrey wanted to see his horse off and Jody and Patty decided to go along for the ride. Jody could not help but admire the riders in their finery, sitting astride excited horses, casually reaching down for a sausage or a whisky mac as the trays passed by. She knew hunting kit would suit her and almost wished she had the nerve to go out with them. Adam was incredibly sexy on a horse, Velters looked very distinguished, Ted was lit up with laughter as Geoffrey's horse pranced frighteningly underneath him. 'Thanks, Geoffrey, I'm going to have a good day, I can tell,' he said. 'Oh, she'll be all right, once you're off,' said Geoffrey, hoping it were true. He had only dared to ride her out to hounds a couple of times and he was beginning to wonder if he had done the right thing in buying her. Julia would not be too pleased if his horse killed her son . . . *Julia, how can we meet today?* he thought with a sidelong glance at his pale-faced wife. *It's going to be soon, I must make plans . . . there's no way around it, I have to have her . . . keep it quiet from Patty, that's all, but I can trust Julia, she won't want to upset anything either.* Geoffrey had plenty of experience of women like Julia, bored, idle, open to offers. Hampshire had been full of them . . . *it won't be long now.*

He took a sausage, put a five pound note in the cap being passed around. 'Not hunting yourself?' he asked Jody.

'No, I'm a real townie,' she said with a self-mocking laugh. 'I used to ride a bit at my cousin's – Dulcie's – when we were children, but I never really got the point.'

'More of a clubber?' he asked. *That's a pretty girl, Adam's done well, but then he would, wouldn't he, wouldn't have to try too hard. Bit pale, though, doesn't look too well.*

'I suppose so,' she agreed and wondered for the first time whether that was such a good thing. She always felt raw and edgy these days. God, she was only twenty-two and sometimes she felt thirty.

'And Adam? Take you dancing?'

'Yes, of course.' *What's it to you, you old lecher?* she wanted to ask, noticing the appraisal in his eyes.

She looked at Adam. He did look good on that big black horse, but he did not look well. His face was pale, he dabbed endlessly at his nose with a handkerchief held in a hand that shook, and not from fear of the horse . . . It was all getting out of hand. Beside him, Ted looked dare-devil and light-hearted. He sat his horse as though it were part of him, its antics only made him laugh. Dulcie also looked completely relaxed, neat and trim and at ease. Jody walked over to her, pushing down her fear of walking between these huge, nervous animals around her.

'Excited, Dulce?'

Dulcie looked down, grinning. 'Yes, this is the scary bit, though.' The hounds began to give tongue, ignoring commands to stay, to shut up. Dulcie had to shout to be heard above them. 'Will you be all right?'

'Of course. I might go back to bed, I'm knackered. I'm not sure I like that Foster man, dirty old bastard if you ask me. I'm glad his wife's here, I'm not sure I'd like to go back alone in the car with him.'

'You can look after yourself, Jode,' Dulcie laughed. 'Don't be too bored – make us some drop scones for tea or something.'

Jody stuck her tongue out at her cousin. 'I'll never be that bored,' she promised.

'Hello, Dulcie, nice to see you out again. Hello, Jody.' Jody did not immediately recognise the young man greeting them, but Dulcie did.

'Hello, Colin. I know, I'm getting spoiled. Geoffrey Foster lent Ted his horse so I could come out too.'

'Nice of him,' Colin said, and turned to the girl riding a small bay beside him. 'Sal, this is Lady Yeoworthy's god-daughter Dulcie – I'm sorry, I forgot your surname.'

'Stanley.' For some reason Dulcie felt a little piqued to see Colin with a girl – a pretty one at that.

'This is my sister Sally. She works for Lord Yeoworthy too.'

'Hello.' Dulcie smiled warmly.

'Ready for the off?' Ted was beside her, barely controlling his horse. 'Foster's horse is a right bugger, Colin, why didn't you warn me?'

'You didn't ask me, Ted.'

The horn sounded out and the hunt moved off. Jody moved back to Patty Foster's side and the two women stood together

watching the hounds stream out across the field, followed by
the horses, Geoffrey's bucking all the way downhill under Ted
who appeared unmoved by the performance.

'Oh God, the last thing I need is Geoffrey's bloody mare killing
Julia's boy,' Patty said. 'I can't ever believe that everyone will
come back whole. Still, we all make our choices in life.' She
turned back towards the car, followed by Jody. 'And ours appears
to be being women who wait at home.'

Jody could not understand the bitterness in the older woman's
voice. 'Well, you're only waiting for a horse,' she said. 'Your
husband's not risking life and limb today.'

'Not life and limb, no,' said Patty. 'But I don't suppose he'll
be spending much of the day with me, either.'

Jody had no idea what to say and walked down the lane in
silence.

'I'm sorry,' Patty said after a moment. 'I didn't mean anything. I
must be pre-menstrual, woke up in a terrible mood this morning.'
And she laughed what was meant to be a light, girls-in-it-together
sort of a laugh. 'If you're at a loose end today, why don't you
come over to the Dower House? Come for lunch if you want.
I'm sure Julia won't mind. Or come for a drink. Whatever.'

'Thank you,' said Jody, who did not want to spend more time
with Geoffrey than she could help. 'I think I'd better go back
to the Manor first, but maybe I'll wander down later. It would
be nice.'

Julia checked everything was under control in the kitchen and
wandered back to the drawing room. She thought she wanted
to read the paper, but could not sit still. Irritably, she rearranged
a vase of early daffodils, straightened a cushion, failed to add
anything to the jigsaw puzzle set out on a card table in a
corner of the room. The drawing room was at the back of the
house, not overlooking the courtyard but down the long drive
an eighteenth century Yeoworthy had thought necessary to add
to the house. Sheep grazed in the park he had laid out at the same
time, the spring sun shone with a false promise of warmth. The
Dower House could just be seen, a pretty but unremarkable late
eighteenth century house built by another Yeoworthy, who had
married very young a strong-willed north-eastern heiress who

had refused to spend the first forty years of her marriage with a long-living mother-in-law. Julia stood at the window, looking out at the view, and wondered if she would move down to the Dower House when Velters was dead and Adam married, and if so what would happen to the Fosters.

She did not think she would be able to bear the move. The Dower House was lighter, had bigger rooms and huge sash windows rather than the leaded ones which blocked out so much of the sun at the Manor. There were fewer bedrooms, she would not have to fill the house with people not to feel alone. But Yeoworthy was home now. Of course she would have to go one day, if not when Adam married then when he had children. That was the way it had been done for generations and Julia had been a part of this family for long enough to know that Tradition was the most important word in the language. (Followed, perhaps, by Discretion.) She realised for the first time, as she thought about her future, that she believed in Tradition now almost as much as did Velters. She could not, after all, accept the bounty given her by Tradition and not respect the duties that came with it. Perhaps it would be rather restful being Julia, Countess of Yeoworthy, handing over the reins to some young Countess, having the grandchildren to tea when it suited her. But she knew herself better. She would be bored, she would dislike the changes brought in by any daughter-in-law, but she would behave properly.

The telephone rang and she jumped. 'Hello?'

'Julia. Geoffrey here.'

'Hello.' This was what she had been expecting, but now the call had come she was at a loss for her next move. There was a pause, while each waited for the other to speak.

'I saw the hunt off.'

'Oh yes? Good. Everyone all right?'

'Delilah was giving Ted a bit of a hard time, but he didn't seem too worried.'

'I don't worry about Ted. Perhaps I should, but he can ride anything.'

Geoffrey felt an implied criticism and did not answer. 'Well, it's very kind of you to lend her,' Julia added, lamely.

'Up to anything this morning?' he asked, hopelessly casual.

'Well, I've people to dinner,' she reminded him, but they both knew how little that meant. 'And Jody's here.'

'Yes, she said she'd walk up the lane or I'd've dropped her.'

Another pause. Geoffrey was at a loss. He was an old enough hand at the game, but seemed to have lost control. Perhaps he had misread the signs, but then he never had before.

'I'd love to see you,' he said, and in her hesitation he read compliance. 'I'll probably drop by before lunch. Or maybe I can buy you a drink somewhere – not the Yeoworthy maybe we could go down to the sea for a change, it's a lovely day.'

More hesitation, more acquiescence, then a laugh. 'I have guests. Jody . . .'

'Oh, she's a bright girl, she'll manage. She can't have expected you to wait on her all day. Leave her lunch and make an excuse . . . Julia?'

'Oh, all right. But I must be back by tea. Where shall we meet?'

Now it was Geoffrey's turn to hesitate. To move everything along would require tact and skill – and discretion, Julia could have told him. This was always the tricky bit.

'Shall I pick you up?' she asked blithely.

'No,' he said quickly, too quickly. 'Um, no . . . perhaps it would be better if we met . . .'

'We haven't decided where we're going, have we?' She laughed, sensing weakness. Yes, he was coming to the point.

'Well. Why don't we meet at the Falconer's Arms?'

'It's a horrid pub!'

'I know, but we can meet there, it's got a big car park off the road, and then go on together in one car.'

'I see.' And she did. Of course it was more complicated in the country. Where to meet, what to do with the cars, whether they would be noticed. Taxis moved freely throughout London, cars could be lost in NCP car parks or on meters for hours. Nobody noticed your comings and goings, a face was a cheque, nothing more, in most restaurants. Yes, it was a different game down here. *Well, I thought I needed a change,* Julia thought, and her spirits lifted in anticipation.

'All right. In half an hour?' She checked her watch. 'And remember, I must be back in time for tea.'

A click behind her startled her, and she turned to see Jody standing against the door. 'I've just got back from the meet,' Jody said, clearly at a loss.

'Good-bye then, and thank you for your call,' Julia said down the telephone. *Well, the lying's started in earnest now.* She turned with a smile. 'Was it fun? Good. I must say when I see them all set off I still feel a bit of a pang – quite miss it. In theory, of course. Now I'm afraid I have to go out for an hour or two, pick up a couple of things, sort a few things out. Oh Lord, is that the time? I'm frightfully sorry, I might not be back in time for lunch. Mrs Tout will have it all ready for you at one, in the dining room, and I'll try and get back. Don't wait for me, will you? You'll be all right, will you? So sorry. I must fly, I'll see you later.' And she was out of the room with only the tiniest trace of guilt. *Well, she's Adam's guest, not mine, and if he can go out hunting all day I don't see why I shouldn't get on with my life. They're all grown up now, I've spent years looking after other people and now I'm going to look after myself for a while.*

Jody, left on her own, knowing that something was up but feeling cross at being lied to so feebly rather than at being left on her own, wandered around the house for a while. Mrs Tout offered her coffee, which she accepted because she thought it would be rude not to, and then did not drink, and she flipped through the *Daily Mail*. She went up to her room, which she had not slept in, and tried to cover some of her pallor with lipstick and blusher. Looking out of the window across the park she saw a white house which she realised was the Fosters' and remembered Patty's invitation. Perhaps she should go down there – it was something to do – but then she remembered that Mrs Tout was cooking lunch and Julia would probably not be back. She could not just desert the poor woman.

She went back down to the kitchen and pushed the door open. 'Mrs Tout, Lady Yeoworthy said she probably wouldn't be back for lunch. D'you think she'd mind if I asked Mrs Foster up? She asked me down there but . . . if you don't mind . . .' She was not really sure why she had thought of it, except that she was bored and never very good at being on her own for too long at a time. Neither did she like the idea of sitting alone in the dining room, lunch prepared for her and probably served to her. Mrs Tout was all smiles, said she was sure it would be all right, no she did not mind at all, what a shame it was that Jody did not hunt, Adam looked such a fine figure on a horse . . . and Jody smiled back and chattered and felt happier than she had all day. It would be embarrassing if Julia came back, but then judging by the tail end of the conversation she had overheard there was not much danger of that. She wondered fleetingly where Julia had been in such a rush to go, but did not really mind, just wished that Julia had been more honest.

Patty was delighted at the invitation. 'Are you sure it's all right?' she asked, almost giggling. 'It would be nice. Geoffrey's gone off somewhere with his gun – says it needs to be balanced or lengthened or something – I wasn't really listening, can't think why it was suddenly so urgent – but anyway, I'm at a bit of a loose end. Julia won't mind, will she? Well yes, that'll be lovely. I'll be up in twenty minutes or so? See you then.'

They met in the far corner of the car park, one car a few spaces behind the other. Julia sat in her car for a moment, steadying herself. As soon as she got out of the car and met his eyes the die would be cast. Maybe this time she was being stupid, maybe she should stop and think, drive away before it was too late. But why should she? All the tired old arguments came back: *Velters does not know, doesn't care; as long as I am discreet it will be all right; I'm not breaking up any marriage, mine or his, that's the last thing I want.* But this was so close to home. He was her tenant, after all. If everything went wrong Velters would throw them out. But it wouldn't, would it? *Velters won't know, Velters doesn't care* . . . And Geoffrey made her laugh, talked to her, flirted with her, flattered her . . . She opened the car door and slowly stepped out into the bright cold sunlight. Geoffrey heard the thunk of her car door and, looking in his rearview mirror, saw her. He too left his car and they looked at each other and knew they shared the same intent and took the few steps that separated them and then they kissed.

And that, to all intents and purposes, sealed his fate.

# 16 ∫

So Henri was not as indifferent to his wife as he had implied. He wanted to be with her on her birthday, to spoil her, to buy her presents – the earrings, had they actually been bought for her, his wife, and then handed to Carol on an impulse, a placatory rather than amatory gift? And there she had been, planning the flight back with him, the hotel room which had briefly seemed so romantic and now seemed only sordid again . . . but he could not be blamed for that, she had been so hard to pin down, how could he be expected to know that she was ready for him now in every sense? But then why had he come at all? It had been unexpected, traumatic, not without its pleasures, but then so fraught with complications. Susanne was his sister-in-law . . . he was mad, mad. Perhaps Susanne had got it wrong, wanted her sister's marriage to be happy – wish-fulfilment or something. But he was going back, wasn't he? Back to Paris, not back to London. Back to her, to Celeste . . . what was she like? Carol had not worried about Celeste until now. Believing Henri, thinking that Celeste was happy with Henri's freedom, she had managed to feel no worry or guilt about her lover's wife. All those emotions had been reserved for her own family, Martin and the children.

She had been deluding herself, of course, living in a fool's paradise. Once again, mocking her, she heard the echo of Tony's voice down the years: *I'm only half way to Paradise* . . . She was being punished now – half way to Paradise indeed, but a mirage of happiness, nothing more.

As she sat on the aeroplane home she wondered if she had ever been more unhappy, if it were possible to feel worse. And she knew it was possible, because she still believed that Henri loved her. He had not been entirely straight with her, but was that really to be expected? Had she been entirely truthful to him? Of course not, by omission at least. She had never told him that she still loved Martin, had implied that she was still with him through laziness or convenience rather than affection. If Henri had only been wanting a quick affair he would have given up on her by now. She had been shilly-shallying far too long, she had been unfair.

Wearily she collected her bag and left the airport. She normally took the tube but in her current mood could not bear to be forced into company with anyone, friend or stranger. She found a taxi, but once inside could not decide where to go. She could not face home, not yet, nor work, where she would have to be enthusiastic, tell the others about the manor, check up on other jobs in progress. She needed to think. She had to force herself to be truthful with herself, to face the facts. On impulse she asked the driver to take her to Syon House. She had always wanted to visit the butterflies there; perhaps they would calm her.

There was Martin. There was Celeste. There was Henri. And there was herself. All four had to be taken into consideration, their needs and emotions weighed up.

She needed Martin. She would be lost without him, she loved him, he was her home. She needed Henri. She needed his touch on her skin, his laughter in her ears, his eyes on hers. She could not think of him without a lurch in her middle, without whispering his name to herself.

Martin needed her. He would be finished if he lost her, she knew that. His previous rages would be as nothing if he knew about Henri, and a small shudder ran down her back at the very thought of what might happen should she ever leave.

And Celeste? It turned out she was more important to Henri than he had admitted. Obvious, really. She was his wife. Carol tried to imagine how she would feel if she were Celeste and Martin were Henri. The thought made her feel sick. It should have made her feel sick ages ago; she should have thought. She had always been told that many couples were perfectly happy with an open marriage, that it was nothing to do with the seventies ethos, that it had been going on successfully since time immemorial. She had never believed it, though, not until it suited her. And now, try as hard as she could, she could not think of a single so-called open marriage in which both halves of the arrangement were happy – at least not at the same time.

She remembered Susanne, who had seemed so innocent, so good, until she had shown the steel behind her eyes. Was Celeste like that? A more sophisticated version perhaps – after all, she was married to Henri, had lived in different countries, was a Parisian rather than a countrywoman. Did she look like Susanne? That small, neat dark head, straight pretty nose, slightly heavy jaw . . . what did it matter? This was the first time she had ever thought to wonder about Celeste. Perhaps because until now she had seemed irrelevant.

The taxi driver let her out at Syon House, and she asked herself why she had come. Never mind. With the apathy that had taken over so much of her life in recent months she paid and followed the signs to the Butterfly House. For a short while she forgot her problems. She had come here to think, but the butterflies engaged her attention entirely. You could not think of other things when you were faced with something so fragilely beautiful as these insects. Carol moved through to the tropical room. Small paths led the visitors through the jungle plants and the steamy heat was almost visible. Tiny, jewel-like butterflies rested, opening and closing their wings on dripping leaves. Carol wondered that she had never been here before, and at the impulse that had brought her here now. She stopped and stared at a yellow and black striped beauty with bright blue splashes of colour on its wings. There was an object with no worries. She must bring Piers here some time. Didn't boys like insects? Was a butterfly an insect anyway, or was it something else?

She was standing still, smiling at her ignorance, when she heard her name called, hesitantly.

'Carol? You are Carol aren't you, Carol Pearsall?'

She stood still a moment. She knew that voice, knew it so well . . . but just could not place it. She turned, smiling politely, to see a middle-aged man holding a child by each hand.

'Carol?' he repeated.

'Yes. Yes, it is – I am. I'm sorry, but—?'

A look of acute disappointment crossed the man's face, and this somehow made him even more familiar, but still she could not place him. Then he laughed. 'Well, I have changed a lot. But you look wonderful, the years have done you no wrong. I'm—'

'Tony,' she interrupted, amazed. 'Tony Bell.'

'Yes. You do remember?'

'Of course, Tony. It's been years.' She could not quite believe this. She had come here on an inexplicable impulse and there was Tony, who she had not seen for so long but who had been so much in her mind recently. She had not recognised him, though, which showed how pointless memory was. She had assumed, in some half-baked way, that he would be the same, slightly greyer perhaps, marginally stouter. The Tony that faced her had not aged well, but not through greyness or fatness. He seemed to have shrunk somehow, morally if not physically. He was very bald, but this gave him a mean rather than a distinguished look. She remembered him as being good looking in a rather beaky way. Now he was all beak. He looked distinctly cadaverous, a long thin lugubrious face with shifty eyes. He smiled – there was no doubt of his pleasure at seeing her – and Carol glimpsed a shiny set of what could only be false teeth. Cheap ones at that.

'Long time no see.' *He couldn't have said that, he just couldn't.*

'Well, yes.'

'Why don't we go and have a drink together?' He checked his watch. 'Well, it's a bit early but we've some catching up to do.'

It was the last thing on earth that Carol wanted, but she knew it would be churlish to refuse. 'What about the children?'

'Oh yes. These are Tom and Olivia. Products of my second – union.' He laughed. 'Their mother's away and they're staying with me this week. A little holiday, eh, kids?' He spoke in the hearty voice of a man not used to children. 'They live near Manchester, so I thought I'd show them a few London sights.' The children shuffled their feet, clearly bored, and Carol felt agonisingly sorry for all three of them.

'Yes, of course. I'd love to. But why don't we go somewhere the children would like? My niece told me about an American diner type place she goes to sometimes in the evenings after work – she said I should take Piers – my youngest – sometime. It's just down from Notting Hill. We'll take a taxi and have brunch.'

'I thought diners weren't licensed,' Tony said doubtfully.

'Maybe not in America. This is London.' Carol firmly took charge and led the way from the tropical room without a backward glance at the butterflies which had so entranced her.

Life had not been good for Tony in the years since they had last met. He had had three wives, four children and two failed businesses. He had, as he delicately put it, had a slight drink problem, been dried out, was now in control. Watching him downing glass after glass of red wine, Carol wondered if this was indeed the case. Seeing her watching, Tony let it be known that he never drank spirits, drank sherry very occasionally, stuck with wine and beer. His children were polite, monosyllabic, cheered up by the diner, the chips and the enormous cokes, loved the free baseball hats given them with the third bottle of wine, seemed totally characterless. Tony appeared to be manifestly uninterested in them – and yet, there he had been, trailing them around the Butterfly House like any other concerned divorced father.

Tony did not whine about his misfortunes, he almost boasted about them, as though he thought they had in some way made him a better man. He had a new idea for a business, was looking at the possibility of importing yurts from Kazakhstan. The new money was with the New Age travellers, see, they were all upper-class drop outs with enormous private incomes which were against their principles. So he was only doing them a service by helping to relieve them of some of it. These yurts were almost as comfortable as a semi-detached in Surbiton, he explained earnestly, but had the credibility of tents.

Carol did not speak much. She would have felt uncomfortable telling him about her three children, her successful business, her one, successful marriage *and it is successful isn't it, despite everything?* So she watched him drinking the wine, and made encouraging noises about the yurts and sympathetic noises about his previous failed entrepreneurial ideas and felt very sad.

What had happened to the Tony she had known? How could time have been so cruel? When she had known him he had been full of wit and vigour and humour. He had been free and happy and sought-after. Why had it all gone so wrong for him? He still had enthusiasm, she supposed, but looking at his eyes she was not so sure. He was going through the motions.

Something had to occupy him, and right now it was yurts, that was all.

The children wandered off to the fifties style juke box at the back of the diner, came back and asked for money, drifted off again, and Tony went on talking.

'I think you'll remember my first wife. You used to know her. Phoebe – Phoebe Rhys Jones?'

Carol nodded. 'Of course I do. She was beautiful. She worked at Harrods at the same time as me, and someone spotted her and she became a model.'

'That's her. Yes, she was lovely. So is our daughter. Emma. She's in the middle of a divorce, poor thing. Works as a window designer for Harvey Nichols. Doing quite well.'

*In her work, maybe*, thought Carol, trying to work out how old this child could be, saddened at the thought of such an early divorce.

'So what went wrong?'

'With me and Phoebe?' Tony looked uncomfortable. 'Well, I suppose you could say I was a bit over-indulgent. My first business was doing quite well, but it meant a lot of long lunches, business meetings – you know the sort of thing. And Phoebe said she couldn't put up with it. I came back from work one afternoon, woke up from my afternoon snooze on the sofa and found she'd packed her things and gone. Just like that. Taken Emma with her. Nothing I could say would change her mind. Said a lot of rubbish about how Emma wasn't safe around me, I'd drop her or something, well it had only been the once and anyone can make a mistake, and it turned out not to be a break, just a chip to the bone . . .'

Carol looked at him, trying to hide her horror. 'Do you mean—' She did not know how to put it.

'Well, yes. I supposed it had all gone too far. And in the end the work suffered too, that's when the business went under, a few months after they left. I'd been importing shoes from Spain, very cheap. So that's when I went to dry out. I didn't really think I needed it, but I thought it would make Phoebe come home. It didn't, of course. By the time I was out she had found someone else and was living in World's End with a viscount and a nanny and being flown all over the world to be photographed.'

For the first time Tony sounded bitter, and Carol put her hand across the table to touch his. 'I'm sorry.'

'Don't be. At least not for that.' There was an indefinable change to his voice which gave Carol some tiny warning of what was to come. 'The marriage wouldn't have worked anyway. The – drinking' he said the word with difficulty 'was just an excuse. Or a symptom. Or both. I was still in love with you when I married Phoebe. I think maybe she knew that. I did. But you were a lost cause and she was beautiful and she loved me and I honestly thought it would work. I suppose she was what they'd now call a "trophy wife". But it wasn't meant to be like that. I wouldn't have been so cruel. Or not then.'

Suddenly he looked like the Tony Carol had known. His eyes were honest now, filled with pain but honest.

'No, you wouldn't. I knew you well, you couldn't have been cruel.' She could not admit that at some level she had always known that he had loved her, she thought that somehow that would be even more hurtful than claiming ignorance.

They sat silently for a moment, heads filled with different memories.

'Hey, Dad, listen.' Tom and Olivia were back, tugging at Tony's arm. 'It's one of your faves, we put it on for you.' And from the juke box came Billy Fury's voice:

> I want to be your lover
> But your friend is what I stay
> I'm only half way to Paradise
> So close, yet so far away.

Carol felt herself blush furiously, looked down at the table, fiddled with her wine glass. She could not look at Tony, but when she heard him say, with no trace of his new brashness, 'So you do remember?' her eyes filled with tears and she nodded.

'Yes, I remember.'

Carol left her suitcase in the hall, and went straight out again. No shopping would have been done in her absence, and she wanted to cook Martin and the family a good dinner; Sainsbury's was the place for her. It took her a few minutes to find her car – Jody had

obviously been borrowing it in her absence, but at least had not
taken it to work today – and once she had belted herself in she
felt the familiar comfort take hold of her. Carol loved her car.
It was nothing very grand – a small Peugeot – but it was new
and it was hers. She felt safe in it, at home in a little mobile
capsule. She opened the window to let out the smell of Jody's
Marlboro Lights and made her way through the traffic with her
usual efficient aggression.

She parked neatly inside the painted lines and ran through
the rain to the shop's electronic doors. Shopping without a list
was a pure extravagance, as Carol had only eaten an omelette
in the diner she was hungry, so her trolley soon filled up
with expensive extras. She thought she was concentrating on
the food, but of course she was not. She was thinking about
Tony and Henri and Martin and her own failings.

*So that was it . . . the romance of my life. The man who loved me,
who could sing without shame. And look at what he turned into. A bore.
A failure. A drunk. Three wives. So much for his fidelity. I suppose it's
just weakness . . . his drinking is a self-indulgence gone too far, so are
all those wives. Oh poor, poor Tony . . . he was so full of hope. Could
we have known it then? He was always full of extreme ideas, plans to
make millions – but we thought they were clever, that he was funny
. . . He always drank a lot, but was it more than any of the rest of us?
(I must get a bottle of gin, we were nearly out when I left.) I suppose
it must have been. Or maybe it was just that he drank too much more
often than the rest of us, maybe that was it . . . was he that much of
a womaniser? I don't know . . . none of his girlfriends ever lasted that
long . . . but he loved me, and at last he's admitted it. (That cheese looks
surprisingly good, silly of me not to have brought any back from France,
though.)* 'A half of Brie please, no, that one, yes, and a quarter of
Parmesan.' *Oh God, the poor man, and those wretched children . . .
the boy was about Piers's age, perhaps I should ask them – no, that
wouldn't be a good idea, I don't think I want to see Tony again.*

*So that's romance. (I might take some brioche and make that pear
pudding.) Romance. All these years I've remembered Tony as a romantic
hero, and look at him now. He wouldn't have gone on singing to me.
He'd have divorced me by now. Or me him. Although I'm not really
the divorcing type. We'd have clung together, weathering every storm,
I'd have pretended not to mind as everything went downhill, pretended*

*to believe in his yurts, pretended not to notice his face getting meaner. Or maybe I just wouldn't have noticed. Maybe my mouth would have got pinched and my eyes shifty. Yes, he'd soon have stopped singing.*

She stood looking at the paperbacks on sale by the checkout. She loved books being on sale in supermarkets, could never resist buying one, but today nothing tempted her. Tales of divorce and loneliness and adultery and passion. None of it appealed. It was all too close to home. She picked up an American thriller, looked at the blurb, saw it was set among the rednecks of Alabama. That was far enough from Pimlico, perhaps it would engage her interest for a while, stop her thinking about herself.

*But I have to think about myself. I have to face up to – everything.*

*I've been like a schoolgirl for too long, getting on with my life, my marriage, dreaming of some romantic alternative, relying on my past to make my present brighter. And that's a mug's game. It was unfair to Martin, apart from anything else.*

*Maybe that is why he's always been so jealous. I've never had a lover, but he's known there was a bit of me that went away sometimes. To dream about Tony holding a candle for me, and to imagine a tall dark stranger coming to gallop me off on his white charger. And Tony was getting drunk and married, and then came Henri.*

*And he was romantic, he really was.* She paused in her unloading of her trolley, looking into the distance and letting herself dwell on Henri, until the assistant coughed and said, 'Excuse me, madam,' and Carol blushed and apologised and finished the job.

She could see now with a blinding clarity what she had known all along. *This won't do. It is not a state of affairs that can go on, and nor do I want it to.* Her hand shook as she signed the cheque and tears pricked her eyes. *I don't belong with Henri, that was a fantasy, a schoolgirl wish, not mine. I belong at home with Martin who loves me and deserves better. What do you get when you step out of line? Wild happiness – sometimes. And the rest of the time stony eyes staring at you, disapproving of you, maybe even hating you. Susanne is a good woman, she was only wanting to protect her sister. I don't want to be the kind of woman who deserves to be looked at like she looked at me. And what else? The guilt, the hiding, I can't live my life like that. If I thought Jody was having an affair with a married man, however detached his marriage, I'd do everything I could to stop it. And they*

*never are semi-detached, are they, there are always those links that
bind you together. Even when you are actually divorced. But that's
not the point. It's not to do with Henri – and Celeste. It's to do with
me, how I am.*

*It was nice to be wanted . . . I won't forget him . . . he brought me
something, even if it was only good sense . . . I shall miss him . . .*

As she unloaded the trolley into the back of the car the tears
streamed down her face, mingling with the rain. She was going
back home to Martin. It was over.

## 17

Dulcie was sitting on the Aga warming plate hugging her knees and talking enthusiastically to Jody as Carol walked in lugging the shopping. Both girls seemed pleased to see Carol, although Dulcie thought she looked washed out.

'Hi, Carol. Is there any more to bring in?' she asked.

'Yes, quite a lot in the car. It's outside the front door. Here are the keys.' Jody and Dulcie left the room together and Carol wearily began unpacking the bags. This was it, this was what she had decided upon and she would stick with it. She heard her grandmother's voice: *if you are going to do something, Carol, it's not worth doing if you don't do it with a good grace.* She was not going to repine. The interlude was over and she was going to re-enter her real world. There was going to be no mourning, no weeping. She would do what must be done.

The girls came back into the kitchen, weighed down, laughing with each other. Carol told herself not to be sour.

'You two look very cheerful.'

'Well, you know, Spring is coming.' They looked out of the window at the steadily dripping rain and laughed again.

'Actually, Mum, Dulcie's in love,' Jody said.

'No, I'm not.'

'Well, she's thinking about it.' They laughed.

'Oh? Who with? I rather liked Giles.'

'Mum!'

'Yes, sorry. Who is it, Dulcie?'

'Ted.'

'Ted? Do I know him?'

'Ted Yeoell.'

'Lord, I should have known it would mean trouble, Julia having all those boys. So how long has this been going on?'

'Not long, it's hardly going on at all. I shouldn't listen to Jody.'

'No. But it does seem to have cheered you up.' *How lucky they are to be young enough for a new love to be an uncomplicated pleasure.*

'Well, it's quite complicated. He lives in Barnstaple, miles away.'

'Yes, I do see that causes complications.' *They don't know they're born, really.*

'Mum, don't you get? It's brilliant. He's the one who's going to be a farmer, just what Dulcie wants, but he's, you know, a proper person, likes dancing and all that, Adam and he get on really well, we have a good time together.'

'So your romance is still going strong?' *It feels as though I've been away months, not days.*

A slight shadow crossed Jody's face. 'Yes, he's great.' *It doesn't look it, I wonder what's the matter . . . oh, later, when I'm stronger.*

'Does Ted get up to London much?'

'No, but he's never off the phone; you'll soon see, Mum,' Jody said before Dulcie could speak. 'And you'd be amazed how fond Dulcie suddenly is of her godmother.'

Gradually the girls' high spirits percolated through Carol's fog of misery. She could not help but respond to their easy good-humour and, in that hour of normal family kitchen life, her recovery slowly began.

Dulcie was not in love, but was in a fair way to become so. Ted did seem to embody everything she could hope for in a man. He was relaxed, cheerful, had the same outlook on life as she did. She liked him for his stubborn insistence on wanting to farm despite his father's reservations. She liked the way he had found his own job and stuck to it. She had not asked, but she gathered that all the boys had a private income, left in trust by their paternal grandmother which alone would not have made them rich, but was enough to live on fairly adequately. Adam would, of course, be much richer one day, and was already richer from his own earnings. Ted wanted to prove to his father that he could run a farm. Dulcie suspected that he hoped his father would contribute, if not buy him one outright, and she knew that Julia felt he should, but for the moment he was happy in Devon.

Life was perfect for Dulcie right now; she had her job which she enjoyed, her new romance and, through Ted, more access to the countryside she loved. She did not go back to Durham very often at the moment, but her parents were not the types to lay on the moral blackmail so she escaped with only occasional twinges of guilt. She knew that with her and now Luke in the south they must be feeling quite bereft, but they all talked often and for a while at least that would have to do.

Molly had sounded pleased that the Yeoell family had become so much a part of Dulcie's life. 'I was very fond of Julia,' she said, 'I knew she'd be kind to you. And Velters is a good man.' Dulcie, who still found it hard to understand how her mother and Julia had been quite such firm friends, said little about her godmother but spoke warmly of Velters. Secretly she had begun to have dreams of a future with the Yeoells; if she was not yet sure whether or not she loved Ted, she knew she loved Velters.

Ted rang that evening to say he had tried to ask himself down to Yeoworthy for the weekend, but that his father had said they were going away. 'Odd, they never do that. Still, Adam says I can stay with him – are you around this weekend?'

Of course she was. It occurred to her to wonder about his gamekeeping, but she decided it was none of her business.

Jody knew that Adam was in trouble, and that he was taking her with him. Although she was dozy, she was not a coward, and although it had taken her a long time to face up to the problem, she knew now that she must.

She rang him up one Sunday morning after a particularly heavy night on the tiles, and said they must talk. 'Jody, I've got a terrible head,' he groaned.

'I know, but we'll get rid of it. Take some aspirin, we'll go and have a pub lunch and take a walk in the park. That'll clear your head.'

'I thought you didn't like walking.'

'Come on, Adam, it's different in London. The ground's even for one thing. Anyway I look on it as medicine.'

He laughed. 'All right. But what's the big deal? We're always talking.'

'No, I mean it, Adam. Really talk.'

'This isn't one of those where-does-the-future-lie-for-us conversations, is it?' He sounded wary.

'No. Well, not how you mean it. Look, I'll see you at midday in the Churchill in Kensington Church Street, OK? They do good Thai food at the back which'll help wake you up. OK?'

'It sounds as though I've no choice. See you there.'

Surprisingly, Adam was already sitting in the pub nursing a Bloody Mary when Jody arrived. She stood and looked at him for a moment before he spotted her, and she felt like crying. He looked dreadful. In the months since they had begun their affair he had completely changed. He was pale and sallow, his hair was now lank rather than floppy. His hands shook as he lit a cigarette, and he constantly dabbed at his nose with a handkerchief.

She took a deep breath and walked into the bar. 'Ads.'

'Hi, Jode. What'll you have?'

'A Bloody Mary, please. Large.'

Adam came back from the bar with two Bloody Marys, although his own was only just begun. Jody noticed, but said nothing and for a while they sat, stirring ice with their fingers and making desultory conversation about the evening before. They studied the short menu and both chose the same special: it seemed the easiest thing to do.

It was Adam who opened the conversation, 'So what is it you needed to say so suddenly and urgently and privately?' he asked.

'It's not really sudden,' Jody said slowly.

'Well?'

'Adam, I'm really worried about you. Look at yourself. You look dreadful. You're shaking, tired – you're not well.'

'It was a late night last night.'

'Yes, but it's always a late night, isn't it?'

'We have fun, don't we?'

She paused. 'I'm not sure that we do, any more. It's always

such a rush – rushing to the next place or the next line or the next tab. And it's all piled on so much. There's never any breathing space.'

'What do you mean?'

'You know what I mean, Adam. You know me, I'm all for a good time, but it's getting out of hand. I don't think I can keep going any more. It's got to slow down.'

'Oh, for Christ's sake, Jody, you're sounding like Giles now.'

'Giles?' Giles had said he was going to keep out of it – unless Adam's work was affected. Oh God, it was worse than she had thought.

'He got all square and told me a lot of old maidish things about "pulling myself together". I'm perfectly together. Honestly, Jody, get off my back about this. I'm holding down my job, doing well, but I need to relax. If I were drinking you wouldn't be so po-faced. It's Dulcie, I suppose, who's turned you all into prudes.'

Was it Dulcie? Were they prudes? Looking at Adam's white face Jody did not think so. 'It's nothing to do with Dulcie. She's said nothing to me, nor me to her.'

'Maybe not, but she's come down here with her rural attitude and middle class morality and turned the whole lot of you into boring farts.' He was working himself up now, and Jody began to feel nervous. But having come so far there was no point in retreating.

'I don't think that's fair. She's not a prude, and she hasn't changed us. She may be straight, and she may have middle class morals, but what's wrong with that? If middle class morality means you don't want to watch someone you love come completely unstuck, then I'm all for it.'

'Middle class morality means being frightened of having fun yourself and stopping other people from having fun. Partly because you're jealous, partly because you're nervous. It's nothing to do with right and wrong.'

'If you're applying that to Dulcie you're being totally unfair. You know she's not like that.'

'I'm surprised at you. I didn't know you were such a fan.'

'You're being foul, Adam, and you know it. Dulcie's good fun and has fun. She just doesn't overcook it all the time.'

'All that fresh country air,' he sneered.

'*Adam.*'

Jody was so angry she almost stood up and walked out on him. But she could not do it. Adam was being horrible, but he was not being himself. She knew he liked Dulcie, knew he enjoyed dancing with her more than almost anyone – they were both very good and tireless dancers. He was delighted at the burgeoning relationship between her and Ted, had even been talking of the four of them taking a summer holiday together.

'I'm sorry, Jody,' Adam said. 'You're right, I'm being foul. If you want I'll say Dulcie isn't middle class or moral or anything. I'm just not feeling well today, I've a terrible hangover, it'll pass soon.'

'Oh Adam, Dulcie *is* middle class and moral. I suppose I am too in the end. I don't see what's wrong with it. You know I don't want to stop other people having fun, unless it starts getting out of hand.'

'But, Jody, I'm not hurting anyone else. Anybody's code of morality is based on not hurting other people. OK, I admit it, maybe it's all going a bit too far. Giles irritated the stink out of me, but he made me realise that perhaps I should cut back a bit, I have been overdoing it. But it's only a bit of self-indulgence, Jody. Who am I hurting?'

'Me,' Jody said in a very small voice.

'You?' Adam looked so surprised Jody could not help but smile. 'Why?'

'Because I'm worried about you. You're changing, Adam, you're nervy and aggressive and ill. You say you've got a hangover, but when did you last feel really well? Really relaxed. Really have fun?'

Adam thought a moment. 'At the end of the day when I went hunting last time I was at Yeoworthy,' he said.

'Exactly.'

It was Adam's turn to smile. 'Don't tell me you're a convert to the countryside, Jody. It'll be happy clappy Jesus next.'

'Be serious, Adam. It's not to do with the country – well, only a bit. You looked dreadful at the meet. Compared to all the others, Ted, Dulcie, that Colin, all of them, you looked awful. And then you spent the whole day in the saddle with what, a packet of sandwiches and one flask of whisky mac or whatever? You didn't have to think about work, or where you

were going to score, or how long you could last until your next
line, and when you got back you looked completely different.
You came down from your bath, changed for dinner – and you
looked like a different person. You looked like you did when I
first met you.'

'If I remember I'd been out dancing with Dulcie and was not
in very good shape.'

'Well, you know what I mean.'

'Yes, I suppose I do.'

'So what next?'

'What do you mean?'

'What are you going to do about it?'

Adam played with his food, not wanting to face up to the
question.

'Well?'

'Jody, I'm cutting back already.'

'Not last night you weren't.'

'Well, in the week. If I have to be honest, I suppose Giles did
make me a bit nervous about work. I made a stupid mistake the
other day – luckily I was able to sort it out – I was tired . . . so
I'm cutting back in the week.'

'Adam, it's not a question of cutting it back, you've got to cut
it out. You've gone too far to do anything else. It's like giving
up smoking.'

'I'll cut back now,' he said stubbornly. 'And when I move
down to Yeoworthy I'll give up entirely. I'll take up hunting and
shooting and fishing, I'll be nice to my wife and father children
and go to the House of Lords. I'll drink nothing stronger than
beer at lunch time and port only on Saturday nights when you
ask the neighbours round—'

'Me? What have I got to do with it?'

'Well, you'll be there too, won't you?'

The stillness between them was absolute. Jody was too
astounded to speak, and Adam was waiting. 'You sort of
implied you loved me,' he said finally.

'Adam, your father may live for another twenty-five years. If
you go on the way you're going there won't be any question
of my being with you. You'll be dead long before him. I wish
I wasn't saying this but unless you give up – really give up –

I won't be around at all. I can't keep going like this, Adam. I want to stay alive and enjoy my old age.'

'With me?'

'If you're still around. Maybe.'

'Then I'll have to try, won't I?'

'Yes. Yes, you will.'

# 18

It was Thursday morning and Julia was on the telephone making
inane conversation to Emma Poole when Velters walked briskly
in to the house, calling her name loudly.

'Julia? Julia darling?'

'Oh, heavens, Emma, Velters is bellowing for me in the hall,
I'd better go,' she said, vastly relieved. 'Yes, well, maybe, I'll be
in touch. Yes, yes. Goodbye. Goodbye.' She finally disengaged
herself and hung up.

'Velters? I'm in my sitting room,' she called. It was her favourite
room in the Manor, a small panelled room in the corner of the
house where she had her desk and an armchair and a richly
worked carpet that she had designed and had had handmade
in Ireland. It was a dark little room, but this was offset by the
flowers which always filled it and the fire which burned there
almost all the year round. In the summer the windows, which
opened on to the flower garden on two sides, were always open
and honeysuckle and roses bobbed lazily in the summer breezes,
giving both colour and their sweet scent to the room. It was a
real retreat, a place to which no one came unless invited. Even
Velters knocked at its door. 'Yes, come in.'

Velters's face was red with excitement. 'I've got a surprise for
you, darling,' he said. *It's a long time since he's called me darling,*
Julia noticed, *What's going on?* 'You've been looking down a bit
recently,' he went on. *Down? I'm on a complete high. He is a dope,
why can't he see . . . well, maybe it's just as well.* Julia smiled at her
husband. She had no idea why he had decided to cancel the
Everetts, who had been invited for the weekend, but it suited
her admirably. Patty had been called away to her father, who

was ill again, and at last she and Geoffrey had laid their plans
. . . he knew a pub in Mere, in Wiltshire. Far enough away to
be safe, near enough to be easy. It was all fixed.

'I'm fine, Velters. Don't worry about me.'

'Oh, of course I do.' Velters's face turned even more red. He
hated this kind of conversation. 'Julia, I've been thinking, here
we are, the house is always full of people, we never actually see
each other. Well, not like the old days.'

'Oh, but we do.' Gradually Julia was beginning to understand
him. *He's eight years too late, why can't he just let things be?* Eight
years of lying and assignations and being minimally dutiful.
Jamie Saunders had been the first, had seduced her, taken
advantage of her loneliness once the children were all away
at school and Velters seemed always to be off on one of the
foreign trips organised by the Lords. After Jamie it had been
easy, what remained of her conscience conveniently pushed to
the background. Until now. Now Velters seemed to be trying
harder to meet her more than halfway and although she was
longing for Geoffrey, she was finding it somehow more difficult
to leave her husband entirely out of the picture.

'Julia, it was you who set me thinking. I know I'm a bit slow
sometimes, but – anyway, here I am, and we have the rest of our
lives together and it occurred to me that we're in such a – routine
– very nice too,' he added hurriedly, 'nothing wrong with that –
but maybe sometimes we should be more – spontaneous.'

Julia almost pitied Velters his struggle, and thought she should
help him out a little. 'Well, the weather's clear. Why don't we
take the Labs for a walk? I'll come and look at your planting at
Witches' Walkway if you like.' He had seemed very excited about
this new project, and maybe it was time she took an interest.

'Yes, that would be nice. But I was thinking of – of having fun.'

'Having fun?' Julia laughed. 'You sound like Adam or Jody.'

To her surprise Velters looked almost hurt. 'Don't laugh, Julia,'
he said. And then he put the envelope he had been holding all
the while down into her lap.

'What's this?'

'Open it and see.' His momentary hurt was overtaken by
excitement again.

Slowly Julia opened the envelope and pulled out the two airline tickets.

'Where to?'

'Look and see.' Julia looked at Velters first. His colour had returned to normal, but his face shone with pride. *He really is quite good looking,* she remembered.

'Rome,' she said. 'Oh Velters, how lovely, it's been years since we went to Rome.' She had gone there with Archy once, but Velters was not to know that.

'You said – oh, ages ago – that you felt we should have a weekend away somewhere. I'm sorry I didn't organise it sooner.'

'You've been busy.' She was genuinely touched at the gesture, wanted to make it easier for him. Life was going well for her, she could afford to be generous.

'I'm always busy – doing nothing,' he said. 'Don't tell me you haven't noticed that.' She had, but did not think he had. Nor had she thought that he had it in him to sound so bitter.

'Well, Velters, it's a lovely idea. Thank you. When are we going?' She squinted at the ticket and as she saw the date her heart sank.

'Yes, you'd better go and pack your bags,' he said, mistaking her silence for delight. 'The flight's in the morning, so we ought to spend the night in London. Let's leave earlyish, so we've time to spare. I'd like to take you out to dinner somewhere really good – the Connaught? Or Tante Claire? Anywhere you like.'

'But Velters, I can't!'

'What do you mean, you can't? Of course you can. Why did you think I cancelled the Everetts? It's all arranged, I've given Mrs Tout the weekend off. All you need to do is pack.'

Julia was furious. 'What do you mean, you've given Mrs Tout the weekend off? I run this house. So who else knows? You can't go keeping secrets from me with Uncle Tom Cobbleigh and all.'

'Julia, you're being silly. Mrs Tout isn't Uncle Tom Cobbleigh.'

'Well, I can't believe that everybody in Yeoworthy knows my moves before I do.'

'It wouldn't have been much of a surprise if I'd asked you to book the tickets, would it? And you wouldn't have done it yourself, would you? You'd have asked Sally to do it, so it would have come to the same thing.'

'Oh, so the Webbers are in the secret too, are they? Anyone else? The Fosters?'

Velters looked at her sharply. 'No, why would the Fosters need to know? I haven't told the Pooles, either.'

That brought Julia up in her tracks. What did he mean by that? She must not panic. Velters was right, she was being unreasonable. *I must pull myself together. He mustn't suspect. But I can't go – I just can't, not this weekend.* She took a breath and tried to sound more calm.

'Velters, I'm sorry. You just caught me off my guard. It's a wonderful idea, and I'd absolutely love to come to Rome. But this just isn't a good weekend. Couldn't we possibly just put it off for a week or so?' She managed a regretful smile, and did not let herself notice the look of hurt on his face.

'What is the problem, Julia? There is nothing arranged this weekend.'

'No, but there is. You see, when you cancelled the Everetts I thought how lovely, a quiet weekend, but then out of the blue – this morning – Rachel Croker rang – do you remember her? Dark girl, was our next door neighbour in London, moved to Wiltshire – anyway, she said she was sorry it had been so long, usual sort of thing, but her husband's just walked out on her, at a time like that you think back to happier moments, she thought of me, wondered how I was – etcetera etcetera – *anyway* on the spur of the moment I suggested going over to see her, hold her hand, all that, and as this weekend was blank I thought I could go over for the night – on Friday, which is tomorrow – so you see I can't possibly be in Rome and Newbury at the same time.' She had expected more time to work on her story, but thought it would do. *Maybe I talked a bit much, though. I don't think Velters will notice.* She looked at Velters with the open eyed gaze she had long since perfected for moments when she needed to declare her innocence.

'I thought you said Wiltshire,' was all that Velters said.

'What?'

'Newbury's in Berkshire.'

'Berkshire, Wiltshire, it's all the same.'

'Yes, I do remember Rachel Croker. I'm surprised she chooses you as her confidante after all these years. I don't remember that you parted on the very best of terms.' He paused a moment to let the picture of a tearful Rachel Croker sink in to Julia's memory. *Oh God, I completely forgot, she accused me of flirting with her bloody husband – what was his name? Peter or something. Said he was weak and at least she expected her friends not to encourage him. And I hadn't, anyway. And Velters and I laughed about it, about the lunacy of anyone supposing for a minute I'd go off with their husband, when I had Velters . . . oh, we did love each other then . . .* She flushed and looked at Velters, put her hand out to touch his arm, withdrew it when she saw the total lack of love or even tenderness on his face. But she had to go on with the lie, she could not back down now.

'Yes, I was surprised too. She said she knew I'd had nothing to do with – er – Peter, but that it had seemed easier to fight against someone she knew than all the rest.' *I'm going to talk too much again*, she knew, and shut up.

'Rachel Croker's waited a very long time to see you. I think she can wait a little longer. I won't change the tickets,' Velters said, and walked out of the room. Julia was left sitting alone, the tickets on her knees, the sound of a labrador scratching filling the room.

*So what am I to do? It was all planned, it seemed so straightforward. And now this. But it's true that I asked to go away. And Velters looked so pleased. Oh hell. It would have been nice. But I can't not go. It wouldn't be fair. Oh God, it's taken Velters twenty something years to come up with a surprise and he has to do it now, the one time I've got something planned. Well, maybe not the one time . . . and what was that about the Pooles? He couldn't have meant anything by it . . . could he? I'm going to have to go. He'd be too suspicious if I didn't. Rachel Croker was a stupid one to pick. We might even have quite a nice time. I do love Rome. And Velters looked so pleased.*

*But what about Geoffrey? He'll already have left. I couldn't ring Patty's father, even if I could find him. He'll be in the car – but how can I talk to him? Patty will be sitting beside him – they may even have the telephone on loudspeaker. Oh, God, this is complicated. He said he'd drive her up, have lunch and drive back this afternoon. He can't possibly be back before we go. I'll have to try and ring him from the flat. Or the Connaught, that would be better, don't want the number on the bill. This is ridiculous. But otherwise he'll turn up at the pub tomorrow night and find he's driven two hours to be stood up. I suppose I could ring the pub now, before we go. But then he'd still have to drive there. And I don't want to leave my name. No, I've got to stop him going. Or disappoint Velters. But I've never seen him so stubborn. He won't change his mind. And I almost want to go with him. He did look so pleased.*

*I've got to make up my mind. The longer I leave it the worse it's going to be whoever I throw over. I don't want to let either of them down. But I'm going to have to, and it shouldn't be Velters. I'll get hold of Geoffrey somehow. We'll refix it. I wonder how long Patty's away for?*

*Rome is lovely at this time of year. Velters did look so pleased.*

Velters did not look as happy as Julia had expected when she apologised, but, chastened, she worked hard at making preparations to leave in an excited, cheerful way. By the end of the journey to London he was mellow again, looking forward to his treat like a small boy. It seemed a long time since they had been alone together in such a concentrated way as they were side by side on the Jaguar's leather seats. Julia remembered how much time they had spent together in cars in the early years of their marriage, driving out of London most weekends, enjoying the companionship of the long journeys. Surprisingly, this journey went quickly too. They talked to each other as they so rarely did these days – not about anything in particular, but easily and jokily. Every now and again Julia found herself swerving away from a dangerous subject, but they arrived in London relaxed, and in an excellent humour with each other.

Julia bathed and changed, then, while Velters was shaving, she quietly lifted the telephone from the hook and – first dialling 141 so that her number was withheld from the records (Patty should not be at the Dower House for a few days but it was not worth taking the risk) – rang Geoffrey. Thank God! He was back.

'It's Julia. I'm in London. I can't come, I'm really sorry. I'll ring you from Rome, I'll explain then,' she said, not giving him a chance to speak at all. As Velters walked in she was standing in front of the mantel mirror putting on lipstick.

'Was that the telephone? I didn't hear it ring.'

'No.' Her back was to him, but of course her face was reflected in the mirror and she saw him watching her.

'I thought I heard you talking.'

'No. Or to myself. At any rate my lipstick. I couldn't find it.' She turned to him with a laugh. 'You look nice, Velters. Shall we go? I fancy proper cocktails first.' He did look handsome, a proud man ageing gracefully. A man who did not make a fuss but could be counted on. Julia was suddenly rather looking forward to the evening, and the few days in Rome, with her husband.

And, do you know, she walked across the room and hugged him.

Of course the Roman holiday was not a honeymoon – how could it have been, between Julia and Velters, with all those years of silence between them? But they both enjoyed themselves. They walked what seemed like miles through the streets, stopping at bars, laughing together at the posturing Italian youths strutting through the evening streets. They did their sightseeing in an energetic but disorganised way, ate well, slept well. They enjoyed each other's company.

Somehow Julia did not manage to ring Geoffrey from Rome. Occasionally she felt guilty, but at least she had managed to stop him from driving all the way to Mere for no reason. She was looking forward to their deferred assignation, but it was not at the forefront of her mind.

Velters was also relaxed. He looked at Julia and saw echoes of his younger wife, and it made him contented. He told himself that he had been imagining things, that Julia had been tired, that he had been right to start to pay more attention to her. His wife was a good-looking woman, it was only natural that she enjoyed a bit of attention. He put all thoughts of Rachel Croker and Geoffrey Foster out of his mind. Being Velters, he put most thoughts out of his mind and enjoyed the moment. Julia knew what was right, he was sure of that.

On the last day they went to St Peter's and stood silently together in front of the Pietà. 'If I could have any one great work of art that would be it,' Julia said softly. 'You know, ever since I first saw it I have kept a postcard of it in my desk. I look at it every now and then.'

'Where would we keep it at Yeoworthy? There's not really enough space.' Julia looked at Velters. He was thoughtful, completely serious.

'Oh Velters, honestly. If we owned the Pietà we'd move to a house that did have a space.'

Velters rose to the bait, but then laughed. 'Fair enough. You're right, of course. It's in its own class.'

'Somehow it puts other things in perspective. Makes you realise what's really important in life.'

'Perhaps you should look at the postcard more often.'

Julia looked at her husband, guilt once again making her sensitive to his tone of voice.

'And what do you mean by that?'

'Nothing, I suppose. Sometimes, Julia, I think that we're not challenged enough.'

'Challenged? What's got into you, Velters, you're getting to sound like one of those New Age self help groups.'

'Am I?' Velters retreated into his amiable-gent pose. 'I don't know. We have quite an easy life, you know.'

'Of course I do.' Julia was irritated. *I know I'm lucky, blah blah blah, I'm very grateful etcetera etcetera, but that's the way it is.*

'We don't have to do anything we don't want to. Ever. Or nothing worse that a minor irritation. I suppose we're in danger of getting spoilt.'

'By our age we're either spoiled or not. And we do lots of dreary things we don't feel like doing.' Velters made as though to speak, but Julia did not give him the chance. She put her arm through his and gave his a quick squeeze. 'I know, we're spoiled rotten, and I have been especially spoilt these last few days. But as we are anyway, let's enjoy it instead of feeling guilty. We'll buy some more postcards of the Pietà – mine's getting tatty and you could do with one too – and then let's go and have lunch. If we're much later we won't have time before the plane.'

Half way home Julia began to think rather more about Geoffrey. Her short holiday was over, she and Velters had had a much happier time than she would have expected, but that did not mean she was not going to meet Geoffrey as soon as she reasonably could. There had been enough pussyfooting around and she was longing for consummation. That was always the hardest part of a new affair, anyway. Once they had got over that everything else would fall into place.

'What are your plans, Velters?' she asked over an unnecessary gin and tonic.

'When?' He looked at his brandy and soda with distaste.

'When we get back.'

'Well, it's Tuesday but there's nothing of much interest at the Lords this week. I thought I'd go straight home with you.'

'Oh. Well, I wasn't sure I was going home. I thought maybe I'd go to the flat.'

'Any particular reason?'

'Yes. You know, Rachel Croker.'

She could see the shutters go down behind his eyes and was almost frightened, but not enough to change her mind.

'I see,' he said, pleasantly enough. 'All right. So you're not going to go straight to Hungerford?'

'Well, no – um, Newbury,' she corrected him, but certainly too late.

'I hope I'll see you at the weekend?'

*Velters is being too damn polite. He knows – or suspects. Oh, bloody Rachel Croker. Why did I ever drag her into it? But he caught me on the hop. And I won't be bullied.*

'Of course you will.' She was too gushing, and knew it. 'And, Velters, thank you for a lovely trip. I really enjoyed it. Really.'

But not enough to stop her doing exactly what she wanted. She would go to London, and ring Geoffrey. She had no doubt at all that he would drop everything and come, and then – at last – they would meet in Mere, spend the night there and make their separate ways back to Yeoworthy. She loved the subterfuge, the intrigue. It was the breath of life to her. And she had a feeling Geoffrey liked it too.

# 19

For the first time, Dulcie noticed an unpleasant atmosphere at Yeoworthy. She could not quite put her finger upon it, but something was wrong. Velters and Julia had just come back from a break in Rome, and both seemed to have enjoyed it thoroughly, but they seemed very out of balance with each other. Every time Dulcie had stayed at the Manor until now she had felt for Velters who seemed – if in an offhand sort of a way – to be much more affectionate towards Julia than she was towards him. But now he barely looked at or talked to her, while she seemed almost over eager to please him. Velters walked around the house with a distracted air, looking alternately angry and hurt and Julia was on her most amusing, gracious, hostessy form.

It was also Dulcie's first visit as Ted's particular friend and she was flattered by Velters's pleasure in this turn of events. 'Ted's a sound boy, the best of them in some ways,' he said. 'I always knew he'd pick a good one. Keep hold of her, Ted, don't want to make any silly mistakes at this stage.'

Ted laughed and looked pleased with himself. 'Steady on, Daddy, I've only invited her to stay,' he protested, and Dulcie blushed. *We've barely kissed and Velters is already treating me like a daughter-in-law elect. One step at a time . . . but it's not a horrible idea.* And she looked at Ted, handsome and healthy and laughing with his father, and thought, *well, one thing is that this is a proper family. They do like each other, go out of their way to see each other.*

She asked Ted if he had noticed anything odd about his parents, but of course he had not. 'Mummy's on very good form; I think Rome's done her some good. Daddy's probably just worrying about missing a few days at the Lords. You know how set in his ways he is.' After her experience with Martin, Dulcie knew better than to say anything more.

After dinner on Friday night Ted took a bottle of whisky from the drinks tray and led Dulcie into the billiard room. 'I'm going to teach you how to play – not enough girls do and it'll stand you in good stead,' he said.

'All right,' she agreed, wondering vaguely if it was rude to Velters and Julia but somehow not minding. They were Ted's parents, it was his home, it was his idea. He could take responsibility.

As soon as the door closed behind them, though, it was clear that billiards was the last thing on Ted's mind. He put down the whisky and glasses, turned and took Dulcie into his arms and kissed her thoroughly. After a while she pulled back. 'Ted, shouldn't we be bashing balls about or something? They'll get suspicious.'

Ted gave a dirty laugh, then, 'Don't be silly. I'm sure we're the last thing on their minds,' he said, trying to kiss her again.

'No, I mean it, Ted. What if someone comes in? Your father said he might join us.'

'Of course he won't. He's not a total idiot. He probably thinks we're doing a lot more than kissing,' and he pushed her back against the table, grinning lasciviously.

'Ted!' Dulcie wriggled free.

'Sorry.' He smiled again. 'Are you telling me you'd really rather play billiards than—'.

'No, no of course not. But, you know, this is the billiard room, not the bedroom.'

She looked so worried that Ted laughed and took her hand. 'Come on then, let's go to the bedroom.'

'What, now?'

'Well, why not? It's eleven o'clock, perfectly respectable, if that's what you're worried about.'

'But your parents—'

'Have probably gone to bed already themselves. We'll go to the drawing room and see, and say goodnight to them and go to our beds like good little children and then I'll tiptoe down the corridor to your room and – and well, heigh ho.'

'No.'

'No?' He looked affronted. 'What do you mean? You seemed keen enough a minute ago.'

'Yes, of course. But not here.'

'I don't get.'

'We can't go creeping around your parents' house like that. I don't know, it's – it's not right.'

'Don't be ridiculous, Dulcie, it's how it's done.'

'How what's done?'

'You're being thick. It's within the rules. You just don't get caught. Nobody minds, everybody does it. It's an unwritten plot of weekends in the country. And anyway, Dulcie, it's our only chance for ages. Come on, we both want to, there's nothing wrong in it.'

'I don't know, it just feels wrong.'

'Oh, come on, don't play the innocent. What do Jody and Adam do in London? And you, come to that, with that Giles bloke you went out with? You all creep around, play the game, don't get caught. Everyone pretends not to see and nobody minds. Please, Dulcie.'

'But I'm a guest. What about your mother?'

'Oh, stuff my mother. She does it herself.'

'What?' Now Dulcie was really shocked. 'Your mother corridor creeps?'

'Well, almost. Of course, Emma was always here so even she couldn't go the whole hog. But I caught them in a steamy clinch once, and she saw me, too.'

'How can you talk about your mother like that? It's disgusting.'

'So was she. If she had to do it, she could have been more careful.' Ted had let go of Dulcie and was sitting on a bench against the wall, head back, legs outstretched, looking a little bit drunk and very dejected.

'Who was the man?' Dulcie could not help being curious.

'I don't think you've ever met him. A posy designer or painter or something called Archy Poole. Drippy little wife who Mummy had to pretend was her friend. Sickening really. Don't see much of them any more, now I come to think of it. Suppose she's on to pastures new.' Without asking, he poured two glasses of whisky, and handed one to Dulcie.

'Does your father know?'

'I don't think so. He wouldn't say if he did. Not to me anyway.'

'Does he have a girlfriend?'

'I don't know. But you see,' he tried to lighten his tone, 'this isn't exactly a very *moral* house, so I really don't see why you and I – who are unattached, and grown up, should not spend the night together. If you still want to.'

'I do want to, Ted, very much. But I'd just much rather not here. I'd be too nervous, or worried. Do you mind? I'm very sorry.'

'Of course I mind. But I won't push it. As long as you promise me that next time I come up to London, you'll go back to your London ways and let me in to your room.'

'I'll look forward to it.'

'Then I must take some days off and come up straight away.' Fleetingly, and not for the first time, Dulcie wondered how Ted managed so much time away from Barnstaple, but then he kissed her again, a warmer, more friendly kiss than before, and she forgot to wonder about anything.

There was no hunting the next day, so after a late breakfast Julia suggested some tennis. Dulcie was not very good, and not very keen, but she could not stand up against Julia's enthusiasm and agreed. 'We need a fourth,' said Julia. 'Shall I ring—'

'I've already asked Colin and Sally, do you mind, Mummy?' Ted said, and Julia had to give in gracefully.

'What was all that about?' Dulcie asked, as they left the house carrying rackets and balls. 'You haven't asked the Webbers, have you?'

'No, but I said we'd call in. Mummy's too competitive. She's got no idea how to be nice to beginners and she would only have put you off.'

'And?'

He smiled. 'Quite right. And. And I knew she'd only ask one of those bloody Fosters, who practically live here as far as I can work out and will probably be here for dinner tonight. I can't stick them.'

'Why on earth not?'

'She's very good at tennis, but she's so keen to please she muffs things on purpose. And she wears the most dreadful tennis whites with horrible little glittery bits sewn on.'

Dulcie laughed. 'That's quite a good reason to hate her. And him?'

Ted smashed a dandelion's head from its stalk with his racquet. 'Nothing special. I just don't like him.'

They found Colin and Sally sitting down to coffee and home-made lemon cake, and were welcomed in warmly. *It feels like home*, Dulcie realised, and felt very happy with the world. 'I love this time of year,' Sally said. 'It's the one time of year Colin can take a bit of time off.'

'Just a breather before we make the silage,' Colin said, stirring sugar into his coffee.

'Good, you've time to come and play tennis then,' Ted jumped in.

'Well, I don't know about that, Ted—'

'You've got to,' Dulcie chimed in. 'He's told his mother the most enormous lie and she'll probably be squeezing lemons at this very minute for home-made lemonade for us all between sets.'

'Or asking Mrs Tout to do it,' said Ted and they all laughed. 'Or more likely doing something entirely different and not thinking of us at all. But still, it would be fun if you came and played. And it would mean I hadn't told a lie.'

'No, it wouldn't,' said Dulcie. 'You told a whopper all right. It'll just mean you won't get caught, you'll feel better about it and you'll have more fun.' But she laughed.

'Oh, all right then,' said Colin. 'You're on, aren't you, Sal?'

They split up – Ted played with Sally and Dulcie with Colin. 'I know I beat Colin, and you're not much good, are you, Sally?' he said over his shoulder. Dulcie felt embarrassed for him, but Colin and Sally just exchanged glances and laughed.

In fact Sally turned out to be excellent, miles better than Dulcie and faster and more accurate than Ted. Ted grew more and more cross as the set progressed. Although Sally was playing with him he was incensed at her skill. From the beginning of the match he had shown a streak of unbridled competitiveness which Dulcie did not like, but as the set went on and it became clear that he and Sally would win he appeared to be competing more with his partner than his opponents. He counted aces and double faults as eagerly as Dan Maskell, but rather less accurately. He lost all interest in what was happening on the other side of the net, except in so far as it provided him with balls to show off his shots. He began leaving balls for Sally, making as though to run for them and at the last minute calling 'yours' in a nonchalant voice. He commiserated with her effusively when she missed, and scowled when she returned. Sally played elegantly and concentrated on the game – she seemed unaware of all the aggression being directed at her by her partner. Dulcie on the other hand was embarrassed and disgusted by Ted and played increasingly desperately, longing for the game to be over.

Colin was the very opposite of Ted. He was nowhere near as good as his sister, but played well in an energetic and enthusiastic way. He obviously minded about winning, but never made Dulcie feel hopeless even when she played her worst. She thought how much more enjoyable the game would have been if Ted had been more like Colin.

'Played at school, did you?' Ted gasped to Sally at the end of the second set. 'How do you have time to keep it up?'

'She played at Junior Wimbledon when she was fourteen. Had to withdraw after two matches – it was when Mum died,' said Colin.

'Well, why didn't you say?' Ted asked.

'You didn't ask.'

'You just told her she wasn't any good,' added Dulcie.

'I did not.'

'You implied it. You just assumed she wouldn't be. I'm surprised you haven't played before anyway.'

'Yes, well, I suppose . . .' Ted tailed off.

'I should get back, anyway,' Colin said, zipping up his tennis racquet in its holder. 'Dad'll go spare that I just wandered off in the middle of the morning and I've a few things to do before lunch.'

'You've got time. I've lunch to get,' said Sally. 'Thanks for the game. Bye, Dulcie, Ted.'

Ted was still in a temper as they walked back to the house.

'I saw she had an expensive racquet. I suppose I should have guessed.'

'What does it matter? It was a good game – except for your temper.'

'I was not in a temper. I'm just pissed off that she conned me.'

'She did not con you.'

'Well, what's she doing being so good? She's – she's—'

'Go on, say it.'

'She's my father's secretary. She went to the local comp. which can't have more than four courts, and I bet they're hockey pitches or whatever girls play in the winter.'

'So?'

'She must practise on our court – who with? And if she belongs to the club, how can she afford it?'

'Ted!'

'Well, honestly.'

'I didn't think you were so snobbish.'

'I'm not.'

'You are. That's all you're being. You didn't expect her to be any good because she's a girl and because she and her family work for your father. That's pathetic. And why haven't you played with her before?'

'I – we – didn't like to ask her when—'

'When you had your friends here, but Colin would do when you were here on your own and felt like a set. Honestly.'

'It's not like that.'

'What is it like, then? It doesn't look too good to me.' She stomped ahead of him through the field and let herself through the door in the wall without looking back at him.

'Dulcie.' He caught up with her and held her arm. 'Come on, I'm sorry.' She could see he did not know why he was apologising. 'I mean, you wouldn't want me to be too interested in her, would you?' And he kissed her and despite herself she laughed and kissed him back.

'Ow!' The garden door swung inwards, its latch knocking into his back and they jumped apart.

'Sorry. I didn't see you were there.' It was Julia, carrying a picnic blanket. Suddenly aware of herself, she flushed and darted between them. 'Lunch will be in a quarter of an hour,' she said over her shoulder and almost ran across the lawn to the house.

Dulcie had seen that expression on another woman's face quite recently. Of course. It was Carol's face in Kensington High Street.

She sighed and linked arms with Ted, her anger with him forgotten entirely. 'I don't know,' she said. 'Being grown-up – really grown up, I mean – doesn't seem as easy as I had supposed.' And they walked slowly across the lawn together in silence.

Patty stood outside the back door, looking out at the hills and wondering why she and Geoffrey were not doing anything this weekend. Her cup of coffee was getting tepid but she could not be bothered to go inside and add more hot. She was only drinking it for something to do, anyway. It was going to be a lovely day; already the sun had a promise of warmth in it and a bird was singing like mad in recognition of the fun it was going to have during the day. *Fun!* thought Patty bitterly. *Bloody birds having fun. It really is too much.*

Perhaps she should do some gardening after all. Not much point, though, if they were not going to stay here and Patty was beginning to wonder if they would. *But I can't keep moving on, it makes no difference, there'll always be someone. Each time the problem comes with me. I've told him twice that once more and I'd go, but I don't, do I? It makes me as pathetic as he is, that's the trouble. And I don't know, do I? Not for sure.* But she did. She knew the signs by now; nothing that he could do could fool her.

Their lease was six months, renewable: they were into their second six months and it had been assumed that they would stay indefinitely, at any rate until the Lloyds demands finally dried up and they could take stock of what, if anything, they had left.

*Where would we go, anyway? Or where would I go if I left him? What would I do? I haven't worked for years, wouldn't know how to set about it, now. I'm damned if I'm going to do a secretarial course while he's living it up with Her Ladyship. Suki took out a franchise with the Tie Rack when she left Richard, and did pretty well, but that was the Eighties, things were different. And I don't want to be a shop girl, anyway. He's going to have to support me somehow. If I leave. If. How often I've been through this. And every time it's the same old story. I forgive him, I'm left a bit sadder, more lonely, and off we go again.*

She heard the telephone ring and turned, but it was picked up immediately. She could hear Geoffrey's voice – but not what he said – floating out of the study window. He sounded happy, light-hearted. *Like the bloody bird*, she thought. And then, *he's planning some fun too, isn't he?*

No sooner had the idea come into her mind than she felt the old sick jealousy stir in the pit of her stomach. *I'm being silly, he wouldn't – but he has before. He promised – but he did before. This is our chance, our new start, but why should that stop him? He just can't fight it; he's weak, that's all, and so am I, to let it go on and on. I'm only forty, there must be a different future for me . . . But I'm being ridiculous.*

She stepped quietly into the hall and looked at the telephone sitting so innocuously on the hall table. *I've only to pick it up, say oh sorry have you already got it and I'd know who it is. Know I was being silly. Or not. It's too late for that. He's been talking for five minutes. I could just pick it up, very quietly, and listen. I've never sunk so low, I can't do that. If only I knew. Maybe he isn't having an affair with her – but where was he on Tuesday night? I rang and rang, I can't think of anyone he could have gone to stay with without mentioning it to me. In passing. He thinks he's got away with it. I suppose he has. Shall I pick up the telephone? I mustn't. I can't. Oh God.* She did not. She was not going to start that sort of thing now. There was no need really. She knew.

She left the half-full cup of coffee on the hall table beside the telephone and, trying to distract herself, went upstairs to make the bed. Of all the jobs she had to do now she had less help in the house, this was the one she hated most. She did not like to think of beds during the day. Somehow it embarrassed her.

The bed made, she moved around the room, half-heartedly tidying. Geoffrey's socks were as always left in the middle of the room, his dirty boxer shorts from the day before lay on the floor by the bath. *They wouldn't all find him so attractive if they knew what a pig he is at home.* Straightening from picking them up, she saw a movement outside that caught her attention and took a step closer to the window. It was Geoffrey, carrying some kind of rug, walking gingerly around the edge of the garden towards the gate into the field. *What the hell is he doing?* She saw him look back towards the house as he opened the gate, and automatically stepped back, although there was no chance he could see her. He stepped through the gate, latching it behind him and then scurried – *how could he be so undignified?* – across the corner of the field and into the little wood beside it. The squawk of a cock pheasant disturbed in his strutting tore the air and made Patty jump. She looked up towards the Manor, half a mile away up the hill but strain her eyes as she might saw no sign of movement. Maybe there was just a faint flutter of blue by the wall, but she could not be sure. *The bastard. How dare he? Playing away from home is one thing, that's almost traditional by now – but this. I won't have it. Not any more. I won't bloody have it.*

She looked down at the boxer shorts balled in her clenched fists. *This is what our marriage is to him. Someone to pick up his fucking pants.* With a howl of rage she threw the cheerfully striped pants out of the window and sat on the floor and sobbed.

Geoffrey, all unknowing, sauntered into the house. 'Patty?' She was not in the sitting room, or kitchen – but her bag was there and the keys of the car were in their usual place on the sideboard. 'Patty?' *Where on earth has she gone?* He felt a prickle of unease, but ignored it. *She hasn't gone and done anything silly, has she? She seemed all right at breakfast.* 'Patty?' She had left a cup of coffee on the hall table, he saw, and irritation replaced anxiety. 'Patty! What are you playing at?' How like her to go and spoil his good mood. But he had better go and look.

He took the stairs slowly – he was not going to be hurried by her silly games. 'Patty? Have you done lunch? I thought we might go down to the Yeoworthy and eat in the garden. What do you say?' He walked into the bedroom and stopped dead. Their biggest suitcase lay open on the bed and Patty, with a white, unmade up face, was packing it furiously.

'Is it your father?' he asked. He remembered the cold cup of coffee by the telephone. 'What's happened, is he worse?' She shot him one look of pure dislike that stopped him in his tracks. 'Patty?' he asked, more feebly. 'What's happened?'

'I'm packing,' she said, as though the words hurt her.

'I can see. Where are you going?'

'I'm not going anywhere.'

*She's gone mad, she's finally flipped. Oh God, here we go*

*again*. He stepped round the bed, put his arms out to take
her.

'Don't you fucking touch me!' she said. *Why isn't she shouting?
She always shouts.* And then he saw that the suitcase, now nearly
finished, was full not of her clothes but his, and he began to
understand.

'What are you doing?' he asked, and his voice was tight, not
with anger but with fear.

'I'm packing your things. You're going. Now. As soon as I've
finished. I'm not going to be made a fool of any longer.'

'But – I don't want to go.'

'Well, I'm not going anywhere. You always find a nice cushy
spot to fall into – go and find one again. You've taken me out
of one home, I'm not leaving this one.'

She went into the bathroom and began packing his washing
kit. She did not throw things, or stamp or cry or shout, but there
was pure anger in every jab of her body. He followed after her,
unsure of how to behave but sure he would win her round.

'Patty, darling, what's upset you?'

'Don't be so bloody stupid. I've had enough, Geoffrey. I'm not
putting up with it any more. It's not even worth talking about. I
told you – I've told you before and it's gone on, but believe me
this time – that once more would be once too much. And this
time it *is* true. You're going – to the Yeoworthy Arms, if you
want. Isn't that where you've just come from? Or perhaps her
arms weren't really the bit of her body you were most interested
in. That's it. I'm packing for you for the last time.'

He remembered the telltale coffee cup by the telephone. 'You
bitch! You eavesdropped.'

'No, I didn't. I didn't need to. You're so bloody arrogant,
Geoffrey. I don't need underhand methods to catch you out.
You give yourself away all on your own. Creeping out of the
gate – with a picnic rug! – for a Saturday morning fuck! You're
not invisible, you know. You promised me you wouldn't touch
her. You said all that was finished with, and like an idiot I believed
you. You just can't help yourself, can you?' She was beginning to
shout now, she could not help herself, and Geoffrey was relieved,
things were returning to normal, he would be able to calm her
down, he would have to be more careful in the future.

'Patty, I'm so sorry. It won't happen again. It's only just started, I'll end it, she'll understand, it was obviously foolish, it just was such a sunny day, you know, the sun always makes me silly.' He tried a self-mocking laugh but she was having none of it.

'It rained last week when I was with Daddy,' she said. Hearing him repeat the lying promises she had heard so often calmed her down rather than angering her more. She knew she was right. She had fought for long enough.

'You mean? – well, yes, it was last week. I was lonely while you were away, it was just once. Patty, you mustn't go—'

'I'm not the one who's going,' she reminded him.

'Well, whatever. Patty, please—' Once again he tried to put his arms around her, but she side-stepped him and went back into the bedroom.

'Geoffrey, something has happened to me today which means your normal route to forgiveness is not going to work. Quite simply, you disgust me. I've known you were weak and susceptible and generally quite despicable for some time now. But for the first time, when you walked into this room, you disgusted me physically as well. You know, when I decided this was it and started packing I was only frightened of one thing. Not being alone, or what Daddy would think, or anything like that. I was frightened you'd walk in here and look at me and say sorry and put your arms around me and I'd forgive you and want you all over again. And when you walked in and I looked at you and realised that I never wanted you to touch me again I was glad.' She snapped the suitcase shut. 'So take that with you and go. Ring before you come back for the rest. I'll make sure I'm out.'

She stood and waited. And Geoffrey, stunned into obedience, meekly hauled the suitcase from the bed and walked away, down the stairs and out of the house.

Not until she heard his car starting and driving away down the lane did Patty collapse on to the bed. She wept for the end of her marriage, but she was proud of herself for the first time in a very long while. And then she pictured Geoffrey walking out, back stiff, dirty candy-striped boxer shorts flapping from his pocket, and her tears turned to hysterical laughter.

She wondered if she need ever see him again.

# 20 ∫

'I don't want to pry, darling, but you have been looking so gloomy recently that I just want you to know that if there's anything I can do . . .'

Jody looked up with a wan smile. 'Oh, Mum, I don't think there is,' she said, but she put her book down beside her on the sofa which Carol took as a signal that the conversation was not yet over.

Carol had come back from work to find Jody already home and lolling on the kitchen sofa with a Mary Wesley. Jody had looked up and greeted her mother but had said nothing more as Carol made herself a cup of tea. Leaning against the Aga, drinking the tea and watching her daughter, Carol felt that she could not let this state of affairs continue. While Dulcie was clearly in the happy opening stages of her new affair and Martin and Piers were as usual in their own worlds, she and Jody were wandering around the house like wounded animals looking for a quiet place in which to lick their wounds and wait for death. She could not discuss her own unhappiness – that was part of the deal she had made with herself – but she should be able to help Jody. That was what mothers were for, she thought. Years before, in a rage at some childish crime, she had shouted, 'I honestly don't know what you think mothers are *for*!' and Jody had answered matter of factly, 'For hugs'. Carol remembered that now, and though she was not very good at hugging, she thought it was time she tried the mental equivalent.

She took another sip of tea and let the silence hang in the air for a moment before she tipped the tea down the sink, and, crossing to the fridge, took out a bottle of Oyster Bay and waved it at her daughter. 'Forget the tea. Let's have a glass of wine. It's nearly seven, after all. You look exhausted, and this'll cheer you up.'

Jody said nothing but she roused herself enough to fetch two glasses while her mother opened the bottle. Drink in hand, Jody returned to her place on the sofa while Carol sat at the table.

'So what's gone wrong?' asked Carol, although she guessed the outline if not the details.

'I've broken up with Adam.'

'My poor darling. What happened?'

'He asked me to marry him – sort of.'

'Jody!' Carol was not a snob, but she could not help a gleam at the thought of what came with Adam. 'And you refused? I don't understand.'

'I didn't really. Well, I don't know if I did or not. But the end's the same.'

There was a pause while Carol tried to work this out. Then, 'Jody, why don't you start at the beginning, tell me all about it. It may make you feel better. And, sweetheart, you can trust me.'

Jody's eyes filled with tears and then, slowly at first, but faster and faster, the story came out. The drugs, the clubbing, her conversation with Giles, her worries, the confrontation in the Churchill, his implied promise that he would stop the drug-taking.

'And he did try, Mum, I know he did. You should have seen him. It – oh God, it was awful. He was so jumpy, so goddam twitchy. He was horrible to me, but I knew why so I didn't leave. But then, I don't know – something got to him and he started on the coke again. Not the E, I don't think, not yet anyway, but he will, won't he? And that girl died and there was all that stuff in the papers, but he just said it was a chance in a trillion and it was just media hype because the Princess of Wales hadn't done anything they could put in the papers that day . . . anyway as soon as I knew he was back on the coke I said I'd warned him and that was it and I haven't seen him since and oh Mum I thought he loved me . . .' and then she really wept, snivelling and snuffling and looking six years old again.

Carol held her (so she did still know how to hug) and wondered at her own selfishness that she could ever have dismissed the young's problems as uncomplicated. Poor, poor Jody. And she thought, as she smoothed Jody's hair, that her daughter had grown up enormously through all of this, even though Carol had only just noticed it.

'Tell me, darling,' she said when Jody's sobs had subsided a little, 'have you ever taken drugs?' And she did not know whether to be horrified or heartened to see Jody begin to laugh through her tears.

'Of course, Mum. Everyone does.'

'Everyone?'

'Of course. It doesn't hurt. Or at least that's what I thought . . .' She looked as though she were going to cry again so Carol quickly interrupted.

'What?'

'What drugs?'

'Yes. And who?'

'Mostly coke, E – Ecstasy – fairly often, dope sometimes. All my friends.'

'Not Giles.' Carol thought of the most sensible-seeming of Jody's friends.

'Yes.'

'Not Dulcie.'

Jody hesitated. 'Yes, a bit. Mum, you're not to tell Aunt Molly. You promised.'

'God, Jody, she'll kill me if she finds out.'

'Well, she won't. Come on, Mum, you know Dulcie, she's OK, she's not like Adam – oh, Mum, I didn't know coke was addictive. I thought – I suppose we all thought – that if we steered clear of smack we'd be OK. I want to help him but I can't.'

'You can start by giving up drugs yourself.' Carol could not help but sound school-marmish, but she was shocked at what she was hearing.

'I have, of course I have. But Adam just said it didn't count because I didn't mind as much as him, which was true, but he didn't realise how frightened I was at how much *I* missed it. That's what really scared me, Mum; how's he going to manage if I found it so tricky?' She cried a bit more while Carol tried to think.

'You need to get him into some kind of clinic, get him proper help.'

Jody nodded, 'I know, but I rang two of them, ones I'd read about and they asked who would pay and they're incredibly expensive and he won't let me ring his parents, made lots of excuses and then they said people can't be forced and he has to make his own decisions, it wouldn't work anyway if he didn't want to come, and then they said I sounded distressed and did I need professional help, they could offer counselling for families, and oh Mum that wasn't the point. I want him to get better and he just won't and it may sound silly but I do love him, or what he was, and what he is when he's trying and he's really fantastically *brave*. And then they said something about Toughlove which means if you love them you're horrible to them and that'll make them stop or something but I don't want to be horrible to him and I just don't know what to do.'

Carol felt some of her own pain diminish in the face of her daughter's. Throughout all of her own anguish she had been putting her own position, her own quest for romantic love, first, before Martin, before her children, before even Henri. *I could have learned a thing or two from Jody, struggling on her own all this time, making all those dreadful calls to patronising professionals – for someone else. And I thought she was selfish.*

'Mum, it was so humiliating. They treated me like – I don't know, as though it was all my fault when all I was trying to do was get him out of it. They said a lot of words like enabling and stuff which I just didn't want to hear. I just want to help Adam get better,' she wailed.

'Jody, they're trying, but they can't provide all the answers.'

'Then why do they pretend they can?'

Carol got up and refilled her glass. Jody's was hardly touched. 'Mothers are meant to give advice and all that, and I suppose I've been too busy getting on with – with my own life recently to do enough of that. But about the only good advice I can give is to warn you that no-one can give any one else the right answers. You just have to work them out for yourself. And they may be – they certainly will be – different for each person. You know, I think I've only just, after all these years, worked out what is the right answer for me. Silly, isn't it?'

Jody looked at her mother with interest. 'What is it? Your right answer?'

Carol looked away. 'That's another story, really. But I was looking too far afield. It was here all along. Right under my nose.'

'It can't be Adam's right answer, going the way he is. He's got so much.' Jody was thinking of his humour, his verve, his happiness in living.

Carol, thinking of his inheritance, his family, said, 'He'll live up to it all. Everything. As long as he sees in time. And you're doing the right thing. If he's asked you to marry him, he does love you. And if he loves you he'll want you enough to give up his other love. You've just got to take that gamble. You've no choice really. Oh darling Jody, I wish you'd talked to me before.'

'I thought you'd be shocked.'

'I was. I am.' Carol was honest. 'But it doesn't mean I don't want to help you out of it.'

'You do now, you probably wouldn't have when I was still in the thick of it. And you've been tied up with that French house and I don't know what.' Jody smiled. 'We've been a right pair, you and me, Mum, moping around the house.'

Carol wondered what Jody knew or suspected. 'I'm sorry Jody. I'm really sorry. It's all over now.' And once again the mother and daughter hugged and maybe some bridges were repaired.

Ted was in London again. 'Don't you ever do any work?' Dulcie laughed. 'Well, some of us do and no, I can't meet you until late, I'm on until nine o'clock on Friday.'

'Can't you just bunk off?'

'Of course I can't. I'm a bookseller. I can't do that from a pub.'

'Oh, come on Dulcie, it's only a job. What'll they do?'

'At worst they'd fire me. And I don't want to be fired. I like it there, you know I do.'

When they did meet in the Uxbridge Arms at nearer ten than half past nine, she found Ted surrounded by cheerful youngish men in suits with noisy girls in tow. He sat alone looking morose.

'Hi, Ted, sorry I'm a bit late. I'm starving, I'll have a Guinness, thanks. What's the matter?'

'I've been sitting here for an hour and a half,' he grumbled. 'Surrounded by people having fun, on my own, and this is my weekend off in London.'

'You knew I wouldn't be here until half past nine,' she reminded him, determined not to be irritated. 'Why did you come early then? Or you could have rung someone else.'

'I was going to have a drink with Adam, but he's all over the place. He's no fun to be with at all. I hear he and Jody have broken up.'

'Yes, how is he?' Jody had now told Dulcie most of what had happened, and had asked her to find out from Ted how he was. Dulcie was glad Ted had brought him into the conversation.

'Feeling sorry for himself. He's not going anywhere, sitting at home, drinking whisky and taking coke.'

'But that's dreadful. Isn't he going to work?'

'No, he's rung in sick.'

'At least he had the sense to do that. Is he eating?'

'You sound like Nanny. How am I supposed to know?'

'Ted! You've been there, you've seen him. What does he look like?'

'I don't know. I went there, dumped my bag, had a drink with him, realised he was out of it and went my own sweet way. I don't think we should go back there tonight, though. The flat stinks. Don't think he's bathed for days. Oh, all right then, no I suppose he doesn't look too good. Don't look at me like that, Dulcie. What am I supposed to do? I'm only here for the weekend.'

'He's your brother, Ted, you should help him.'

'How?'

'I don't know, make him bathe, for one thing, eat, get back to work, stop the drugs. Not to mention the whisky.'

'You know I don't do drugs, Dulcie. I told him ages ago he was an idiot and he laughed at me and look where he is now. He'll get over it.'

Dulcie was disgusted at how comfortable, how indifferent Ted sounded to his brother, but she had promised Jody not to do anything, just to find out what the position was. Oh God, she was not going to like this.

'What do you want to do tonight then?'

'Go back to your little basement room with you.'

'You go straight to the point, don't you?' she laughed.

'I was only asking. Please,' he added. 'I've come an awful long way.'

Dulcie did not give him a direct answer. She was not liking Ted very much this evening. 'What about supper?'

'This is your patch, you tell me.'

They settled on fish and chips at Geale's, and after they had finished their drinks wandered down Uxbridge Street together. Dulcie was feeling more friendly by now, but Ted's attitude to his brother still niggled at the back of her mind. She was sure none of her brothers would be so cool if she were in such trouble, but the more she saw of other people's families the more she thought her family must be the exception rather than the rule.

Tucking into their plaice and chips, a bottle of house white wine on the table between them, Dulcie decided to tackle Ted about something else that had been bothering her.

'Ted, how do you manage to get away from the Verneys so often? Don't they mind?'

'I don't really know. I just tell them I'm going and go.'

'You can't do that!'

'I can,' he grinned, but his charm was lost on Dulcie. 'Here I am.'

'But it's a farm, it's not an office.'

'Not everyone's like you, Dulcie. You're too strict with yourself. Like I said, a job's just a job. They've got plenty of people working on the farm. The others cover for me. I'd do the same for them.'

'I *would* do, rather than I *do*?'

'What do you mean?'

'I mean that they don't ask you, do they?'

'I suppose not. But it's different. They've nowhere they want to go.'

'Don't be stupid, of course they do.'

'They're all local.'

'So? They must have girlfriends and wives or whatever too.'

'Not much of the whatever down there,' he laughed. 'That's why I'm up here, my lover.' He affected a Devon burr which, though perfect, irritated Dulcie. Once again she found herself biting back a quick answer. It was true, he had come a long way to see her and she did not want to fight.

'Anyway, I won't be there much longer,' he said, helping himself to more tartare sauce. 'My master plan is about to come off, I think.'

'What's that?'

'Well, you know Mummy's been on at Daddy to buy me a farm – small maybe, but something of my own? I talked to her the other day and it looks like he's coming round to the idea. I'd have to put some of my money from Granny into it but that's fair enough. I did the degree and I've been working a few years and in the end Daddy's quite sensible. Why work for someone else when you could be working for yourself?'

'That's good news. Where will you buy?'

'Well, that's the beauty of it. By luck the Webbers' lease comes up in another year and I'll probably take it over for the next five years, during which I'd do the farm manager's job as well, and buy it from the estate then. My plan is to get Daddy to knock the value of it off whatever he has set aside for me, so in effect I'd get it now when it's useful rather than when he dies when I'll be too old to care.'

'You can't do that.'

'Mummy says it might be quite difficult but she's sure a good lawyer could sort it all out. Trusts and things, you know, quite complicated.'

'I didn't mean that. You can't do that to the Webbers.'

'What?'

'Throw them out. How long have they been there?'

'Oh, for ever. I think Colin's grandfather was born there. His father certainly was.'

'And you'd throw them out?'

'Of course not. We'd give them another cottage. Mrs McGilligan at Stag's Harbour must be going to die soon. They can have that.'

'But what would Mr Webber do?'

'What do you mean? He's near retiring age. A few years here

or there, what's the difference? And Colin and Sally would still work for us.'

'Farmers don't retire. At least not proper ones. Why don't you live at Stag's Whatever?'

'It wouldn't do for me at all. It's too small.'

'But there are three of them. You can't mean this, Ted. You'd take away their farm, their house, their work. Colin's meant to be your friend.'

For the first time Ted looked a little uncomfortable. But he retaliated. 'It's not their farm, it's ours. They've always had it on five-year leases. Of course we'd give Webber a pension.'

'It's immoral. I just don't believe it. What does your father say?'

'It's not immoral. It's like Hong Kong. The lease runs out, you take back what's yours. And we're not the Chinese.'

'The way you're going, you're not much better. The Communists might have a point – don't let anyone own anything, it's not good for them.'

'Well it hasn't done them much good anywhere else, has it? Look, Dulcie, I obviously just haven't explained it properly. It all makes perfectly good business sense. Nobody's going to be done out of anything. OK, the Webbers might be sad to lose the house, but they'll get over it, it's just a house. We'll look after them all right. It's the way it works, don't you see?'

Once again Dulcie was being told to accept something she instinctively loathed because it was 'the way it worked'. Creeping around between bedrooms in the dark, throwing friends out of their houses – all, it would appear, the way 'it' worked. Whatever 'it' was she was disliking 'it' more and more. And she was having grave doubts about Ted. She suddenly thought of Giles and knew that whatever his faults he could never be as morally indifferent as Ted was showing himself to be. She felt quite sick at the thought of the Webbers being shoved into some small cottage to suit Ted and pushed away her plate. Oblivious, Ted started picking at her chips.

She realised he had left one question unanswered. 'What does your father say?' she persisted.

Ted hesitated, a chip halfway to his mouth. 'Mummy isn't entirely sure she can make him go along with it,' he admitted.

'She says he's very attached to the Webbers. She also says that one of the reasons he's come round to helping me is that a farm next door is up for sale. The old man died and the daughter doesn't want it. He's quite keen I should have that. She says he might not want to break up the estate, but the farm next door would be a good thing. I suppose she thinks that if I don't have any children it could go back to Adam's or whatever and make the estate even better.' He laughed. 'But once I've persuaded Mummy she'll be able to talk Daddy into it. You see it'll save me money. Have you finished? Shall we go dutch?'

And Dulcie, who never minded paying her own way, looked at him and knew there was no chance at all of letting such a one into her small basement room. Tonight or ever.

# 21

News of Geoffrey's departure reached the Manor by Monday lunch time. Mrs Tout's niece, whose boyfriend mowed the lawn at the Dower House, told Mrs Tout who told Julia when she brought in the lunch.

'Mr Foster's left the Dower House.'

Julia was surprised – she thought Geoffrey would have mentioned any plans to her on Saturday morning – but she was careful to give nothing away. 'Oh? Anywhere special?'

'No-one knows. He left on Saturday morning with a big suitcase, heading down the valley road.' Mrs Tout put the shepherd's pie onto the sideboard. 'Davey says he heard Mrs F crying.'

'Surprised he could hear anything over the noise of that mower.'

Mrs Tout paid no attention to the implied put-down. 'Looks like Mrs Foster's staying put, though. She was weeding like anything this morning.'

'Thank you, Mrs Tout,' said Julia.

She was left alone, picking at her lunch. *So what is going on? Everything seemed fine on Saturday morning. I thought Dulcie and Ted might have noticed something was up – idiotic of Geoffrey to forget his blessed rug – but no-one said anything. Oh God, how can I find out? I suppose I could call on Patty, neighbourly cup of coffee – no, no, not that.*

For a while at least all she could do was wait, and stew in her own juice.

She did not have to wait for long. Velters had had lunch at the Yeoworthy with a neighbour from a few villages away who he had been hoping to persuade to take a gun for next season's shoot. Julia had been thinking too much of her own position to consider Velters's but as soon as he walked in to the house she knew something was wrong.

'Did Gerald bite?' she asked, hoping to divert him.

'Foster's gone. Some say he's done a runner, some that poor little Patty has thrown him out. What do you know about it?'

'I don't know what you mean.'

'Don't fool about, Julia. I asked you a straight question.'

*He's not shouting. I don't know if that isn't worse. Oh God, what do I do now?* 'Nothing.'

'Don't lie, Julia. I may have been a fool for years, but I'm not going to be any longer.'

'Nothing, Velters, I swear. Mrs Tout told me at lunch time. That he'd left with a suitcase. That's all I know.'

Velters looked at her and decided that she was telling the truth. 'All right. So do you have any theories about why he left?'

One last desperate attempt. *It might just work* . . . 'Maybe money? Is the rent up to date? . . . Lloyds . . .'

'You can do better than that, Julia. I walked into the pub with Gerald and do you know, nobody could meet my eye. In my own pub, dammit. That pretty Josey that serves blushed so much I thought her eyes would pop.' He paused, searching for words in which to express his disdain for his wife. 'I would never have believed it of you, Julia. I would have thought you'd have more self-respect than to want your name bandied about the local pub like the village whore.'

'How dare you, Velters!' Now she was as angry as he, but where his rage was cold, hers was white-hot. 'I will not be spoken to like that!'

'But you don't mind being spoken *about* like that?' he sneered. 'As long as it's behind your back it's all right? As long as your "relationships", as I expect you like to call them, are behind my back they're all right?'

She realised how hurt he really was, but she could not resist trying to justify herself. 'I don't believe a single person mentioned my name in the Yeoworthy today.'

'Not in front of me, no. But they said they'd heard another woman was involved, and couldn't look at me. Poor Gerald had no idea what he'd flown into. Thought he was in for a bit of local gossip. Couldn't understand why no-one was more forthcoming to him.'

'I have never done anything that could lay me open to cheap comments in the Yeoworthy Arms,' said Julia proudly, believing herself.

Velters looked at her with disgust. 'I'll talk to you later,' he said. 'I'm not entirely sure that I could trust myself now.' And he left her alone with her thoughts.

At half past six Julia was sitting in the drawing room reading the newspaper. She had decided that her best method of approach was to behave as though nothing had happened. No specific accusations had been levelled at her, she had admitted nothing. Maybe when Velters had calmed down she would be able to persuade him that he had been making a mistake. *If only Geoffrey would ring me and let me know what happened. Where on earth can he be?*

At a quarter to seven Velters walked into the room and, polite as ever, asked her what she would like to drink. He poured her a gin and tonic and himself a whisky and soda and sat down on the sofa opposite her. *He's not going to say anything. He's realised how he over-reacted.* Julia could not believe her luck. She put the paper aside and took a sip of her drink. 'So did Gerald take a gun?' she asked conversationally.

Velters looked at her, his face tight. 'I think we should sort a few things out,' he said. 'I don't want details, but I want the truth. Are you having an affair with Geoffrey Foster?'

Julia wondered whether she should try one last ditch attempt at lying, but she knew it had all gone too far for that. Her hand tightened on the glass. 'Yes,' she said. Velters winced, and the grimace made her feel much worse than any rage would have done. 'But—'

'I don't want to know any buts,' Velters interrupted. 'Is he your first lover?'

She paused, but again she realised that now there was only room for the truth. 'No,' she said quietly, and could not meet his eyes. She looked down at her hands, at her left ring finger which bore the broad platinum wedding ring and the Yeoell emerald. *Oh God, what have I done?*

They sat together in silence. Julia did not dare to speak, and Velters could not. His mind was full of images of their years together, but he could pinpoint no moment when it had all gone wrong. Unless he knew when it had started, the suspicions were going to sour every moment of the last thirty-odd years. But he had promised himself not to ask for the details. The only way through this was to forgive the past – give a general amnesty – and start again with the future. If he could. If she would let him.

'Has Foster been in touch with you since he left?' he asked at last.

'No,' she said. 'Velters, I know no more than you. The last time I saw him – on Saturday morning—'

'I said, no details,' he interrupted, remembering his wife's flushed gaiety at Saturday lunch.

'– there seemed nothing wrong. I mean—'

'I know what you mean. Did he ask you to go away with him?'

'No! Velters, this was all – very new, there was no question of—'

He nodded. 'And when he rings? Which I suppose he will—'

'I – I don't know.'

Another pause, in which Julia longed to leave her chair, to drink her drink, to pace the room, anything rather than sit waiting for judgement to be pronounced, but she was frozen in place.

Velters sighed. 'What you have done sickens me. Literally as well as figuratively. I thought – I thought you were better than other women. I used to pity the poor fools whose wives played around. I thought we believed in the same things, you and I.'

'You never asked me what I believed.'

'I did. Years ago. I suppose I thought you wouldn't change. But you did, anyway, and I was too trusting – too stupid to notice. How could you do it, Julia?'

'It just – happened.'

'I let things run their course, I didn't pay attention. It must have been my fault. But I *hate* it, Julia.' Suddenly he exploded. 'I hate my stupidity, I hate your lack of morality, of faith. I hate seeing the sniggers in the pub—'

'You mind what people think of you,' she fired back.

'Yes, a bit. Of course I do. No man wouldn't. But I hate what they think of you, and I hate that they're right. Although you're not like that, not really, you can't be—' For a moment Julia thought he was going to cry. But not Velters. He had never cried in front of her. She did not suppose he ever would.

'I've kept faith with you all these years, Julia. And don't think there weren't times when I nearly didn't – so nearly.' Suddenly, vividly, he saw in his mind's eye the red-headed South African diplomat he had met on a tour of the country he had undertaken for the House of Lords. She had accompanied his group throughout the trip, a funny, elegant, self-deprecating woman, much more clever than him, he supposed, and God he had wanted her. She had given all the right signals, he had been tempted, almost beyond endurance, but he had thought of Julia at home with the children and kept faith. A year later Cheryl, whose name was the only ugly thing about her, had come to London and they had looked at each other and known the pull was still there, the opportunity not lost, and yet he had gone back to Yeoworthy to put himself out of temptation's way. *Had Julia started all this then? Was I already being faithful to some image I invented in the sixties?* He turned to the window to hide his pain.

'I don't know what you want to do, Julia,' *I obviously haven't known for years*, he realised, 'but I'll tell you where I stand. I won't put up with you and Foster – going on – while you live under my roof.'

*My roof is it now, it's been my home for more than twenty years and now he's taking the 'my roof' line. How dare he?* she thought, but she could not make herself feel angry. She almost felt chastened, but not quite, not yet.

'If your – affair' – how hard he found it to say the word, but he resisted the temptation to sneer – 'is too important to you to stop, then you must go. Either way, I don't want to talk about it.' (*Don't you see, you never wanted to talk about anything,* Julia wanted to cry, but could not.) 'You must make up your own mind.'

Velters began to leave the room, but turned back. 'Julia, if it makes any difference to you, I want you to stay. Not because of the neighbours,' *although who are the neighbours but the Fosters, the enemy* 'but because' he gestured at the walls and then, very slightly, at himself, 'you belong here. You know, you can trust me. Do you ever think you'd be able to trust Foster? I'll see you at dinner.' And he left.

Patty was back at her weeding the next morning, vigorously turning over the almost clear beds with a trowel, kneeling on a little cushion, almost enjoying the feeling of the sun on her neck, her mind a blank, when she heard her name spoken.

She sat up on her heels with a start and turned to see Geoffrey standing hesitantly at the fence.

'I didn't hear the car,' she said.

'You look engrossed,' he answered.

She pulled off her gardening gloves and dropped them in the little gardening basket she always affected. 'What do you want?' She sounded weary more than anything else: not angry, not tearful, just very tired. *I suppose it was madness thinking I could get away with not seeing him again. We're going have to go through it all once more.*

'You.' He hoped to sound loving, apologetic, tender. He sounded querulous.

'You've had me for twelve years and four months. Neither of us has been especially happy. Not together, at least. I think that's enough.'

'You can't do this, Patty.' He sounded firmer now, but he still had not come in to the garden.

'Why not?'

Geoffrey did not know how to answer. This interview was not going as planned, not at all. He tried a different tack.

'Of course we've been happy.' He edged closer to the gate. 'Patty, I don't think we should be having this conversation out here. Can I come in?'

'I don't think we should be having this conversation at all. I've made up my mind, Geoffrey. I'm sorry if it comes as a surprise, but you've had enough warnings.' She stood up and looked at him thoughtfully. 'Maybe that was my mistake. Anyway, I've been in touch with the lawyers. I want a divorce as quickly as possible. I won't be greedy. I just want to be free. I suppose you had better tell me where you are staying. No, don't come in. Please go.'

To his horror but not hers – she was still too numb to notice much – his eyes filled with tears. He tried for a moment to stop them, but could not control himself. 'Please, Patty,' he snivelled. 'Please don't do this. I love you. I've always loved you. What will I do without you? I'm sorry. I've been a fool. It won't happen again. Not ever. Not with Julia, not with anyone. Please. I've learned my lesson this time.' Now he lost all dignity and clung on to the fence, openly sobbing. Patty looked at him with no emotion, only a mild curiosity. 'Don't do this to me,' he begged. 'I need you. I'm sorry.'

Patty stared at him. She did not see a lover, a friend. She saw a man whose dirty socks and pants she had picked up for twelve years and four months, who never knew where his tie was, who never made her laugh. She saw him blubbing and realised what a poor, cheap weapon tears were. She disliked herself for having used them so often, and she despised herself for having wanted to hold on to this excuse for a man for so long. She knew the months, perhaps the years, ahead were not going to be easy for her, but then neither had the past been easy. She would manage.

At last Geoffrey pulled himself together enough to look at Patty and realised that he was going to achieve nothing for now at least. He blew his nose and wiped his eyes. 'Sorry,' he said, referring to the last ten minutes rather than the last twelve years. She nodded. 'I never knew you could be so strong,' he said as he turned away.

'You made me strong,' she answered, and he turned back, a gleam of hope in his red eyes. 'In the end,' she added, and without another word walked into the house.

*Funny, I could swear that was Geoffrey's BMW*, thought Julia as she sped past the Dower House on the way back from shopping. *Perhaps he's gone back.*

She was not quite sure how that idea made her feel. She was still totally at a loss about what had happened to her control of her own life. One part of her thought that perhaps she should ignore the whole Geoffrey episode, pretend it had never happened, but she knew that was too easy. He was bound to contact her one way or another, and meanwhile there was Velters, scrupulously polite, following her with eyes that looked sometimes angry, sometimes hurt, sometimes puzzled, waiting for her next move.

She parked the car carelessly in the courtyard and wandered through the house to the garden. If Geoffrey asked her, would she go? She could not pretend to herself that it was a grand passion. It was a lusty companionship, a bit of fun to while away her life with – but her whole life? *On the other hand it would be a grand adventure, to leave all this for a new love, to have no responsibilities. We could travel, make new friends, see new places . . . it's quite tempting really. Perhaps we could live abroad for a year until the dust settles . . . somewhere exotic . . . Samarkand, Zanzibar . . . or a city, Budapest, Constantinople, Paris, Rome. Rome . . . Velters . . . Oh, God.*

She looked out across at the quiet fold of the hills. Sheep scattered the fields, horses grazed as though modelling for Stubbs. The sun shone in an English, polite sort of way. It was not too hot, not too bright, it was a let's-have-a-picnic sort of a day. She thought of all the picnics that had been carried out of this house to adjoining fields. She thought of children falling into the lake, being stung by wasps, arguing over strawberries. *If I go, I'll never see any of this again,* she realised. *Maybe in ten years' time I'll have been forgiven enough to be allowed back to Miranda's wedding. Maybe.*

She looked at the garden she had more or less created and then back at the house, the splendid stone house which she had loved for so long. *And after the year in Samarkand, then what? A rented cottage, away from here, away from Hampshire, somewhere where neither of us knows anyone. Where no-one knows either of us. Where the children may or may not be willing to come. With Geoffrey. Who makes me laugh, who knows how to have fun. (Who is persistently unfaithful to his wife.) Would he be unfaithful to me? (Velters isn't.) I don't think so. (Not at first.) I think he might be in love with me. (But I'm not with him.) It would be an adventure. (Maybe it's time I stopped having adventures.)*

Standing in the sunshine, looking at the beautiful house in the middle of the most beautiful place in England (*perhaps the world, but then I haven't been to Zanzibar yet*), Julia suddenly felt a sense of the most terrible loss. Either way, the choice once made, she would lose. All this – and her family – or Geoffrey. *It just isn't fair.* But it was, of course.

She heard footsteps in the house and saw Geoffrey coming out of the darkness of the hall and into the sunlight of the garden. He smiled and held out his hands. 'Julia.' It looked incongruous, Geoffrey standing there in Velters's garden, looking so possessive.

'So it was your car,' she said.

He looked surprised. 'Yes. I was just picking some things up.'

'What's happened?' she asked, still without moving towards him, and he dropped his hands.

'I've left Patty,' he said stupidly.

'So I've heard.'

'I'm sorry. I couldn't get in touch with you. I didn't know what Patty had been saying. I knew Velters would be in London today. I came here as soon as I could.'

'Actually he's not. In London.' She smiled as he jumped and looked nervously over his shoulder. 'He's gone to Wellington. He'll be back for lunch.' She relented and moved over to him, kissing his cheek. 'It's almost twelve. You look as though you need a drink.'

'Thank you. A glass of wine would be nice.' Julia left him in the garden and went into the house. She was playing for time, but she needed it.

When she came back into the garden carrying a tray with two glasses and a cold bottle of white Burgundy she found Geoffrey had moved over to the garden seat.

'You look very beautiful today, Julia,' he said as she walked across the lawn towards him.

'Don't you think you should tell me about you and Patty?' she answered, handing him the bottle and corkscrew.

'I suppose I should have gone years ago,' he said, not looking at her but appearing fully engaged in his task. 'But I've always felt I couldn't. She's not strong, you know, mentally I mean. But being with you made me see the difference between truth and lies and I thought I couldn't go on. It will be better for her in the end, she can't have been happy either.'

He poured two glasses of wine and handed one to Julia, but he still did not look straight at her.

'So you woke up on Sunday and decided to go – just like that?' Julia asked, sitting down opposite him, her eyes not leaving his face.

'Er, Saturday afternoon, actually,' he said.

'But we were together on Saturday morning. You said nothing then.'

'No. I hadn't decided.'

She waited.

'I left you, and I felt so happy. I remember I was whistling as I walked through the wood, and the bluebells were all out and the sun was warm . . .'

'Yes,' she said, remembering.

'And I got back and felt in such a good mood. I thought I'd take Patty out to lunch, give the poor girl a bit of a treat. I went into the house and found her upstairs, tidying the room or something, and I looked at her face and it looked so sour and mean, and I remembered yours and I thought I can't go on and I said I'm sorry I'm leaving you and I turned and walked away. Cruel, perhaps, but best in the end.'

'Just like that?'

'Yes.' He sipped his wine.

'Someone said you were carrying a suitcase,' she said slowly.

'Well, yes, I thought it would be sensible to take a few things.'

'Where did you go?'

'Not far. I went over the moor, to the pub in Molland. It's got a couple of small rooms they let out. I didn't think anyone would look for me there.' He laughed, warming up, suddenly pleased with his adventure.

*It's not quite Zanzibar. Molland.* Thought Julia. 'So what next?'

'Julia – will you come with me?'

'To Molland?'

'No. Away. Anywhere.'

'Zanzibar?'

'What?' He looked alarmed. 'Well – oh Julia, it doesn't matter where. We'd be together. We've both been in dead marriages for too long. Shouldn't we have a last chance of happiness before it's too late? Come with me, now, pack up and come. We could be so happy together. I need you, Julia. We need each other. Let's take this chance before it's too late.'

Julia sat quite still and watched him. *He's said nothing about love*, she noticed.

As if reading her mind, he added, 'I know this is all new, but isn't that the way to do it? Grab our love while it's young, not waste it in furtive meetings, in lies and complications. Come with me.'

*He really is begging me, he really does want me*, thought Julia. She looked at him, wondered why his eyes looked so puffy and why his need aroused no tenderness in her. *He's lying*, she thought suddenly. *I don't know how much, to what degree. But he's lying. And if he's lying now . . .* she looked past him, back at the hills. *He wasn't picking anything up from the Dower House. He was asking Patty to take him back and when she refused he came on up here.* She did not know why she was so sure, but she knew. *He wouldn't have left Patty, not just like that, not for me. He doesn't love me. It's not me he wants, he needs a woman in his life. That's all.* She looked at his pleading face. *Velters doesn't plead*, she realised. *Velters would never look at me like that.*

She wondered how Velters would manage without her if she went and knew with a shock that he would. It was not just a question of money, of the stuff that would make the running of his life easy. Velters would probably miss her – the Roman holiday had made her realise that despite the day to day irritation she and Velters did still like each other, had a vast store of affection that was usually hidden under the sameness of everyday life. He would miss her but he would not pine. He would get on with his life.

She did not answer Geoffrey at once. She looked at his handsome – *perhaps he is just a little bit coarse looking* – flushed face and thought how different he seemed now from the laughing man who had seduced her, *or did I seduce him? I'm not really sure.*

'What will you do?' she said at last. 'Where will you go?'

'I haven't thought.'

'Shouldn't you?' Perhaps that was cruel, but she needed to know – if he was asking her to join him she had a right to know.

'I'll rent somewhere, maybe a bit further west. Or maybe in

Dorset. You'd like to be nearer London, wouldn't you?' he asked hopefully.

'What about Patty?'

'She seems to want to stay here, but I doubt I'll be able to afford it. I don't want to owe Velters money as well as everything else.' He laughed, but it jarred and he fell silent.

'Geoffrey, this has all got just a bit out of hand. I thought we knew where we stood. Neither of us claimed to love the other. We were having fun. And it *was* fun.'

'It still will be. It will be an adventure.'

Julia sat twisting the stem of her glass. 'I wondered about that. But it wouldn't be. A rented cottage somewhere in England, bickering about money with Patty—'

'And Velters.' He wanted Julia to bring something to the arrangement after all.

'Not Velters, he'd never bicker about money,' she said proudly. 'We'd hate each other by the end of a year.' *Or I'd hate you*, she knew, letting her eyes follow the curve of the hill in the distance. *Give up all this beauty, give up the last thirty years of my life, because of an affair that went wrong. Zanzibar indeed. More like Basingstoke. No, it won't do, it won't do at all.*

'I'm sorry, Geoffrey,' she said. She tried to sound gentle, but to him it sounded as though she were dismissing a daily woman. 'I'm sorry it's ended up in such a dreadful mess. Go back to Patty, tell her you're sorry, have another try,' *if you haven't already.* 'We wouldn't last together. I think we may have been stupid. I'm sorry for my part in it. But no. Thank you for asking,' now she sounded like a well-mannered five-year-old, 'but I don't think I'll come with you.'

For the second time that day Geoffrey cried. He snivelled and wept and finally came out with the truth. 'I can't manage alone, Julia. What will I do?'

'You should have thought of that. Mend your bridges with Patty. I don't know.' *If I were Miranda I'd tell him to 'get a life'. That would be too cruel.* 'Geoffrey, Velters will be back soon. I think you should go. Again, I'm sorry.' She felt she should kiss him goodbye but could not bring herself to touch him. *Anyway I don't know why I should keep apologising. It's his fault as much as mine. More, really. What did he think he was doing, walking out like that? Unless she did throw him out in which case he must have been really dim and got caught. Oh, I wish he'd go.*

He did, at last. Sodden faced, self-pitying, he drained his glass and stumbled across the lawn. Julia felt no emotion at all as she watched him leave. Only the realisation that it was going to be rather embarrassing when she first bumped into Patty.

She waited until she heard his car leave and then carried the tray of drinks back into the house. *Thank God that's over*, she thought. *I hope I never have to see him again.*

As she crossed the hall the front door opened and Velters came in. Julia saw him take in the tray, the two glasses, and she put it down on the hall table and walked up to her husband.

'He's gone, Velters. He won't be coming back.'

'And you?' Velters was perfectly still.

'I'm not going anywhere.' She sensed his body relax. 'That is, if you'll keep me. Velters, I'm sorry. I've been – very stupid.' He knew how much that cost her. She stood straight, not making any move. It was up to him now. For the moment at least.

He bent and kissed her forehead. Then, almost despite himself, he put his arms around her and held her close. 'Thank you,' he said, and released her. He looked at her again, as though he had not seen her for a very long time. 'Shall we have lunch?' he said, and led her into the dining room.

After lunch Julia took the dogs for a walk. She needed to be alone for a while, needed to realise what she was feeling. She avoided the track down the hill through the wood to the Dower House, and instead set off at a brisk pace up the hill, towards the rough ground at the top where the dogs could chase rabbits and the wind would blow her head inside out.

Lunch had been silent and polite, but some of the tension of the last few days had gone. Life was not going to be easy for a while, but there was no question that she had made the right choice. Velters would not mention it again, she knew that. He would ask no questions about the past, nor would he check on her in the future. He had decided to trust her and he would try his hardest to make sure that he did. Perhaps his lack of imagination, which had so infuriated her in the past, would help now. Or perhaps she had misjudged him all along – he had imagination enough but the strength of will not to allow it to rule his life. She did not know. But was beginning to care.

She thought of the two men she had seen this morning – the pleading, weeping man in his too new, too loud tweed jacket, tottering away from her blaming everyone but himself, and her husband, dignified, forgiving but ungiving. *How could I have looked at Geoffrey when I had Velters? He may be difficult, he may even be a bore sometimes, but is four times the man Geoffrey is. Geoffrey's cheap. Cheap emotionally.* She suddenly realised that although Geoffrey had drivelled on endlessly about himself, about a love he could not possibly feel, Velters had done neither. *But Velters is the one who loves me. He would not have behaved as he has otherwise.*

She stopped to catch her breath and looked back down at the grey roofs of Yeoworthy Manor laid out below her. *I didn't not go just because Geoffrey isn't good enough*, she suddenly knew. *Or because of the children, or Yeoworthy. I didn't go, because I didn't want to. Because of Velters.*

She set off up the hill again, trying not to think until she reached the level land at the top. She did not like the thought that was trying to express itself, wanted to put the realisation off for as long as she could.

*Velters isn't just better than Geoffrey. He's a much nicer person than I am. Why has it taken me so long to notice it? I've been a fool. He's given me another chance and I must take it.*

And then: *Oh Lord, it's not going to be easy. I do hate being in the wrong. But if I try, really try, it will be worth it.*

# 22

A month later, bluebells had given way to roses and honeysuckle. Summer had arrived.

Yeoworthy was at its most beautiful in the summer. Roses of every colour, from the gentle yellow of mermaid, through Albertine's pale coppery pink to the rich dark pink of Zephirine Drouhin climbed the grey stone walls of the old house. The garden was heavy with competing but never conflicting sweet smells.

'It really is heaven on earth,' said Carol, burying her face in a honeysuckle and breathing deeply. 'I wish I could make a garden as beautiful as yours, Julia.'

'We should make a team,' Julia said. 'You doing the insides of houses, me the outsides. Although to be honest', which she was much more these days, 'I have the ideas, but I don't really know how to put them into practice. Vellacott really deserves the praise.'

Life at Yeoworthy had, on the outside at least, settled back into its old groove. The weekend parties, the visits to London (but Julia never stayed any longer than Velters now), the estate office, the farm, the house, the garden.

This weekend the Morecombes had come with Dulcie and Piers. Jody had been asked but had decided Yeoworthy without Adam would be too painful. Julia had rung Carol, warm, apologetic for the missed years. 'But now our children seem to spend their lives together, wouldn't it be nice if we saw each other again? It's been too long. The Sonnington-Crowthornes will be here, I think you'll like her, she's very funny and he's dim but worth it because he's so good looking.' Carol laughed, thinking how little Julia had changed over the years.

In fact she found Julia had changed rather more than she had expected. She was still funny and gossipy but she seemed somehow more gentle than Carol remembered – or than Dulcie had led her to believe. Friday evening had been fairly sticky, conversation about their shared past seemed to be the only way they could make a link between them, but as Saturday progressed the two women refound their friendship. Velters seemed a little baffled by Martin's eager enthusiasm but the two men liked each other more than either had expected.

Dulcie lay on the lawn half-reading *The Horse Whisperer* and wondering why it was quite so successful. *Children and horses, I suppose. What a combination. Perhaps I should write a book. I can't stay at Waterstone's for ever. I need some sort of a goal in life.* But it was too hot to think about career moves.

She propped herself on her elbows and watched Julia and Carol walk together round the garden, stopping here and there to sniff at or admire a plant.

*I think Carol must have got rid of that man. Whoever he was. She looked so miserable for a while – seems to be better now. Of all people . . . Ma used to say how happy their marriage was, how much they loved each other. If she knew . . . but I wouldn't tell her. Why upset her? I wasn't supposed to know. It was all an accident. Funny though. Ma always thought they had one of the strongest marriages she knew. Perhaps it is. Otherwise I suppose she'd have gone.*

*I don't know about all that . . . marriage. It just isn't as easy as the grown-ups want you to believe. I went off Giles after ten minutes, Ted even less. I wouldn't stand a chance of lasting forty years or whatever you're meant to do.*

*Julia and Velters though, they seem all right. They've got a pretty good life. I wouldn't mind that . . . she's changed since I knew her, she's nicer, nicer underneath, I think.*

Velters came out of the house with Martin and Fiona Sonnington-Crowthorne. 'There's a slight movement in favour of a jug of Pimms,' he said. 'Any takers?'

Julia crossed the lawn and put her hand through his arm. 'Why don't we go for a walk first?' she suggested. 'It's so lovely. Round the orchard and back through the woods. Just a stroll.' *She never used to ask him, just tell him what she was doing*, thought Dulcie, and watched as Velters patted his wife's hand, smiled and agreed. 'Can you hold off awhile, Martin?' he asked.

'Of course, what a nice idea. I love going for walks,' said Martin and he looked across at Dulcie and they both laughed. 'Will you come, Dulcie, or is it too metropolitan a pastime for you?' he asked.

'Oh, Martin, I'm feeling far too lazy. I'll stay here and do something useful,' she said, secure in the knowledge that there was nothing useful she could do.

She sat up and watched while Fiona called her husband, Quentin, and Julia called the Labradors and the six wandered lazily off on their walk, followed by Piers.

*I suppose things are happening all the time in a marriage, no-one else can really guess. They just look at the obvious things. Children and divorce. I wonder if the ones in the marriage know much more than the outsiders. Those six are all still married. Ma and Pa. Loads of other people, whatever the papers say. I suppose I will be one day. I wonder what really went on with Carol and that man. What Martin knew. He seems much calmer now.*

She thought of her boyfriends, imagining them as husbands. Christian at secondary school – you could not judge a fifteen-year-old, she had no idea even where he was now. Greg at Durham, that had been just good fun, she could not imagine him as a real grown up. Will and Oz – Will would be good, he was very kind. Someone had told her that Oz had come out since Durham, which was taken as a bit of an insult by all his ex-girlfriends. David, her most serious boyfriend at university. He had finally gone off with someone else, was doing well at Architecture School now apparently. *Funny how close you can be to someone and then suddenly they disappear and after a while you don't even feel a hole where they should be.*

*Giles. There's still a bit of a hole there. I do miss him. I can't imagine ever being married to him, though. He'd always be at work, say he was doing it for the family. And then we'd have children and he'd go all obsessive about a son. And I can't be a stay-at-home type of a wife, I'd want to be involved. Either in whatever my husband was doing or in something of my own. It was a shame, really. I wish I could see him more often. He did right by Adam. He is kind.*

*Kinder than Ted. Ted's just good fun. But hard. I should never have*

*got involved with him. I got carried away. What with Jody and Adam,*
*and Julia being my godmother. And here. And hunting.*

'Dulcie!'

It was Ted, coming laughing out of the house. 'Where is
everyone?'

They had not seen each other since the evening in Geales.'
He had been furious with her – perhaps with reason. He had
after all come all the way from Devon on the implied promise
of their relationship being taken a step further, and at the last
minute she had reneged, said she was sorry, she had made a
mistake, no he could not come back with her to the basement
bedroom.

She shrank at the sight of him – no-one had told her he was
coming. 'Hey, Dulcie, forgiven and forgotten,' he said, bending
over her and kissing her. 'Sorry I got so het up. Friends?'

Relieved, she smiled, kissed him back, began to apologise until
he shut her up with a hug.

'Let's not mention it again. One of those things,' he said, and
in his good humour she saw why she had liked him so much
in the first place.

'So where are they all?'

'Gone for a walk. There was talk of Pimms. Are you here for
the rest of the weekend?'

'No, just lunch. I promised I wouldn't be back late.'

'How's it going?'

'I've handed in my notice.' She gave him a sideways look.
'I'm not going to be Chinese,' he said. 'I suppose you were right.
Mummy was iffy about the whole idea and the only time she flew
it past Daddy he gave it the thumbs down. And Colin is my friend.'
He smiled his quick, charm-filled smile. 'I got carried away. We're
buying Lock's farm. It's going at a good price, but don't look like
that, they're not being robbed. A bit of a mortgage, a slice from
Daddy, some of Granny's capital loosened out of the trust. We
can do it.'

'Good. I'm glad, Ted.'

'I'm going round there after lunch with Colin to have another
look. Want to come?'

'I'd love to.'

'How are the old folks?'

'Your parents?'

'All of them – you were worried about your aunt when I last saw you.'

'They seem all right. It's funny, though, they all seem to have changed places since I've known them.'

'How do you mean?'

'With each other.' She thought of Julia asking Velters if he wanted to go on a walk, of Carol and Martin, he so relaxed, she somehow edgy and eager to please. She spent more time at home than before, but when she went off on a job it was she who cast the regretful backward glance, while Martin let her go with a kiss and a wave. 'They've all adjusted in some way. I thought you did all that at the beginning of a marriage.'

'You read too much.' Ted was not really interested. 'Shall I go and start making the Pimms?'

They were about to go indoors together when the telephone rang and Ted rang ahead to answer it. Dulcie sat down on the bench and picked up her book again.

A few minutes later Ted came back out, his expression entirely changed.

'That was Adam. He's ringing from Broadway Lodge.'

Dulcie frowned. 'That sounds familiar. Who lives there?'

Ted laughed bitterly. 'Every rich junkie in the land. It's a rehab place, Dulcie. He said he's trying to be cured. He wanted to talk to Mummy. I'm going to have to tell her. Oh God, this is serious.'

Dulcie thought immediately of Jody. 'Thank God,' she said.

'Thank God?'

'Oh Ted, I told you how bad it was, how worried Jody was. If he wants to be cured he can be, he'll be better again. Jody was right, she said he was brave.'

'He said would I ask you to tell Jody. Said it was important.'

'It is. I will. It'll be all right.'

They heard laughter and saw the others come back, Piers at the back throwing sticks for the dogs. Dulcie and Ted stood side by side as the others emerged from the wood into the sunlight. Ted went forward to his parents and Dulcie watched as they stood stock still in shock and heard Julia's cry and realised their life was not as easy as she had thought.

\*     \*     \*

Lunch was a fractured affair, everyone trying to act normally, Julia trying hardest of all but continually on the verge of tears. Carol and Dulcie, who had known much of what was going on before, felt like traitors, but knew they could have done nothing to help. Velters looked totally bewildered. He had no idea such things happened. 'I thought all that sort of thing happened in tenement flats in Glasgow,' he said, 'although I suppose Jamie Blandford . . .'

'And John Bristol,' said Julia. 'They're endlessly in the papers for this kind of trouble.' Neither of them could say 'drugs', not yet, neither wanted to know the details. They were having enough trouble trying to understand the outline. Julia felt totally betrayed – how had her son not come to her, asked for help?

'He didn't know – wouldn't admit – he needed help,' said Carol. 'He'll need you now, when he comes out.'

Julia rang Broadway Lodge and talked to Adam but was told not to come, not for a while, and so they sat and ate fish pie and peas and tried to pretend this was a sunny Saturday like any other.

To that end Ted and Dulcie went to visit the next door farm as planned. Colin was waiting for them in the courtyard as they came out of lunch and the three of them set off, Dulcie and Ted's spirits rising as they left the gloomy houseparty. Dulcie wondered for a moment whether Colin had any inkling of Ted's original plan and caught Ted's eye. He shook his head, the tiniest shake, and nothing was said.

There was nothing pretentious about the farmhouse – a white Devon longhouse, not as nice, she had to admit, as the Webbers', but perfectly respectable. A big, stone-floored kitchen with an old coal-fired Aga, a small study, two small sitting rooms, and a downstairs bathroom made up the ground floor. Upstairs were one big and four small bedrooms with a badly-converted lavatory jammed into the corner of the landing. 'This house hasn't been touched for years,' said Ted. 'It's not brilliant, but with a bit of money spent on it it will be fine. Perhaps I should get your aunt in.' They stood upstairs, looking out of the small landing window. 'Look at the farm buildings. They're in excellent nick and the roof's fine. There's four hundred acres, which will do to start. What do you think?'

'It'll be lovely,' said Dulcie. 'Don't get Carol, she's miles too expensive. Turn one of those bedrooms into a bathroom and get rid of the horrible loo. You don't need a bathroom downstairs, just a loo would do. You could have one big sitting room like you said and then the bathroom could be turned – I don't know – into a parlour or telly room or something. You are lucky, Ted, it'll be really nice. Stables and everything.' She hugged him in excitement.

Ted unrolled the map of the farm he had brought with him and he and Colin pored over it while Dulcie wandered around the house again, looking sadly at the remnants left behind by the old man's daughter. An old table, an armchair gone beyond the point of worn-out comfort, a toothbrush in the sink, 1950s kitchen units, once someone's pride, now battered and dated.

'Like the Yongy Bongy Bo,' she said.

Ted looked blank, Colin smiled. 'Have you found the old candle yet?'

'No, but I will,' she said, and did.

At last Ted looked at his watch, 'Oh God, I should have gone,' he said. 'Can you two lock up, and Dulcie, give the keys back to Mummy? She said she'd deliver them back to the agent on Monday. I'll see you soon.' And with a kiss for Dulcie and a slap on the shoulder for Colin he was gone.

Colin and Dulcie locked the house and walked out into the farmyard together.

'So you'll be down a fair bit, I suppose?' he asked. 'Helping him sort it out and that.'

Dulcie looked at him in surprise. 'I don't think so,' she said. 'Well, of course, if he needs help.' Then she realised what Colin meant and blushed. 'Oh, it's not like that,' she said. 'We're not, er, going out with each other.'

It was Colin's turn to look surprised. 'I'm sorry – I thought—'

'Well, nearly, you know,' she laughed awkwardly. 'We're just good friends – the genuine article,' and she felt that indeed they were, and would remain so.

She walked along the lane with Colin, thinking about Ted, trying to puzzle him out.

'He's a good lad, Ted,' Colin said, as though reading her thoughts. *If only you knew*, thought Dulcie, but kept quiet. 'Gets a bit carried away, mind. Maybe you've found that.' Colin's face was humorous, and Dulcie nodded agreement. 'Comes up with all sorts of schemes.' Colin went on. 'He's got an eye for the main chance, but he's all right underneath.' They walked together in silence, until Colin said, 'Had his eye on Rattle's Cross, you know,' and Dulcie looked at him.

'You mean you knew?'

Colin laughed at her face. 'Ted can't keep his mouth shut about anything. Word gets around.'

'Aren't you angry?'

'We wouldn't have liked it, but he'd have been within his rights. Sally was angry, very. That's why she showed off at tennis that time. But I never thought it would happen. Dad said Lord Yeoworthy would never allow it, but you know I didn't think Ted would push it through. Like I say, he's a good boy underneath.' Colin sounded much older than Ted sometimes, although Dulcie knew that there was only a year or so between them.

Once again they walked in silence, but it was an easy, old-friends silence. Then as they reached the Manor gates Colin turned to her and said diffidently, 'Would you like to come home for tea?' and when she did not answer at once, added quickly, 'I'm sure Sally would like to see you.'

Dulcie looked at him and noticed for the first time how blue his kind eyes were, and she smiled and said, 'Yes, I'd like that very much. Thank you.' And together they turned their backs on the gates of the Manor and walked up the hill to the farm.